PAINTED FIRE

MARK L FOWLER

First published in 2022 by SpellBound Books
Copyright © Mark L Fowler

FOR ROGER BRAMMER, POET AND FRIEND

She had endured much under many physicians, and had spent all that she had; and she was no better, but rather grew worse. Mark 5:26

PROLOGUE
1969

The carnival was buzzing.

I'd spent a dismal hour in the marquee watching my father drinking, my mother sampling the pastries. That was the ritual; trying to look my Sunday best while my parents got on with their day. I was never anything but the dutiful son.

Except that on that fateful day something *was* different. For me everything was set to change.

I was standing close to the entrance to the marquee, catching glimpses of the outside world framed in the late summer sunshine, wild and mercurial snatches of sounds drifting in off the August crowd. The irresistible tug of curiosity was getting the better of me. I wanted to see what was going on; what all the screaming and laughter was about.

I fought the urge to investigate, and was putting up a good fight too; but even a Sunday-best child, in the end, is only flesh and blood. All the promise of fun invading from outside finally over-powered me, and I made my move leaving my parents to their pleasures.

A few steps, I promised myself, nothing more than that. Stay close, just in case; the world, as my parents had so often impressed upon me, could be a dark and treacherous place.

With those few cautious steps everything turned on its head. I ventured out of the tent, cautiously at first, to find a strange reality waiting, though in truth no stranger than the one my guardians insisted on. Characters from the stories I hungrily devoured every night had been set free from the pages. The Seven Dwarfs were failing to stop Snow White from eating the poisoned apple, while across the way Alice was having tea with the Mad Hatter. I caught Goldilocks' eye, and I'm certain that she smiled at me. I didn't even blush.

I didn't much care for the Narnia Witch, and so moved on to watch the Fire-Eaters and the Human Balloon, with enough change left in my pocket to lose twice on the shooting gallery and still buy an ice-cream. I watched the Knife-Throwing Angels, and the Bearded Baby showing card-tricks to a spellbound audience. And no-one was more spellbound than me.

Aware that I had lost track of the time, I started to make my way back towards the marquee, stopping to applaud as Snow White and her friends finally defeated the evil queen. But when I got back to the tent my parents had gone.

The screams from the carousel had, like the clowns and circus freaks, turned grotesque, and a storm of tears was building in my chest. I knew that I was about to cry. Then I remembered, in the nick of time, what my father had told me. That I was too big to cry and to never forget it or else he'd give me something to cry about.

I stood outside the tent trying to hold the panic down. Best to stay put, I knew that much. Wait for them to come back and find me.

The Alligator Girl and the Dog-Faced Boy were looking over, and the Fattest Lady in England was rubbing her belly like she was thinking about eating a little boy lost. I closed my eyes, wishing that the day would quickly turn into tomorrow.

Then a hand snatched mine.

"Come with me, child."

An old fortune-telling crone had hold of me, dragging me past the One-Eyed Pixies and the Tattooed Fairies, and on towards the black tent in the distance, the one painted with stars and crescent moons. Though she looked impossibly old, the crone was strong, and determined with it.

As we approached the black tent I heard a man shouting, "Comes to something when you have to drag your customers in." There was laughter from the man and his friends, though none from the old crone. Opposite the black tent was a refreshment stand. She took me over to it and bought me candy floss.

"Normally you don't take gifts from strangers, do you know that?" she said, offering me the treat. I nodded, taking the candy floss. "What's your name?" she asked.

"Ben," I said.

"A noble enough name, I'll give you that. Is that the extent of it? You do *have* another name?"

"Tolle," I said. "Ben Tolle. I'm here with my parents."

"And how old is Ben Tolle?"

"He'll – I'll be ten tomorrow."

"You get that?" said the witch to the candy floss seller. "Put it through the speakers: 'Ben Tolle, aged ten. *Lost.*' We'll be in my tent. Step this way, Ben Tolle."

Inside the black tent she sat me down at a small table, and took out a deck of cards that looked ancient. The cards had weird pictures on them. I'd seen similar in books and horror films, but nothing quite like the pictures on those cards. I felt nervous looking at them, though a little excited, too. I was certain that those cards held secrets, and that the old crone was about to unlock them.

"I'll give you a free telling to pass the time," she said. "Put your sweet down and shuffle. Don't worry, the cards won't bite you."

I gobbled down the remains of my candy floss and shuffled the cards. When I'd done that, she held out a hand as crusted and veined as old cheese. Taking the cards back from me, she spread them out on the small table between us, and studied them. After a while she asked, "What do you want to be when you grow up, Ben?" I said that I didn't know. "Oh, come on, child. There's more to you than that. Show me some imagination. You've got the spark in you, I can see that. It's in your eyes."

I'd not long finished reading about a boy of my age who had a series of adventures in a peculiar world that was in some ways similar to mine. The book was cool, so I said, "I'd like to be a writer."

"Not a policeman or a fireman?"

I shook my head.

"What kind of a writer would you like to be, Ben?"

I thought for a minute, about the books that excited me the most. The ones that still haunted me long after I'd turned out my bedside light. "I want to make up my own world," I said. "I want to have amazing adventures there whenever I like."

The crone laughed. "Make up your own world, eh? And have adventures? That sounds like a future if ever I heard of one. What kind of adventures did you have in mind?"

A thousand stories shot through my head, though I still didn't know how to answer her question. "I'm not sure," I said. "But I think they would be the best ones ever."

She grinned at that. "I think you might be right," she said, looking at me as if she was seeing right down as far as you could go. "Let's see what the cards say, shall we?"

She studied them closely, and seconds slowly turned to minutes. Then I noticed that her eyes had darkened, and her face, which had seemed so kind, for a carnival crone, had tightened into a hard knot. She shook her head, glancing up at me, before looking back down at the cards. In that brief look I saw something. It might have been pity.

At last she gathered up the cards and suggested that we walk back to the marquee, in case my parents were there already, waiting. But curiosity had bitten, and bitten hard.

"What do the cards say?" I asked her.

"What are you asking, Ben? What do you want me to tell you?"

"Am I going to be famous one day?"

"So you want to be famous now, and rich too, I suppose?"

She became thoughtful for a moment. "Okay, Ben Tolle, three things I can tell you."

I almost smiled. Three things, of course, what else? All of the best fortune-tellers told you three things.

She looked again at the cards. I swallowed hard, feeling my Adam's apple bobbing in my throat as I did so; the excitement swelling up inside me so that I could hardly breathe.

"You will write a book," she said.

"So I *will* be a writer!"

"Indeed you will. But it will take a very long time, and it will be a very unusual book, quite unlike any other. And ... you will marry an angel."

I felt my cheeks start to burn.

"Oh, yes, Ben Tolle. You will set off together on a journey, and on this journey you will meet a stranger in a strange land. He will be a man of great power, a magician, of sorts."

"What does the magician want?" I asked.

The old crone hesitated.

"Will he become my friend?"

She took a deep breath, as though preparing to lift a heavy burden. Then she said, "A book, an angel, a journey, and a magician. I promised three things and I've given you four. There's nothing more to tell."

"But I want to know about the magician."

At that moment, a younger woman entered the tent and whispered something into the old crone's ear. When the younger woman had gone, the crone looked at me. She stood up, slowly. "There is one more thing," she said. "I see a boy eating his meal standing up. My word, you're going to be sore. Come on, they're waiting."

She took my hand, and we hurried back to the marquee, where two angry parents stood, one smelling of carnival spirit, the other of righteous indignation. My father glared silently while my mother thanked the old crone for her trouble, and then reminded me of the strap hanging on the pantry wall.

As I was led from the marquee, I glanced back. That haunted look in the old crone's eyes … I would never forget it.

A silent car ride later, I lay across the kitchen table, my mother handing the strap to my father with all the ceremony of an early birthday present, before holding me down.

I let my imagination take me on its wings, away from that place. I thought of the haunted stare, filling my mind's eye with it, while in another world I heard the distant, dark voice of my father: "I'll teach you to scare us like that, going off with strangers, messing with witches. I'll beat the devil out of you."

I fought against the urge to scream, even as the fire consumed me, until at last I heard my mother shouting, "That's enough."

I lay face down on my bed through the long and sleepless night, thinking of long journeys and magicians in far off lands.

Something had opened.

In a few days the pain had lifted, yet the memory of the old crone's words stayed with me. And when the moment of epiphany finally came, twenty-five years later, thousands of miles from home, boiling up from the desert floor like a scalding mirage beneath a murderous sun, it brought with it the tears that I refused to let fall on that long ago August afternoon ...

CHAPTER
ONE
1994

It was a Sunday night. Kate had spent the week playing Lady Macbeth at the Victoria Theatre, and we decided to waste her night off on some mindless entertainment. The Castle View was showing the latest Hollywood offering starring Hal Tweedie. *Which Way's Hollywood?* The posters were calling it a postmodern comedy, though I didn't hear anybody in the cinema doing much laughing.

There couldn't have been far to go in the film, when Diana Mortis-Mayhew, naked and breathless, leant across the bed, taking hold of Tweedie and breathing hard into his ear.

"Which way's Hollywood, sucker?"

Kate's hand snatched out of mine.

"What is it?" I said.

Kate's expression was blank. She was trembling.

"Are you alright?"

The tremor was subsiding, the blankness lifting. All the life that had drained out of her a moment before was seeping back.

"Hey," she said. "Isn't this the best film you've ever seen?"

People were turning around, and no doubt wondering what movie we were watching.

"Okay," she said, "I give in. It's shit. Fancy a walk?"

It was an hour back to the rented box we called home. Kate lampooned the film all the way, dancing me through the streets. I don't believe that either of us had a thought for the lashing rain. I never laughed so much. We went to bed soaking wet, eventually falling asleep in each other's arms. The next thing I remember was the light from the streetlamps breaking through the thin curtains in our room. Kate was sitting upright, sobbing, a pillow covering her face, as though she was trying not to wake me. I switched on the sidelight. "Hey, the film wasn't *that* bad."

I reached for her hand. She was trembling again.

"What's happening?" she said.

"You've been dreaming. I'll make a drink."

I made to let go of her hand, and she gripped me tightly. "No," she said. "Don't leave me."

"Kate, what is it?"

I held her, rocking her like I was comforting a frightened child. Her beautiful chestnut hair was sticking to my face, and the sweat was running off her. "I don't want to go there," she said.

"Where don't you want to go?"

I wondered if she was still asleep.

"He's too strong for me," she said.

"It's okay," I said. "Nobody's going to hurt you."

We sat up all night, Kate crying uncontrollably for most of it. I suggested calling the emergency doctor, or taking her to A and E, but she wouldn't hear of it.

The morning took forever to arrive, and when it came it offered little respite. Later in the day she slept. But the following night brought more of the same.

After the second night she agreed to see her doctor, for what good it did. A week turned into a month, and the GP filled up our medicine cabinet and did a lot of blowing out his cheeks and looking baffled. He was a founding member of the 'take three of these, four of those, a spoonful of this and a shot of that' school of medicine, and soon we had a box on top of the medicine cabinet and then that was full, too.

I went to see him again, on Kate's behalf, not telling her what I was doing. She never would have allowed it.

"Ah, Mr. Tolle," he said, when I finally got in to see him. "And what can I do for you *today?*"

"I'm concerned about my wife," I told him.

"Concerned? In what way?"

"She's not getting any better. She needs to see someone."

"Is that right, Mr. Tolle? And who do you suggest that she *sees?*"

"She needs a specialist?"

"I see. A specialist in what, though?"

I could feel my blood beginning to warm, my fists curling hard and tight.

"Why do you think that your wife needs to see somebody else, Mr. Tolle?"

"You don't seem willing to do anything."

"And what would you like me to do, exactly?"

He sighed heavily and reached for his prescription pad. "I'm going to try her with some different medication, though in my considered opinion patience is the best medicine. As I have said, *repeatedly*, this temporary aberration will make its exit as quickly as it made its entrance. Bad dreams rarely prove fatal, in my experience." He tapped the side of his face. "They're only in your head, you know."

I wanted to smack the smugness out of him. But that wasn't my style, not then, at least.

"So you won't make a referral?" I said.

"Did you have anyone particular in mind, Mr. Tolle?"

I slammed the door behind me on the way out.

It wasn't only the nightmares. She was experiencing chronic pain, head to toe. She said it felt like her bones were on fire. She couldn't work, and I gave up my job at the pub and stayed at home with her. More pills, more medicine, some with *my* name on it.

Her illness, which had sprung out of nowhere, as likely most illnesses do, was defeating us and no one seemed to be taking any notice. We were screaming through one-way glass, the world not listening, merely walking by minding its own business.

I wrote a letter to an agony column in some thin magazine from the quack's waiting room. They published and wrote back, suggesting that I write to my M.P. I did so, and copied in the local papers for good measure.

Things started to happen after that: an examination by a consultant, a second opinion followed by third and fourth opinions, growing local interest, tests, further tests, and more opinions. Round and round it went, but no more casual dismissals, no more shrugs of the shoulders and professional sarcasm.

There was talk of a wonder drug and our guttering hopes ignited. The drug failed and our hopes plunged back into the dark hole. A second wonder drug was mentioned, and then a third. The third was a sure-fire miracle, according to the finest medical brains in the UK. We kept our hopes at a nervous flicker, rode the grim wind, and steeled ourselves for a fourth wonder drug, which never materialised.

Kate's pains deepened; her dreams blackened. She tried to hide the worst from me, but I could see the suffering in her eyes every day and night.

The case was beginning to cause a stir, the buzz starting in the medical journals, apparently, and eventually interest from the media followed.

Mystery illness baffles the medical world.
Kate Tolle deteriorates as wonder drugs fail.
Irish actress willing to travel in last desperate bid for life.

Nobody actually said that Kate's condition was terminal, because nobody actually seemed to know what her condition was. But our brief news-worthiness had won the public's heart and tugged at purse as well as heart strings. There was money donated from the pockets of ordinary men and women throughout the land, and enough of it to put us on a flight to almost anywhere in the world. We threw our savings into the pot, meagre as they were, and took out loans. Our local paper boasted that nothing would stand in the way of Kate Tolle finding the planet's specialist in whatever her condition turned out to be.

And that was the problem: no one had a blind clue what we were dealing with.

The money continued to roll in. I was shocked by the generosity of strangers. There was talk of travelling to the States, with some rising-star medic in New York keen to have a stab, and queues of medical scientists forming in Boston. New Zealand was waving a few hands too, and there were calls from Tokyo, Sydney and Perth. I wondered if the deadlock would be broken by some esteemed member of the medical fraternity putting on a blind-fold and sticking a pin into a map of the world.

Then an anonymous letter arrived on the desk of the fund secretary. The letter was from California. The writer had been on business in England and heard about our 'situation'. Back in the States he'd made enquiries on our behalf. It transpired that a private medical practitioner in San Francisco, a curiosity going by the name of Professor Buck-Bradbury, was interested in offering his services.

Accompanying the letter was a donation. Our generous benefactor suggested that it was a pleasure and a duty to ensure that we got the best of everything the States could offer, and that the enclosed donation could be seen as a personal contribution to Anglo-American relations. The donation more than doubled the already substantial fund.

Enquiries were made into the practices of Professor Buck-Bradbury, and by all accounts he was something of a living legend on the West Coast. His specialism was the obscure, 'the more bizarre the better', according to one testimonial. Rare psychological conditions were his bread and butter, so to speak, though it didn't sound to me like he was charging bread and butter prices.

The man was deemed a maverick, shunned by mainstream practitioners, and the subject of at least a dozen campaigns to close him down. But people were paying fortunes to visit him, and he seemed our only option if we weren't to spend the rest of Kate's life waiting for the medical world to resolve its differences of opinion.

The aura of mystery surrounding Professor Buck-Bradbury captured the imagination of the press, which gave its unequivocal support:

Kate Tolle's last chance lies in the hands of Californian Witch-doctor.

Kate didn't want to go. On the evening before we were due to fly she said, "I'm too tired for this, tired of tests, of being a lab rat, of having my hopes raised. I can reconcile myself to anything, even dying, come to that. But hope turns the screw. It gives and then it takes away."

I felt the same, though I wouldn't admit it. "You can't talk like that," I said.

"It's the truth, Ben, and you know it."

"Hope's all we have."

"Is it? I thought we still had each other."

"That's not what I -"

She smiled that sunburst smile of hers that could light the darkest corners of the world. Like I was the one who was dying ... and perhaps I was. Without her I was walking dust in the shape of a man.

Insecure old Ben, who met and married the most beautiful girl in all the world and never felt worthy. The imposter, waiting to be found out before it all came crashing down.

"Do it for me," I said. "I know you're tired of all the bullshit. But - you can sleep on the plane."

She took a swipe at me. "And what about the money?"

"The money's nothing," I said.

"Oh, really?"

"One day I'll pay it back."

"And how will you do that?"

"I'll think of something," I said. "But somehow, I'll pay it back."

It wasn't the last time that I failed to tell her the truth.

We headed for San Francisco, our hopes resting with an American enigma paid for by the British public and by an anonymous benefactor from California. At the airport we were treated like minor celebrities. I had to remind myself that I was no longer a child, and this wasn't some prize-draw trip to Disneyland. Nobody expected us to be gone for more than a few days.

We never saw England again.

CHAPTER
TWO

THE HOTEL WAS LIKE NOTHING I'D SEEN BEFORE, LET ALONE SPENT TIME in. It was the kind of place I imagined would be frequented by pop stars and international jewel thieves. Kate wasn't impressed as we walked into the chandeliered lobby.

"Remind me," she said. "Who's paying for this?"

"Some rich American, mainly, and I dare say he can afford it."

It wasn't the most diplomatic statement that I had ever made, and I regretted it as soon I'd said it. I vainly hoped that Kate might let it go, putting it down to the long and difficult journey.

"I don't care how rich he is, or she is, not to mention all of the other donations. I don't like wasting other people's money."

"Wasting? We've come here to find a cure -"

"And extravagance is part of the cure?"

She was exhausted from travelling. It wasn't the time to start an argument, and certainly not one about money. We checked in and I told her that things would look different in the morning.

Eyeing our sumptuous surroundings, she gave me a look. "You mean that this five star fantasy will turn into a no star B and B after a good night's sleep?"

"It is a bit grand, I'll grant you."

"*A bit grand*? I overheard the manager telling Madonna that they could offer her easy terms!"

"Let's just go up to our room and get some rest," I said.

We went up in the lift and walked the short, heavily carpeted corridor to our room.

"Here's home," I said, opening the door and trying to raise the mood.

"There must be some mistake," she said, casting an eye around the bedroom before we'd even closed the door behind us. "I mean, look at the place. We should have checked this out. We can't stay here." She looked about ready to drop. "You could lose your underwear in this carpet."

"Better use the hangers, then. You need to rest now."

She flopped on the bed. I was starting to make my promise again, about paying all of the money back one day. I wasn't convincing anybody, but Kate was too tired to argue. She was asleep before I even had chance to kiss her goodnight.

I got my head down and awoke to the sound of screaming.

I had been dreaming about money; walking through rooms piled high with wads of the stuff, room after room and then out into huge gardens, breathing in the clean, fresh air before the clouds darkened and the coins began to pelt down on us.

It was the dead of night, and I couldn't wake her. The people in the adjoining rooms probably thought that we were rich and artistically temperamental. There was nothing I could do but be there with her, telling her everything would be alright and trying to believe it myself.

I felt the loneliness sweep through me. Suddenly it felt like a long way from home.

As I sat on the bed, my impotence raging, I wondered who had made the arrangements. I understood that it had been the American, the anonymous benefactor. It had all happened so fast, and nothing had been checked out, at least not by Kate or me. There were a lot of things that we should have checked out but didn't.

I thought back over our arrival in San Francisco, the driver of the cab waiting to collect us from the airport, informing us that there had been a change in the arrangements. We had been due to stay at the Indigo, a budget motel providing us with everything that we needed, but due to unforeseen circumstances we had been upgraded, and would now be staying at the International, off Union Square.

The detail of the change in plan hadn't registered with me. We had arrived in a vast, busy city, in a country, a continent, unfamiliar to us; tired, nervous, excited, too. It wasn't until we pulled up at the hotel that we began wondering if there hadn't been some mistake.

But there was no mistake. They were expecting us. Mr and Mrs. Tolle from the UK: *glad to have you staying with us.*

Why would somebody pay for us to stay in a place like the International? I could get my head around some kind, benevolent soul, touched by our story paying for Kate to see a specialist who might be able to help where nobody else had. There were people like that in the world, thank God. But why the unnecessary expense of a top hotel in a prime location? That didn't make sense.

Eventually, Kate began to settle, and the night passed. In the morning a car came to take us to our appointment with Professor Buck-Bradbury.

He was not what we expected, whatever that was. Maybe we had anticipated the Living God that the imposing entrance to his clinic, complete with Athenian sculptures portraying the multi-tudinous sins of mankind, suggested. The reality came packaged in a long, thoughtful beard that he enjoyed scratching; a distin-guished moustache that bore little relation to the hair that made up his beard; intelligent spectacles that magnified tiny peevish eyes; lank hair that surrounded a stupendous bald-patch, and a wrist-watch that looked to me to be worth more than I'd seen in a lifetime. He looked every inch a man in disguise.

His clinic was out of town, housed in its own private valley, and boasting no visible neighbours in any direction. It was techni-cally possible to take a residential option, but only if your assets were of aristocratic proportions. Even our mysterious benefactor hadn't seen fit to extend hospitality that far. It was a blessing, as it turned out.

Buck-Bradbury spent the day asking questions, carrying out tests, examining samples; poking here, prodding there, stopping to scratch at his beard and roll the ends of his whiskers, then a little more blood from here, a spot more tissue from there. He said he believed in a *holistic* approach.

When he'd finished for the day we returned to the hotel. He wanted us back in the morning, but Kate told me that she'd had enough.

"He's just going through the motions," she said as we arrived back at the International. "He's waiting for more lucrative subjects before washing his hands and sending us home."

"How can you know that?"

"I don't trust him."

"You've got to give him a chance," I said. "He comes highly recommended."

"But by who?"

"By the person who's paying."

"I don't like it, Ben. We shouldn't have been rushed into this. He hasn't told me what's wrong. If he's that wonderful, what's taking him so long?"

"Some things take time -"

"And some people like a blank cheque. I think he's spinning it out."

"One more day," I said. "Give the man a fighting chance."

She agreed, reluctantly, telling me that she was too exhausted to argue anymore and wanted to go to sleep. I lay next to her, waiting for the screams, and holding her when they came.

The next day she was in terrible pain, though determined to honour her promise, and giving Professor Buck-Bradbury his final opportunity to prove his worth. Looking back, she was doing it for me. I don't think that she believed in him for a second.

We made the trip back to the valley, where Buck-Bradbury spent the morning in what appeared to be his typical style, asking endless questions, conducting a further battery of tests, devoutly scratching his beard and fiddling with his moustache.

Around mid-day Kate asked him straight out. "What's wrong with me?"

"Patience," he replied.

"I'm sick of these games," she said. "I want answers."

"You think we're playing games here?"

"Yes, frankly."

"And why would I waste my valuable time playing games, Mrs Tolle?"

"Maybe you're fond of the contents of other people's wallets."

"And do I look, to you, like the kind of person who would stoop to stealing loose change?"

"You call what you charge *loose change*?"

"It's all relative."

"Unless you can tell me what's wrong with me, and what exactly you intend to do about it, we're leaving."

Professor Buck-Bradbury wouldn't hear of such a thing. He still had to try this and have a go at that. "I'm just warming up," he said, laughing. But Kate wasn't laughing and neither was I. He asked me to step into his office for a few minutes, *alone*. And that's when I saw his true colours.

It wasn't just the money, it was the thrill of the chase. He was like a lunatic gunfighter, twirling hypodermics instead of six-shooters, hard on the heels of some big-shot, son-of-a-gun disease that would rue the day it ever set foot in *his* town. It wasn't enough for him to have Kate as his experimental rat, he wanted to start cutting into me. Mind games, it turned out, were another of his specialities.

His office felt like a courtroom. "I'll come to the point, Mr Tolle. I accuse you of colluding with your wife's desire to take on the role of the sick and, to put it bluntly, *dying* patient. If you don't persuade her to stay and take more tests, then I'm afraid that you amount to nothing more than her executioner. I question your marriage Mr Tolle and I question your commitment to your wife. Damn you, I question your love for that poor lady."

I was speechless. This three-headed monster - doctor, psychiatrist and prosecutor - took me to the brink of bloodshed and then brought out the Wild Turkey and the President cigars.

"Drink? Smoke?"

Being too British for my own good I thanked him all the same. "Do you have a diagnosis?"

If the man had any sensitivity to body language, my clenched face was telling him to answer me quickly. He merely shook his head, filled a glass, and lit a cigar. "Sure you won't join me?"

I turned to leave.

"You fucking murderer," he shouted.

I hesitated in the doorway. But only for a second.

On the way out we saw the new arrivals, some of them loaded with luggage, clearly taking the residential option. They were welcome to it, and to every ounce of pity. What did Buck-Bradbury need with the likes of us when the high rollers were moving in?

We were taken back to the International to rest up before the flight home the next day. Tacitly, Kate and I shared a sense of relief as we held hands in the back of the cab. Yet the relief was mingled with sorrow and fear. We still didn't know what was wrong with her, or what sufferings lay ahead. Our hope of a miracle had amounted to nothing, and it might have been our last chance.

Kate was deadly tired by the time we got to the hotel. Trying to hold the pain at bay was sapping what reserves she had left. I helped her into bed and made her as comfortable as I could. She was burning up. We hadn't brought any medication with us because none of it made the slightest difference. Her temperatures seemed to come and go as they pleased.

I watched over her as she at last began to relax, drifting slowly into sleep, her eyelids starting to fidget hiding a soul loaded with dreams. I prayed that there might be some good ones waiting for her, and wondered what her thoughts might be at that moment.

If she was simply glad to be going home, relieved to have all the poking and prodding done with.

I felt the fear grow. Was this apparent respite the calmness of acceptance? Was the fighting almost over - the beginning of the end?

How could I know that?

Watching as she slept I became transfixed by the peace radiating from her. I had seen nothing like it since her illness had started, and it was beautiful to witness. Was my wife coming back? Could this, after all, be the turning point? Her illness about to disappear as rapidly and mysteriously as it had appeared: a miracle?

The hope rose in me, I couldn't hold it back. But as I watched her, my brief euphoria was already fading, and I started to edge out into the dark waters of grief, convinced once again that this was the peace that comes before death itself.

She looked so content. How could I sustain the fear of losing her?

Maybe that was my one moment of bravery; my one true display of altruism: that I had it in me, albeit fleetingly, to grant her an eternity of peace without caring that I would be left alone in the world to face what remained of life.

I watched in fascination, her beautiful face resting in the arms of something hidden and unknown to me, beyond me, and I allowed the notion to take hold that perhaps Professor Buck-Bradbury had cured her after all. That he might appear at the door, pointing a fresh cigar at us and ridiculing our lack of faith.

The notion didn't last.

As I watched her sleeping that fateful night, the sound of sirens startled me. Something was happening down on the street outside our hotel.

At first I kept my eyes on Kate, not wanting to miss a second of her tranquility. Then slowly I started to curse the distractions outside, knowing that curiosity was close to shattering my faithfulness.

The noises were getting louder. I went over to the window, the deepest part of my vigil over as I tried to make sense of some tragedy that wasn't mine.

Down in the street below there was a confusion of people, and the flashing lights of the cavalry. I turned back to Kate, dreading what changes might have taken place, dreading that I had missed the last moments of her precious peace.

She hadn't changed, though. If anything her serenity had blossomed. My superstition was broken. It wasn't my faith or faithfulness that was holding her remission. A single blink or turn of my head would not bring about the return of her devils.

I wanted a beer. I wanted to celebrate. But I hadn't it in me to wake her, and shatter what she had and might never have again.

The loneliness was bearing down on me, and I cracked, like the weak man that I am. Slipping out through the door I headed for the bar.

The hotel lobby was buzzing. Whatever had happened outside the hotel had filled the bar with a repulsed excitement. From what I could make out an old lady's throat had been slashed. A vehicle had driven past the entrance to the hotel and the body had been thrown out, landing on the steps, dead on arrival.

That was the core of the story, though the details varied. There was talk of a brutal sex attack, but the specifics were not forthcoming.

I made it to the bar. Behind me, and to right and left, the speculation blended into a quagmire of obscenity.

What was I doing here? Looking for a beer, eager to know the grisly facts about some tragedy that didn't concern me?

And all the while my wife was lying five floors above me, and alone.

I turned to leave, and found myself pinned to the bar by the weight of the crowd. The panic was rising: *she could be awake already, alone in a room in a strange city, the sound of urgent sirens screaming out of the night; in pain, frightened.*

The barman's eye caught mine and I lowered my gaze. Then a voice cut through the crowd.

"This man needs a drink." A hand reached up from out of the crowd and touched my shoulder. "Sometimes a beer's the only thing to do."

The crowd parted and I looked down on a face smiling back up at me. It belonged to a key-ring of a man looking up at a giant.

I didn't move, couldn't. The stranger's eyes pierced me, nailing me to the spot. A drink was in my hand. The crowd had dispersed like the parting of a sea.

"I'm giving you permission to drink your beer," said the tiny man in front of me. "Whatever you've got to do, you'll do it better for giving yourself five minutes. So what do you say - you going to trust me?"

His voice was as calm, as untroubled, as an ocean sunrise. I felt the knot of tension loosen. He watched me finish my drink.

"Sounds like a bad business here tonight, though it doesn't do to believe everything you hear." His eyes glinted, assured of the wisdom behind them; brimming, it seemed to me, with forbidden knowledge. "Sometimes," he said, "it turns out that the truth is far worse."

"Can I get you a drink?" I asked him.

"What's your name?" he said, ignoring my question.

I told him.

"So, Ben, what are your favourite cards in the tarot?"

I shrugged my shoulders. I knew nothing about tarot cards and I didn't care to know. My father's strap had cured me of any curiosity in that direction a long time ago.

"I'll tell you mine, Ben," he said: "*The Magician and the Fool.*"

Again he reached up and placed his hand on my shoulder. "By the way, the name's Merle," he said. "And don't worry ... she's going to be fine."

THREE

THE DAY I GOT MARRIED WAS THE HAPPIEST AND SADDEST OF MY LIFE. ON that day I had everything. Yet such consuming joy cut the moorings and took me up to a lonely cloud, making our happiness seem like a fragile and exposed thing, at least to me.

No family came to our wedding and no friends either. My parents were dead and I was an only child. Friends had come and gone; I was careless with them, not knowing their value, and scared of letting anybody know how desperate I was for friendship. I was my father's son.

Kate was also an only child, and a happy one, from what she told me. Born in Ireland, her parents had moved to Manchester for business reasons, though always vowing to return to their beloved homeland at the earliest opportunity. The whims of business, however, dictated otherwise, and they bore with bitterness the indignity of watching their daughter grow into an English rose with an accent that betrayed them. They took her wish to marry an Englishman as the final insult, and once the die was cast they refused to have anything further to do with us.

And so their only offspring ceased to exist, and we stood at the altar without any of her clan to witness our happiness. The absence of family was something that Kate couldn't bear her friends to witness, and so none were invited. Our marriage cost me nothing; it cost her everything.

She insisted that we were married in church. I hadn't been inside a church in years, and then only at funerals. Churches frightened me, threatening to reveal something about me that I'd kept hidden for a long time. A belief, deep down and seemingly indestructible: that my soul was riddled with darkness. That the face I showed to the world was not that of the real Ben Tolle, but merely a mask hiding the real me: the monster lurking beneath the skin.

So, a church wedding would not have been my choice, not in a million years. It was what Kate wanted, though, and that was good enough for me.

The priest, Father Brian, was clearly a man of compassion. His warm words filled up the empty spaces of that huge church building. I grew fond of him during our pre-nuptial preparations, though in all honesty I didn't understand half of what he was saying at the time.

I remember being puzzled by his emphasis on the redeeming power of forgiveness. He'd brought up the subject during an early meeting at the flat that we were renting. We were going over arrangements, and Kate was making a round of drinks in the kitchen when Father Brian asked about numbers. Without meaning to I'd given him an abrupt account of the state of play in the family department, and he'd picked up on the burden that I was apparently carrying.

"You cloak your anger well, Ben. Maybe you've had a lot of practice. One day you're going to have to let it go."

In our first meetings I found it difficult looking him in the eye, imagining that he could see through me, exposing what lay beneath the light. I felt like that about a lot of people, particularly those in positions of authority. But I don't believe that I ever felt it more keenly than when I looked into the eyes of Father Brian.

As the years passed I often thought about him. I meant to look him up, go back and talk with him. *Anger and forgiveness: a beginners' guide for dummies.*

It never happened. I never did go back. My faith had deserted me a long time already, if it had ever existed in the first place. Faith, or the concept of it, conjured memories of my mother's religious mania; her developing madness throughout my childhood. My father had drunk himself to death for the lack of it, and for the pretence of it. Faith, when I gave the notion headspace at all, was something as cold and lifeless as the grave; dead, buried and beyond resurrection. Father Brian had opened a door; had loosened the coffin lid.

I stood in the elevator, sick to my stomach. I shouldn't have left Kate alone. What if she had woken up and panicked; tried to get out of bed, fallen? Would I find her lying on the floor, a fractured skull, a pool of blood, her last thoughts wasted on a husband who loved her enough to let her die alone in a strange bed in a foreign land while he went down to get a drink?

When the elevator doors opened I expected to see her being carried away on a stretcher, her bearers eyeing me with contempt.

The corridor was empty.

I walked its short, endless length and felt the walls closing in.

Stopping outside our door I listened. All I could hear was silence. My fingers wrapped around the gold-plated doorknob, and I breathed so deeply that I thought I would empty the corridor of air.

Turning the heavy doorknob I went inside.

Kate was sitting up, and I saw the most wonderful smile slowly fade from her face. In the days that lay ahead I would come to remember that smile as the death of summer. But inside the moment, I was so taken with my own confusion that I hadn't even taken stock of the fact that summer had returned at all.

"What is it?" she said. "You look scared to death."

I sat down on the bed. "I'm sorry," I said. "I went down to the bar."

"So, where's *my* drink?" she said, the beautiful smile ousting her frown, telling me, if I would open my eyes, that something miraculous was taking place right in front of me.

"You're sitting up," I said. "You're awake."

She clapped her hands. "I'm thirsty, too."

An image of the strange little man in the bar flashed through my head.

"How are you feeling?" I said.

"Best sleep I've had in months. I had some dreams, though. I'll tell you over a drink, if there's one going."

I poured some coffee from the dispenser.

In contrast to the savage nightmares of recent weeks, Kate's latest dreams sounded like the lifting of a curse. She had returned to the haunts of her childhood, the magical holidays in Ireland which her parents planned for all year long.

"I was there, Ben. I could see it and touch it. I could hear the laughter. God, how we used to laugh! Even my parents laughed in those days. They would troop back to England with tears in their eyes, vowing that next year they would stay forever."

It wasn't the first time that she'd told me about those holidays, but never had it sounded so fresh and vivid, so *alive*.

She was bringing it to life, talking as though she had just stepped off the boat, back from some impossible journey into the past. She told me how her dreams had moved from childhood into womanhood, reliving her apprenticeship as an actress with the Court Jesters, meeting me as I was starting my own apprentice-ship as temporary barman at the boozer next door to the theatre.

"It was like – you're going to laugh at this and slap my face, I know – but it was like I was being taken on a guided tour of my life. It was weird, but not the least bit scary. If anything, it was sort of reassuring. I woke up feeling like we were coming out of a cave into fresh sunlight."

I thought again of the little man in the bar.

By the way, the name's Merle ... and don't worry, she's going to be fine.

I thought of mentioning the guy to Kate, and then decided against it. She might assume that I'd found some evangelical fruit-cake who was working the tourist trade. Or that I'd stuffed down ten beers instead of one.

"Is there something the matter?" she asked. "You've gone very quiet."

"I was thinking."

"A penny for them?"

The name's Merle ... and don't worry, she's going to be fine.

"Maybe," I said, "if we stayed a couple more days ..."

"What's that?" asked Kate, looking at me oddly.

I needed to see the little man again. Ask him some questions. I just didn't know how to articulate the need to my wife.

"I think we should make hay while the sun shines," Kate said, tearing me from my thoughts.

I looked at her, and thought I caught a twinkle in her eye. "You mean you're feeling well enough for ... *that*?"

The laughter erupted out of her. "Oh, Ben," she said, squeezing my arm. "I'm sorry, I'm afraid you'll have to be patient. Soon, though." She squeezed me again, and I felt the current of electricity shoot to all the old familiar places. "I think we should head home," she said, "while I'm feeling well enough to travel. If we can get a flight early tomorrow, we should take it."

"Don't you think you're rushing things," I said. "It's a long flight. You need a few more days. We're comfortable here."

"Comfort bought by other people's money, Ben."

"Don't you think I'd spend my own if I had any?"

"What is it, what's troubling you?"

"I'm thinking about the future," I said.

"And ..?"

"I'm thinking what people will say when they find out that the great Buck-shit-face-Bradbury was only after their money."

She didn't appear convinced. "What's really on your mind, Ben?"

Lying to Kate was as difficult as arguing with her. A few half-baked untruths scrambled through my head, but she would have seen through them in seconds flat and we would have been through the door, heading for the airport. I let honesty rule the day. A kind of honesty, anyway; the best that I had to offer at short notice. It didn't involve telling Kate about the man in the bar, though I did at least shut my brain down and let my heart speak for once. It was the last sensible thing that I did for a long time, though in terms of consequences it was the worst thing I *ever* did, my sincerity closing off our escape route and setting in motion all that was to follow.

"Will you trust me?" I said.

"Of course, why wouldn't I?"

"Will you trust me about something that I can't explain to you?"

"Go on ..."

"I want us to stay one more night. Please, don't shoot me down. I know you feel bad about the money. I'll sort that out, somehow ..."

Her eyes narrowed. "It's not like you to be so melodramatic. Have you been watching American television? I warned you, it's no good for you."

She ran her fingers through the beads of sweat building on my forehead. "Are you alright?"

"I will be," I said, "if you'll trust me."

She frowned, and I prepared myself for the cross-examination.

"Okay," she said. "I can't stand seeing a grown man beg. One more night, if it's so important to you, but then we're going home, that's the deal."

I kissed her, and then flopped back on the bed.

"The beer in this place must be something special," she said.

Later that evening Kate drifted into a peaceful sleep, and I slipped back down to the bar. The place was busy but there was no sign of Merle.

I made a few enquiries. Nobody knew who I was talking about. I had a feeling that he would turn up, though, and so I ordered myself a drink, taking it over to the far side of the bar, where I found a discarded copy of the local paper.

The front page was shocking. I'd forgotten about the old lady, and here she was, barely cold, and already featured in the late edition.

The police department was urgently requesting anyone with information to come forward. There were details given, and they were not pleasant. The poor old soul wasn't complete when they checked her over: heart, lungs, liver and kidneys missing. There was some nut out there on the loose.

I put the paper down, drank up my beer and decided to check on Kate.

As I stood up, the man who held the keys to our future came striding into the bar. He looked even smaller and skinnier than I remembered, and he was dressed in a plain white suit with expensive leather shoes and a wide brimmed black hat to match them. He was wearing a bow tie that mirrored the red rose in his buttonhole, and his face lit up into a ferocious smile.

"Can I get you another, my friend?" he asked, pointing to my empty glass.

"That would be great," I said. "I'll just nip to the toilet, I mean rest-room, I -"

"Toilet's fine," he smiled, "Beer - or should that be *two fingers of red-eye* now that you're in the *good ole U.S of A?*"

I practically ran to the elevator.

When I got back to the room Kate was still sleeping. I shook her gently, repeating her name until she stirred. "What is it?" she said, still coming round. "What's wrong?"

"Get dressed," I said, "there's someone I want you to meet."

"What time is it?"

"We won't stay long, one drink."

She switched the sidelight on, and rubbed at her eyes. "Look, Ben, if you want to stay in the bar and have another drink, that's okay. You're in San Francisco. We'll probably never come this way again, so go and enjoy yourself and tell me about it in the morning."

"I want you to meet this guy."

"I'm tired, Ben."

She switched out the light. "Go and have some fun with your new friend. You deserve it."

I kissed her in the darkness, waited for a few moments as she folded back into sleep, and then I headed back to the bar.

There were a couple of untouched drinks waiting on the table; a beer and a mineral water stacked up with ice. I sat down, nursing my beer, too many things running through my head and nothing coming out of my mouth. Merle seemed intrigued by the spectacle of nervous confusion sitting before him, amused by the way my hands played with my glass, and the way my eyes moved emptily around the bar, occasionally catching his strong gaze.

He never prompted me, and he showed not the slightest sign of impatience. I bullied my imagination to come up with something to say. And the harder I thought the tighter my lips pressed together.

But he wasn't going anywhere. His comfort appeared bottomless.

The Magician and his Fool.

The cards in the tarot.

I read a story once, about a young man who fell under the influence of a con man. The young man was looking for a guide, and looking in all the wrong places. He had no confidence in himself, and he was vulnerable to being exploited. Terminally nervous around silence, he would fill it, wasting words and time, preferring to give away secrets lodged deep in the heart than suffer the traumas of stillness. And all the while the con man would sit and watch, and listen, swimming in silence, basking in it, above it all, circling, watching, *waiting*.

Was Merle looking to exploit me? Biding his time until I was ripe for the picking? I didn't think so. There was something about him ... I was willing to risk it.

The newspaper caught my eye again and I seized on the idea before I'd thought it through. I had to say something.

"Strange case," I said. "The old lady, I mean. There are some seriously sick people ..."

He smiled, as though charmed by my conversational turn. "That's a case the police will never solve, my friend," he said. "And you want to know why?"

I wasn't sure that I did. On the other hand, I was desperate for knowledge. I wanted to know what *he* knew. "Why?" I said.

The faintest smile swept across his face, as though he had knocked on the door and I had opened it.

"Because," he said, "the police don't believe in magic."

I tried to conceal my confusion.

"She's getting stronger," he said.

"The old lady?" I asked, stupidly.

He didn't say anything. He didn't need to say anything.

I said, "How did you know ..?"

He held up a hand. "Listen: I told you that she would be okay. Have you forgotten that already, or didn't you believe me in the first place? Do you think I'm some crank who haunts bars, telling every stranger he meets that he will save the life of a loved one?"

My hand was shaking so badly that I could hardly keep the remains of my beer in the glass.

"So when can I meet her, Ben?"

My mouth moved but nothing came out of it.

"Maybe she's a little nervous of strangers. You're a long way from home, after all. And faith, it seems, has become an undervalued commodity in this cynical age."

I lifted the glass to my mouth somehow.

"It might help," he said, "if I tell you a little bit about myself. Another beer?"

He ordered some more drinks, and then he told me this:

"They found me under a bush on the remote banks of a wild river. You could say I was the American edition of Moses. The authorities couldn't trace my parents; I don't know how hard they tried. It was up north, in Oregon. The day they found me was the coldest in the record books for that part of the country. I was adopted, and in my first two years almost killed three times, though I couldn't say that my adoptive parents were much to blame, except for the fact that they never seemed to know where I was or what I was doing."

An edge came into his voice. It was sheathed but I could still feel the promise of past blood.

"Anyhow, first time was down to bee stings when I crawled into a hive. Guess I thought that some fresh honey on the table might sweeten their sour dispositions. Second time was when I got badly infected by a scratch from a wild cat, and I guess hygiene wasn't one of their strong points, either. Third time was a stray bullet from a hunter's gun that lodged in the barn door six inches above my head, the shot coming from nearly half a mile away - least that's the version I was told. Rest of my early childhood was pretty dull."

He took a sip of water and paused for a moment, as though deciding which course history should take.

"On my thirteenth birthday I met a man in the woods close to where they'd found me as a baby. He told me who my parents were, my real parents, and where I could find them. Told me I had been marked out for great things. He talked about initiation. Told me I had to enter the doorway and how. 'Kill your folks, son.' That's what he said. 'Do this and the world is your reward.' I listened, but I didn't obey. Left Oregon instead, didn't trust him, somehow.

"I left for nearly five years. I wandered out into the desert where I met some Indian folks, natives, and I told them my story.

"They listened carefully and then they explained that it had been a test. Told me I had Indian blood and that the stranger knew it and had tried to exorcise powerful spirits lying dormant inside me, using his feeble magic.

"The stranger wanted me to kill my real parents so that I would destroy my heritage and destiny, closing the door on all the great things that I'd been chosen to accomplish. I had passed the test by not succumbing to cheap temptation. My first reward was that I had at last found my people. Well, if that was the truth, it was more luck than judgment. Confusing for a boy of my tender age, wouldn't you say?"

Confusing for anybody of any age, I thought. I watched him lift his glass once again and take the lightest sip from his drink before continuing with his tale.

"Anyway, they told me that my natural parents had lost faith in the world, and that they had floated me down river in the belief that the white man could give me a better life. They did it out of love. And it would be better, they said, if I left my real folks to their faithless dreams. They'd already suffered enough, turning their backs on their own heritage and future. They would never find rest, and they could never equip me for what lay ahead.

"Then they showed me things, stuff you wouldn't believe - not yet, at least. And after five years they pointed me back to Oregon, telling me it was time to come of age: 'Time to become a man.'

"Well, I'd learnt every kind of magic from those desert people, and I've loved the desert ever since. It's where I belong and I can never stay away from it too long. But there was destiny waiting back in those Oregon woods. My rite of passage, you could say.

"So, this time when I met the stranger, I was prepared. My magic was a thousand times stronger than his. He was awe-struck by what I'd learnt; couldn't fathom the changes in me. I told him it was his turn to face the test, and I pointed him like a gun at the home of my adoptive parents and I watched him act like a wolf.

"And with the blood still wet on his face ... I took him to the river and drowned him like a dog." Merle lifted his glass and took another sip. "It was a curious childhood, but it was a wonderful childhood's ending."

He pointed again to my glass. "Another drink, my friend?"

Lacking the power of speech, I nodded.

"You see, Ben. You start to loosen up once you get to know a person."

CHAPTER
FOUR

WHO IN GOD'S NAME WAS I SITTING WITH? THOUSANDS OF MILES FROM home, in a city where old ladies were hacked to pieces and left like raw meat on the steps of grand hotels, I was sitting with a man who thought he was the American Moses. Listening to a stranger telling me his confusing tale of how he had arranged the murder of his adoptive parents before drowning their killer with his own hands – what the hell was I supposed to make of it? Was this man unhinged, dangerous, or just having fun at the expense of some innocent abroad?

Why was he telling me these things - to impress, to endear him to me? Hardly, I concluded. Who, on hearing his crazy story, would not decide that the only sensible thing to do was to slip quietly away and let him pick some other fool to have his fun with?

Don't worry ... she's going to be fine.

He was coming back from the bar.

Maybe this was it: the pay off. My insides started melting, before congealing around the thought of him revealing the true cost of his time and effort in pouring out his life story. Or else him grinning, slapping my arm: *Just kidding - but if you could have seen your face!*

He sat down, placing a fresh beer in front of me, and sipping carefully at another glass of mineral water again stacked up with ice.

"Some story, eh, Ben? But let me set the record straight. I wouldn't want you getting the wrong idea about me. You see, contrary to what you may be thinking right now, I'm not some parenticidal psychopath graduated to luring innocent travellers to their deaths."

He took another sip, watching me carefully as he did so. Under the subtle yet intense pressure of his gaze, I lifted up my beer and took a hefty swig. As I set the glass back down on the mat, he said, "I'm a healer, is what I am, and I can smell sickness, Ben. I can smell her sickness on you. And that smell makes me angry. Because it ain't right that good people are cursed, while the evil ones among us never get more than a dose of the clap. There's so much injustice in this world that sometimes I swear that I don't know where to begin. And I don't know how we bear it. How do you bear it, Ben?"

I shook my head dumbly. I started to ask how he knew about my wife being ill, and about his promise that she would be *fine*. But with a hand he waved me down.

"I'll tell you how *I* bear it: I do something about it. I change things. I put some natural justice back into this upside down, inside out world. But there's always a price to be paid, and you can never get away from that. At the day's end the books have to balance."

This is it, I thought. *What all of this has been leading to.*

As though he had read my mind, he said, "Which isn't to say, my friend, that I'm about to announce the scam that you might believe all of this is really about. Nothing that I can offer will cost you a penny or a dime. But still, having said that … there is still a price to pay."

I took another drink of my beer, almost emptying the glass.

"Which is to say: if I make Kate well again - *and I will* - then someone else has it coming. Maybe someone more deserving, but someone. And that's the law, the whole of the law."

All of the time that he was talking, his eyes were picking over the people in the bar, as though he was looking for a suitable dumping ground for Kate's illness.

As he watched me finish my drink, he leaned forward. "Another week and she'll be as good as new, better, even."

When he leaned back in his chair I felt his weight leaving me. I looked sorrowfully down into my empty glass, believing in him and at the same time frightened.

"What is it, Ben?"

"I'm afraid that it's home tomorrow."

"Can't wait to get out of town?"

I shook my head. "Money."

"According to our local news, the generosity of the British public should have been more than a match for that money grabbing quack Buck-Bradbury."

I felt suddenly exposed, like a fish in a bowl of polished glass.

"Don't miss much, our news boys and girls," he said.

"They don't seem to."

"Sure as I am that the Buck would have skinned you pretty good, even that old vulture has limits, and particularly where press interest is involved. And after all, you didn't take the residential option, known by many a poor fool as the 'open-cheque route'. Like it or not, you guys are newspaper fodder on both sides of the Atlantic. The Buck wouldn't want people getting the wrong idea."

He seemed to know a lot about us. If Merle was targeting us for a scam, I had to set the record straight. Let him know that he was wasting his time.

"Our own money's gone," I said. "That is, what little we had. Kate feels bad about squandering funds given in good faith, and so do I, as a matter of fact. We don't want to take advantage of the people back home. Most of them are probably no better off than we are."

He raised his eyebrows, pushed out his bottom lip, and nodded.

"Admirable sentiments, I'm sure. But you call saving a life squandering? You have some peculiar ideas over on that little island of yours, and that's a fact. Anyway, I heard there was a benefactor. I heard some business man took an interest in your story and wanted to see you both well taken care of. So, what's with all the guilt? Some of these business guys over here are richer than the president. Listen to me, Ben: you can't go home yet."

"But -"

"You've seen signs of improvement, and you think it's over. Sorry to burst your bubble, but she's walking a tightrope, my friend, and she's only just started walking it. It'll take a good week before she reaches the other side. I hate to be blunt, but I tell you this much for nothing: if you leave now she'll be dead in a matter of days."

"How can you know that?" I said.

"I know it, believe me."

"What's wrong with her?"

Merle shook his head. "I'm a healer, not a doctor. I don't know what's wrong with your wife. But I do know how to cure her. You have to keep faith, that's all you can do. That and keep her here until she reaches the other side."

I caught a glimpse, maybe nothing more than a twitch in his eye, and in that moment it all seemed to fit together like a glorious fake. That he didn't know what was wrong with her - it didn't ring true. Out of desperation I'd let my heart outgun my brain and let the casualties mount high on both sides.

I felt the rage course through me. I'd heard enough and I stood up.

"Smell sickness, do you? I'd say it's money you can smell. Did Buck-Bradbury send you over to finish the job? Leave us alone, will you. We'd rather die together in civilisation."

I left the bar, energized by my little speech and wondering where it had come from. People spoke like that in the movies and in my own imaginary conversations, and occasionally even in the stories that I tried to write and that never got published. Merle had got under my skin, and opened up something deep down there.

Instead of heading for the elevator, I made for the stairs, needing to walk off some of my anger.

Before I'd even made it to the foot of the immense staircase I was already back-tracking, regretting my proud words and doubting my conclusions. After all, there was no getting away from the fact that he had anticipated Kate's recovery. Either he had known it was going to happen or else he had made it happen, and either way that seemed remarkable.

The world was full of strange phenomena which science couldn't explain. Even the Bible was stuffed with miracles, raising the dead, turning water into wine, loaves and fishes.

I stopped walking. It wasn't my unwillingness to believe in unknown forces that had provoked my anger; rather the way his eyes had leaked out something unintended when he told me that he didn't know what was wrong with Kate.

I stood at the foot of the staircase, wondering what to do. I couldn't leave it. He'd said that she would die in a week if we went home.

I started to walk up the staircase as two old ladies, plastered in gold and dripping with precious stones, passed by me. One was holding a copy of the late edition and I heard her say, "Only some stupid old fool getting her dessert, I guess." I watched them laugh their way towards the bar, and carried on up the stairs, all the time thinking that the road to heaven was certainly not paved with gold.

At the top of the staircase I stopped to let my piety reign for a few moments as I watched all the wealth coming and going about its privileged business. Looking from the shadows of the amazing chandelier above me to the dinner-suited ants scurrying below, I wondered again what we were doing in such a place, and who was really footing the bill. I cursed myself for not being more involved in the arrangements, leaving it to others; habits of a life-time. If Kate had been feeling more like her old self, she would have checked everything out herself, and I would have been content to let her. But she hadn't been up to it, and I hadn't stepped up to the mark.

Had the anonymous benefactor arranged this hotel? Did he own it? And why the last-minute change in arrangements?

The day had been too strange to be certain of anything. What or who could I trust? What part of myself could I rely on and how could I begin to talk this through with Kate? I couldn't take her home and watch her die when the promise of life had been given for the price of a few more days. Was one week of faith too much to ask?

That's when I felt the pressure of a hand on my shoulder. I knew who it was without turning around.

Merle placed an envelope into my pocket. "I've booked you both in for another week," he said, "paid in advance. You wouldn't have liked the Indigo rooms. The receipt's in there, along with a little spending cash. See you tomorrow night."

And with that he was gone.

I waited for a few moments before taking the envelope from my pocket. On the front was a message, handwritten:

To prove that everything in the States really is bigger - including the charity.

Along with the receipt for a further week's stay at the International, there was cash doubling what we'd been given in England, benefactor included.

In that moment it was decided: whatever happened, even if I had to tie Kate to the bed, we were staying put. Whatever the coming days held in store, we'd face it, together.

I'd always told her everything, partly because I was such a poor liar. But that wasn't the whole of it. I'd never wanted to sow the slightest doubts into our relationship. Losing Kate would be my death: it's what death and hell meant to me. Since we'd first met it had become, and had remained, the thing I feared most. Honesty had always been my policy, but honesty here was tantamount to an admission of insanity. Unpracticed in the art of deceit, how could I be convincing?

I looked at the money, the stuff of lies; one of the great motivators in mankind's quest for dishonesty. Perhaps if I held the money close to my heart, the perfect lies would ooze out of me like lines of poetry.

And maybe they wouldn't.

What kind of con man gave away that kind of money? What was there to hustle? The money I was holding in my hand was more than the pot, even before Buck-Bradbury and the hotel manager had taken their cuts. So where was the sting? There was no more money, and so Merle couldn't fail to make a loss - so how could he possibly be working a scam?

What was I missing?

The thoughts were circling, and I was staring blankly at the money, when a cough startled me. I turned to see an old gentleman, elegantly dressed, standing behind me. He had a pack of playing cards in his right hand. I saw him discreetly eye the money, which I hurriedly returned to my pocket. Then he eyed *me*.

"You look like you could use a little advice, son."

I tried to smile. "Maybe I could."

"Want to tell me about it?"

"I wouldn't know how to start," I said.

"Try the beginning. It's usually the best place to start, in my experience."

He looked so concerned that for a second I could have blurted it all out. I held myself back, letting the impulse pass.

"Is it stolen - the money?" I saw the cards move in his hand. "Or did you win it? Let me guess: your wife doesn't know you gamble. So why don't you just tell her you stole it?"

"It's not stolen," I said, not very convincingly. *But what if it was stolen?* "No," I said. "It's definitely not stolen."

"Then you *definitely* have nothing to worry about," he said, tipping his hat and making his way down the stairs.

With nothing to worry about I made my way back to the room.

"What time is it, Ben?"

Kate sounded drowsy, like she had just woken up.

"It's late," I whispered. "Go back to sleep."

"Have you had a good time?" She patted the bed. "Come and tell me about it."

"We're staying," I said.

"Staying? I don't understand."

"One week."

She sat up, switching on the side light. "Ben, we've been through this already."

I sat down on the bed. The money felt good tucked away next to my heart, out of sight. It brought with it a confidence that I wasn't used to.

"We're staying, one more week, and that's all there is to it."

She looked at me for so long without saying anything that I thought she must have been able to see the money through my clothes and that she was already busy counting it.

At last she said, "You're not the Ben Tolle who left this room earlier."

"I don't know what you're talking about. Look, how about tomorrow we -"

"Don't try to change the subject. There is no tomorrow, not here. We're going home."

"You already agreed to one more night."

"That was before you got greedy."

My hand twitched. I almost reached for the money and threw it on the bed. *Almost.*

Where had all of that new-found confidence gone so quickly? Could the presence of money only sustain it when you were born rich?

"Kate, trust me."

"God, Ben, how many times?"

"I wish I could explain."

"So do I. If you've something to tell me, you'd better tell me."

The words tumbled out.

"Merle's promised to pay."

A tense silence stretched out, and then snapped. "Merle?"

"He's promised to pay."

"Pay what? Who?"

"Pay for us to stay here until you're better."

"This is the guy you met in the bar?"

"Yes."

"And he's promised to pay for us to stay here, what, indefinitely?"

"Well, not quite."

"Runs a convalescence service, does he, this *Merle?* And doesn't mind paying Hotel International prices? What's going on?"

"One week, that's all."

"Let me get this straight. You meet a guy in a bar, and in no time he's offering to pay for us to stay the week in San Francisco, in a five-star hotel."

"When you put it like that."

"How do you want me to put it? Big drinker, is he?"

"He was sober, as a matter of fact."

"That's even more concerning. And why would he want us to stay another week? I'm glad that you've made a friend, but couldn't you drop each other the odd line from time to time? It would be a lot cheaper."

"I don't want to lose you, Kate."

Her expression softened and her eyes suddenly filled. "I think we *will* stay another night," she said. "I want to meet this guy. I want to find out what's so special about us that would make a stranger spend a fortune keeping us here in this extravagance."

I stood up, and walked over to the window. After a few moments I felt her hands resting across my shoulders, gently massaging them. "I don't want to sound ungrateful, Ben," she said. "I know you're doing what you think is right."

I wanted to take the money out of my pocket and start from the beginning. But a fool doesn't easily change his ways. And anyway, she would have done what I should have done, and questioned the deeper motive.

While she continued to work her fingers into all the tension I had stored up, my hand rested on the money hiding in my jacket pocket, gently stroking it.

"It's not very flattering, you know."

"What's that?" I said, startled out of my reverie.

I turned around and she was naked.

"Not very flattering you standing there with your head in the clouds, when there's business down here that needs taking care of. Come to bed, Ben."

"Are you ... sure?"

Her laughter was sublime, full of strength and vigour. "Yes, I'm quite sure. But don't keep asking. Nothing turns a girl off quicker."

On the bed I started to fumble at my clothes and then, hesitating, I reached over to switch out the light.

"Getting shy in your old age?" she said. "Has it been so long?"

But it wasn't my nakedness I was hiding.

Later, with Kate breathing peacefully beside me, I made myself a promise. In the morning I would tell her about the money. No more deception, no more secrets. It was time that I stepped out of my fool's costume.

I kissed her and she responded with a vague murmur.

CHAPTER

FIVE

I woke up with a change of heart. I decided that I wouldn't say anything about the money. There was nothing to be gained and everything to lose. Kate would demand I return it, and cancel the week's reservation for good measure. It wouldn't allay her suspicions, only serve to heighten them. The money was a gesture, Merle's way of proving that he could be trusted. That he wasn't out to fleece us.

Kate seemed stronger that morning, and we took a stroll before breakfast, out into the gentle San Francisco sunshine. We hadn't gone more than a few hundred yards when we came across a small second-hand bookstore: *Scriveners*.

"Should we?" she asked me.

"Be rude not to," I said.

She loved books, hunting down obscure editions and bargains. I enjoyed the easy atmospheres that pervaded the best bookshops, particularly the second-hand palaces where the aromas of erudition held the promise of wisdom, the perfect book waiting for the random fall of my hand on its spine. Kate thought that I ought to read more, yet I had the curious, stubborn belief that it would taint my latent originality. I'd held onto that notion for as long as I could remember, clinging to the idea that the masterpiece was already inside me, and destined to come out any day of its own accord.

I'd written stories over the years, though I rarely showed them to anyone except Kate. She hadn't seen more than a fraction of my output. It was all part of my sense of being a fraud. That I had somehow won her unfairly, tricking her into believing that I was going to make it as a writer one day, matching her talent. That one day she would see me for the failure I was, and that our days together would be numbered.

A few days before all of this started, she had asked about my current writing ambitions, and I came out with some rubbish about producing a book that might scare people out of their minds. She said to get on and do it and not waste time talking about it. It was after that conversation that I recalled a long-ago day at the late-summer carnival, telling the tarot-card witch that I wanted to be a writer: a ten-year old boy who had happened across a collection of stories by some forgotten storyteller, catching a glimpse of how he might transform a world that he didn't understand.

The glimpses came, through the years, and the stories began to pile up. Attempts, largely, at making sense of my childhood years, transforming the suffering caused by my mother's illness, and my father's demons - or was that the other way around? I could never tell for sure. Still, I knew, down in the core, that the magic of story held the key to bringing clarity out of the chaos of life, and laying a handful of tenacious ghosts to rest.

I wrote that down, once, as a mission statement. And most New Years I reminded myself that time was ticking on, and that maybe this was to be the year when I finally made it happen. I'd long since talked myself out of believing in supernatural monsters, but I still knew their names, and the chills that they were capable of provoking. Sometimes I wished that I did believe in them; wanting to hang on to the idea that there was more to the world than life and death.

Over the years I'd noticed a change in Kate's reading habits. In our first years together she read mainly play scripts, which seemed natural enough given her profession. She could start a new one in the morning and give me a private solo performance - edited down to its essential three, five, seven, nine minutes – the same evening, playing all parts and getting a standing ovation from me every time. Then somewhere down the line her interest began to reach more deeply into the word on the page, and the poetry and fiction sections became her first ports of call.

And so it was on that particular day, the fiction department drawing the change out of her purse. Two bargains from the pen of an American: Mark Twain. Kate had read *Huckleberry Finn* as a child and found it "hysterically funny and unbearably sad." She was like that with books, getting right the way into them so that to watch her reading was an emotional experience in itself. I used to fantasise about one day producing something that could do that. It would be the benchmark of my success, I decided.

The other book that she found in *Scriveners* that day was *A Connecticut Yankee in King Arthur's Court*, also by Mr. Twain. And it changed everything.

We left the bookshop and headed back to the hotel. The walk had tired her, and by the time we got back to our room the energy and colour had drained out of her. While she rested, I looked at her new books. It was the second one that intrigued me: *A Connecticut Yankee*. I opened it up and came across a nineteenth-century factory worker from New England, getting hit on the head with a crowbar and finding himself in medieval England. It struck a nerve, somehow, and when Kate woke up I was already halfway through the book.

"Any good?" she asked.

"The man was from another planet."

"Best thing that ever came out of America."

"This book?"

"Twain in general."

"You're not forgetting the lovely Buck-Bradbury?"

She screwed her nose up and hissed. "I love Mark Twain. But I'd rather take him home and read him there."

I left her favourite American in Camelot, and joined my wife in bed, where we stayed, one way or another, for the rest of the day.

In the spaces made by Kate's intermittent dozing, I found time to finish the book, and then I wanted to go straight back to Page One, thinking that I might understand it better the second time around.

She was still asleep when I closed the book. I kissed her, not waking her; wondering what great roles lay ahead once she was fully recovered. I let my imagination loose over Hollywood, and pictured myself one day writing the screenplay that would launch her film career, watching her walking up to collect the Oscar.

In my fantasy I noticed that there were gaps in the audience, vacant seats. My thoughts turned to Kate's parents, and a wave of resentment rose up. How was it possible for so-called Christian people to abandon their own child for marrying into *the wrong blood?* How could they have kept their distance so callously in their daughter's time of need?

It struck me that Kate must have had the same thoughts, though she'd never voiced them, at least not to me. I thought of my own parents, and wished they were alive. I wished they could have seen Kate and been proud of what we had together. They never knew my dreams, and, in fairness, I never knew theirs, either. They spent their lives in the darkness, submerged in the nightmares of alcoholism and mania. They feared the world too much and it made them afraid to walk in the light, or even to believe that the light existed.

I nodded off, no doubt stupefied by the shallowness of my own amateur psychology, and when I awoke the room was already dark.

The gloom felt oppressive, full of monsters, though not the monsters that had enriched my childhood and adolescence. Those years seemed remote, and the names I had given to fear had changed. If your gun contained the magic bullet, the ending was never in doubt. If you knew where to find the hammer and the sharpened stake, it was going to be a happy-ever-after every time.

Now, though, the stage was set for a world of uncertain evil, with no easy nemesis. I didn't know it, but the show was about to begin. Before the evening was over I would have exposed Kate to the flesh and blood destroyer of worlds.

She looked stunning that evening. My fairy tale princess bore not a blemish. The sleep appeared to have replenished her, and she glowed. An electric wind blew through my soul as we walked along the corridor towards the elevator.

The bar was quieter that evening, with only a handful of people dotted around the tables. Mutilated old ladies might be good for business, but only in the short term. I took a beer and a mineral water to the table by the far window, which provided us with a spectacular view of the huge spires of the financial district of San Francisco, if nothing else. As if I needed reminding about money!

I felt at the wad of notes still hidden away in the pocket of my jacket, and asked Kate what was at the top of her list of tourist attractions in the city.

"I wouldn't mind seeing the Golden Gate Bridge," she said. "You?"

"Alcatraz."

"It wouldn't be the same without Burt Lancaster. Anyway, they make you swim back through shark infested water."

"No sharks, just dangerous currents. Every bit as deadly, though."

She put on an expression of bitter disappointment. "Sharks would be more fun. Imagine what the folks back home would say when you told them how you'd been bitten in half swimming back from prison - talk about green with envy!" She glanced at her watch. "What time's this Merle joining us, then?"

"We didn't arrange a time."

"So he might not turn up?"

"I'm sure he will."

"Regular, is he, or just telepathic?"

I smiled, awkwardly. It seemed the better option than opening my mouth and fumbling my way down a labyrinth of crooked alleys that I hadn't anything like the measure of.

We sipped on our drinks and waited.

A minute later Merle exploded into the bar dressed in the same immaculate black and white, with a yellow bow tie to match his now yellow buttonhole. He marched up to our table and held out a hand. "Kate, I presume? Enchanted to make your acquaintance," he said. "Your husband has told me so many wonderful things about you."

"Has he really?" said Kate, taking his hand cautiously.

"I've built up quite a picture," said Merle, finally letting go of my wife's hand.

"Then I hope that you're not disappointed," said Kate, looking relieved to have her hand back.

"More drinks, my friends?" he said.

He bought a round of drinks consisting of one beer and two mineral waters. It was party night California style.

I moved around the table to sit next to Kate, while Merle sat facing us. It felt like an interview about to commence, though I still hadn't worked out who was in the hot seat. We passed pleasantries backwards and forwards, and Merle launched more successful raids into Kate's seemingly infinite store of laughter than I care to remember. I hadn't heard her laugh so much since that night back in England, when all of this began during that dreadful Hollywood film. His aim was deadly, hitting a bulls-eye every time, with his observations of British life, marriage, the Royals, America, greed, vanity. It was a virtuoso performance. But he had underestimated Kate. She found him amusing, charming, there was no doubt, and on the whole appeared to be enjoying the performance. And that was the extent of it: enjoying a well presented show. I knew it would take a good deal more than that to wrap a fist around her heart. It all seemed too obvious, even to me, and I felt my disappointment growing the longer it went on. I wondered if he wasn't used to dealing with the likes of Kate, and too used to dealing with the likes of me.

As the laughter died down following an impersonation of a string of American presidents selling the Golden Gate Bridge to a hapless British Prime Minister, he changed tracks. "I want to be serious for a moment," he said. "I want to tell you about the future."

I felt my nerves tightening. I didn't dare look at Kate.

"I know that you've been badly treated here in the States," he said. "You came here on the goodwill of your people and found yourselves falling straight into the claws of one of our innumerable and particularly malignant confidence men. That sickens me. It sickens me to my stomach, and I don't want you going home thinking that all Americans have been formed in the likeness of Buck-Bradbury. I want to show you that this country of ours, for all its faults, has another side, and I want you to see that other side."

I was suddenly interested in the grain of the wood in the table between us, and in the froth sliding down the side of my empty glass.

Merle went on. "Buck-Bradbury is the lowest form of life. He sells dreams – dreams of being made well, of being healed. He sells the same dream over and over, and he might as well be selling bridges, or entire nations. Whatever he promises, he never delivers. That would be bad for business. Make one person better and they'll all expect it."

Merle shook his head. "They come to Buck-Bradbury as a last resort, and because he charges top dollar they believe that they've seen The Man and given it their best shot. Then they go back home, content that everything has been tried, having placed their trust in *the best that money can buy*. So they tell everyone at home what a wonderful man Buck-Bradbury is. It's called 'preparing the way' and it's also called 'playing the loser'. Meanwhile, Buck-Bradbury tidies his figures and publishes another piece of academic dazzle with a bottom line of: *Wow, what a wonderful guy Buck-Bradbury is* and ponders what piece of real estate to buy up next. He's going to end up owning North America one day, and I'm not kidding."

Out of the corner of my eye I saw Kate's mouth open. Before she'd chance to raise the obvious point, Merle covered it. "Of course, he was good once, before he got greedy. He may even have cured one or two people in his time, before he saw the light."

"The light?" asked Kate.

"The light of the silver dollar. Believe me, that was a long time ago. And ever since he's just gotten worse and these days *everybody dies*."

I watched Merle take a slow, deliberate sip of water, letting his last sentence quiver on the air.

"But what we have here is something unusual. You two fine people have broken the mould. You two thinking people have had the courage to walk out on Professor Buck-Bradbury, and the intelligence to see him for what he really is. You two have said no to buying an American Bridge: no to the Brooklyn, no to the Oakland and no to the Golden Gate."

"Aw, shucks," said Kate. "It was really nothing."

"I would say you were too modest, good lady, though I would hate you to think that I hadn't appreciated your wit."

I sat back in my chair and played with the froth in my glass. Better to leave the talking to Merle.

I offered to buy some drinks; it had to be my turn. But Kate said she was feeling tired and was going to bed, and that she'd leave us boys to it.

I felt the panic kick in. *Where was the turnaround? What about the money? What about getting on a plane and going home to die?*

Nothing had been said yet. It had all been small talk and preparation. Merle was losing the moment and he didn't seem to realise it.

Kate stood to leave. Merle was on his feet, his hand outstretched. "Goodnight," he said. "It has been a real pleasure meeting you.

You are a brave lady and you have a good husband and I would love to buy you both dinner tomorrow evening."

The relief was profound. The way things had been heading I was expecting him to promise to come and wave us off at the airport and forward an obituary.

"You're very kind," said Kate, "but we're checking out tomorrow."

"What's this?" asked Merle.

Kate turned to me. "Going home, isn't that right, Ben?"

"I'm sorry to hear that," said Merle. "Are you well enough to travel?"

"Well enough to come out to play, well enough to travel," said Kate. "Can't bunk off school any longer, I'm afraid."

There was a pause. Then Merle smiled. This was it.

I held my breath.

"Then," he said, "it only remains for me to wish you a safe journey. Goodnight."

I was too dumbstruck to say anything; deflating like a scissored bladder.

"Goodnight," said Kate. "I'll see you later, Ben."

"I'll see he's not long following," said Merle.

Kate left us, and my confusion turned bitter. I reached inside my jacket, taking out the money and throwing it across the table.

"Thanks but no thanks," I said. "If this is a game then you'd better take your sadistic pleasures elsewhere."

"You can be a touchy fellow," he said, "did anybody ever tell you that?"

"*Touchy*!"

"You haven't enjoyed this evening?"

"I was hoping for a little more, you might say."

"If you want more, I'll give you more. But here's fair warning, my friend. I can give you so much that before you know it you'll be begging me to stop."

"I doubt that."

"Five minutes?" he said.

"What can happen in five minutes?"

Merle laughed so hard that he had to take his hat off, and I was treated to an unexpected sight. His head was completely bald, and covered with the tattoo of what appeared to be a medieval wizard. An image from the Mark Twain book flashed into my mind, but was gone before I could grasp it.

Wiping his face with a handkerchief, Merle placed his hat back onto his head with extraordinary care. "Everything and anything," he said. "That's what can happen in five minutes. Come with me and I'll show you."

"Where?"

"Not far. We can't get far in five minutes. First you put that money back in your pocket and you keep it there."

I hesitated, but there was never any question. He had me and we both knew it. Only he knew it better than I did.

I followed him out of the bar and back into the hotel lobby.

As we approached the entrance a familiar face came in through the revolving door that separated us from the world outside. It was the old man, the one who had spoken to me on the stairs the previous evening. He smiled when he saw me, and winked. As I passed him he whispered, "Everything working out alright?"

I looked back, but he kept walking.

"Who *is* that?" I said.

"Ex-Chief of Police," said Merle. "Carved out a name for himself in the Tenderloin district of this fair city. Gets his kicks these days writing dime detectives. Bet your ass there'll be a mutilated old lady turning up in his next one."

Merle was already through the revolving door and darting across the road, and I wasn't too far from being splattered by the honking, cursing owner of a battleship on wheels as I hurried to keep up with him.

He disappeared down a set of stone steps, not even looking back to see if I was behind.

I followed him down.

At the bottom of the steps was the entrance to a small basement. I waited for a moment, peering into the darkness ahead of me. I called out his name, only to be greeted with silence. At last, and with a deep breath inside me, I went in after him.

Inside the basement was total blackness. I could see nothing at all, not even my own hand stretched out in front of me. I felt my way forward, tracing a damp wall with my fingertips. After a few steps I stopped to listen, hearing something moving, though I couldn't work out what the sound was. Then I heard it more clearly: a scraping sound. My eyes were beginning to adjust to the darkness and I could make out the dim outline of a figure. The scraping sound became quicker and I recognised the sound of someone lighting a match. The darkness was broken by a sudden explosion of light.

Merle was standing in front of me, smoking a freshly lit cigar. As my eyes re-adjusted to the light, I looked to see the body of a young girl lying at his feet.

The match went out, and the level of remaining light was now dependant on Merle's manner of smoking. Inhaling deeply on his cigar he once more illuminated the scene, and with a gesture invited me to inspect the body lying before him. I walked slowly toward the girl and held out an unsteady hand, my heart thudding too fiercely for me to be sure whether there was a pulse in her body or not.

"Well, Ben, what's the diagnosis?"

"I think she's ... dead."

"You mean you don't know?"

I tried both wrists and then the girl's neck. As far as I could tell there was no pulse. Merle pulled hard again on his cigar, lighting up the gloom. "Well?"

"She's dead."

Merle nodded. "So let's see what we can do about it."

Kneeling down next to the lifeless body, he began inhaling deeply on his cigar, gently prizing open the girl's mouth and exhaling smoke into it. After he had done this, he closed her mouth, trapping the smoke inside. Then, after repeating the action, I saw a tremor from the upper part of the 'corpse'.

Had I been mistaken?

I watched Merle blow in more smoke, and this time a weak cough issued. Each time he blew more smoke into the girl's lungs, her cough became stronger, until, at last, she was in the grip of a full-blown coughing fit.

The strange little man moved back to let the fit run its course. "You see," he said, "it's all relative. Smoking, they reckon, is bad for you. But that doesn't always have to be true in every case. Having said that ... if this girl were my daughter, I would beat her black and blue if I found her blowing secretly on my cigars."

I felt his words dissolving, swirling about me as I fell into blackness.

The next thing I experienced was the intense smell of cigar smoke, and I looked up from a faint feeling of nausea to find him kneeling over me, blowing fumes under my nose. "I'm sure many first year anatomy students have the same problem," he said. "But in the interests of advancement, education must out."

I looked around me. The girl had gone.

"Where -?"

"Back home where she belongs."

"But, who was she?"

"One of the lucky ones."

He helped me to my feet, and we headed back towards the hotel. As we entered the lobby he told me that if we could open our minds fully, we would hear, see, smell, taste and feel the suffering around us, and respond to the endless voices calling us every second, pleading for our help. "A million prayers we might answer if we learnt to use the senses we were born with."

The girl, he told me, had not been quite dead in this instance, though her pulse had been too faint, too weak, for the untrained student to detect. She had passed into unconsciousness after overdosing on the profits from a night serving the pleasures of doomed men. She would have died, though the miracle in this case, he assured me, was being in the right place at the right time, and not in the raising of the dead.

"It is always better, my friend, to aim for the lower key miracle than to indulge in needless displays of the upper limits of one's art. That is the sign of the truly gifted magician. History is stuffed full with crowd-pleasers and pretentious conjurors. Beware cheap imitators; you are in privileged company this evening."

He walked me to the elevator, pressing the button that would send me back to Kate.

As the doors started to close on me, Merle said, "We'll be seeing each other. Sleep well, my friend."

CHAPTER
SIX

THE REAR OF THE ELEVATOR WAS MIRRORED. I MANAGED TO AVOID looking into it. *An old habit.*

As a child I loved to watch late night horror movies, Friday nights, as I recall. I preferred watching them alone, getting more out of them that way, extracting the delicious frisson of fear at its most potent. And my parents didn't approve of horror films, though fortunately they were good sleepers. If I kept the sound on our small black and white television set turned low, my taste for lurid darkness didn't need to be added to their list of worries, or causes to take down the strap from the pantry wall.

There was a film that spooked me more than any other. I can't recall the title or much about the film, except for the one scene that I can never forget.

There was a mirror over a fireplace, and something ominous about it that may have been down to whatever camera tricks they were using, and the eerie soundtrack that was playing as the camera lingered over the lighted mirror. The flames flickering from the fire were casting all kinds of grotesque shadow-shapes, when the main character, a boy not much older than I was then, entered the room. I remember sitting bolt upright on our old living room sofa as I watched the boy walk into that room, and silently I was screaming at him to go back. Then the boy saw the mirror, and immediately a look of terror overcame him, and the music went into overdrive. I was feeling sick with dread, and just like the boy I tried to look away, to avoid being drawn into that dark mirror, terrified of what it might reveal. I watched his resistance breaking down, weakening in the face of overwhelming, though still invisible, forces ... *and he looked, and he kept on looking ... and he saw something unspeakable unfolding over his shoulder.*

As clear as yesterday I remember scrambling off to bed that long ago night, walking on my knees towards the stairs, trying to avoid catching sight of the plain, wooden framed mirror that hung on our own living room wall, and vowing all the way up the stairs that I would never look into one again. And every time after that, when a film got to me, whether the monster was the bogeyman, the tooth fairy, the witch or the werewolf, I would ceremoniously avoid the mirror for fear of what it might show me.

As the hotel elevator rose up through the floors of the hotel I tried reminding myself that I was no longer a child, and that the phobia came from a film that I would no doubt laugh through if I ever saw it again.

The lift started to slow down ushering in the conviction that the opening doors would reveal what was waiting unseen in the mirror – the conviction growing inside me like a bubbling curse. When the elevator finally stopped I was expecting to come face to face with the Goat of Mendez. (Another film that I recall from those years, and one I was caught watching, drawing a sermon from my mother about the dangers of the occult, and a visit to the kitchen table to re-enforce the lesson.)

The doors opened and I held my breath. It seemed that the Goat of Mendez was taking the night off.

The corridor was empty. I stepped quickly into it, careful not to catch sight of the mirror behind me, and hurried to our room.

I expected to find Kate asleep. She was moving around in the bathroom, and I sat on the bed listening to her brushing her teeth, wondering what to tell her when she came out.

My head was a tangled mass of exposed wires. There was nothing to gain by reviewing my thoughts because I didn't know how to begin connecting them up. In my head the fantasy was in full swing. It went like this: Kate had returned to the room tired, until Merle's show across the road had rejuvenated her in some impossible way. By blowing cigar smoke into the lungs of a young girl, he had mysteriously blown life back into my wife, and I would find her bursting with energy, ready to celebrate life, with a new attitude towards extending our stay in a city that was not only agreeing with her, but healing her.

When she emerged from the bathroom, I was surprised at how pale and worn she looked. "Are you okay?" I asked.

"I'm tired," she said, "And homesick. I've finished most of the packing."

"I see."

She looked at me, sadness in her eyes. "It's time to go back home, Ben. It really is."

I asked her what she thought of Merle.

"He wants something," she said. "I just haven't figured out what."

"He wants to help us."

"And how's he going to do that?"

"You don't like him."

"I don't trust him."

"Why?"

"I just don't. I can't put my finger on it."

"But -"

"Look, can we hold the post-mortem in the morning?"

Morning came early, ahead of sunrise. Kate woke me, breathing hard, gulping at the dry conditioned air.

I switched on the light. Her eyes were closed in sleep, her face contorted in pain. I didn't need a doctor to tell me that she was back in the thick of it. She cried out in such distress that I could feel it, and still she didn't wake up. Her breathing was becoming more erratic, and then her eyes opened and the wildness in them startled me. I picked up the room telephone and called reception.

"Ambulance. Room Five-One-Seven."

Kate was screaming.

As soon as we reached the hospital they took her down to intensive care and showed me to the seated area with the coffee machine and snacks. I had no change for the machine, only the wad of money from Merle that was still in my jacket from the night before, stuffed with nothing smaller than hundred dollar notes. I was contemplating trying to change one of them, when a kind soul took pity on me with a few coins and didn't expect a conversation in return.

Later, one of the nurses came and told me that Kate's breathing was back under control, though it was too soon to say any more than that. I made myself comfortable and thought over the events of the last few days, little of it making sense.

My wife once told me that the next best thing to marrying an Irishman was to marry an Englishman with an Irish attitude. When I asked her what she meant by that, she went all mysterious on me and said that in a previous life I must have spent serious time across the water. I'd laughed at her sense of drama, though I wasn't entirely without a drop or two of Irish blood, allegedly.

My father, as he was fond of reminding me, was one eighth Irish, though which eighth I never found out. Family wasn't something that we ever talked about. So, whether that eighth part of him hailed from North or South, and whether it was Catholic or Protestant, I haven't the slightest idea and neither do I particularly care. I don't think he did, either, in truth. All the same, it made me forever curious about anything to do with Ireland. It raised questions, possibilities.

I thought about the time I first met Kate. It was my night off and I was spending it at my place of work, in what was grandly called the 'concert room.' Vince was singing sixties songs, building up for his (as he called it) world famous rendition of *Hey Jude*. I was filling in his frequent toilet breaks with a few Irish songs that I had learnt, mainly from my father during his drunken bouts around the weekends. (He used to say that Sunday was the day for rejoicing, and that true rejoicing was done in song, and that all of the finest ones were Irish.)

Kate came in with a couple of the Court Jesters, and I could see them trying to keep a straight face as Vince put the finishing touches to *Ferry 'cross the Mersey*. The Court Jesters were kind, and applauded politely. They knew how tough it was standing up in front of people, trying to entertain, and I'm sure they could imagine how much harder it is to do that with absolutely no talent whatsoever to offer the audience. Vince, of course, was a glorious exception: to my knowledge, having no talent never caused a single butterfly to ever enter the portly domain of *his* stomach.

When the song was over he shot out the back way, as he always did after a big number, though not before he'd bowed to each one of the Jesters. He was a gentleman through and through was Vince, though no singer.

I took up the microphone and wished for a sudden implant of talent, or preferably a power-cut. Beautiful women always made me nervous, and I was in the presence of one that night putting all other contenders in the shade.

It sounds corny saying it like that, but it was the truth, plain and simple. I was smitten in the first five seconds, my poor pride and vanity about to be crucified. I needed something more to parade than painful embarrassment.

I sang *Danny Boy*, though I never heard a word of it. I was too conscious of standing up there like a fool, and trying to avoid catching the eye of the woman with the haunting smile watching. Vince emerged and called out for *Irish Eyes*, telling me, for the room to hear, that I was sounding a little nervous.

Halfway through *Irish Eyes* a group of youths came in, and I could tell they didn't much care for the song or the singer. Two of them left, but the other two heard me out. When I'd finished, one of them shouted, "What's with all this fucking IRA shit?"

"Leave politics out of it," I said. "If you can't appreciate good music then you might as well be six feet under."

Good music might have been stretching it, at least the way I was singing that night. But I stood by the point I was making all the same.

The two of them gave me the finger and drank up, making a few anti-Irish noises as they left. We waited for the window to come through, but they must have found better sport elsewhere. That's when I heard a sound better than any song. Kate was clapping, her friends joining in. "All of Ireland applauds you," she said. "Do you know *Wild Rover*?"

I looked at Vince. He nodded.

"The stage is all yours," he said.

She took me to Ireland for the honeymoon, showed me all the places she could remember from her childhood. Best of all was a small fishing village that I can neither pronounce nor spell to this day. It might have been the place we would have chosen to grow old together, had things had worked out differently.

Her father had taken her there when she was six, during one of the family holidays, and she had returned to the place in her early teens. She told me that she often dreamt about it, and straight-faced even proclaimed a mystical yearning for it, like it was where she belonged. I remember her reddening up when she told me that. She was never comfortable with that sort of thing, which made two of us. I knew what she meant though; the atmosphere of the village was subtly different from anywhere else that I had ever visited. It had legends and stories running through it. I didn't believe any of them, of course. But like watching a good horror film, it never hurt to indulge in fantasy now and again.

Kate told me that she wouldn't have dared take me there unless we were already married, because legend had it that the unattached young woman, visiting the village for the third time from across the sea, would find herself the bride of a mighty magician.

"Call me old-fashioned," she said, "but if I want my husband performing magic tricks for me, then I'll buy him a conjuring set for Christmas."

She took me to see her Aunt Helen in Dublin before we returned to England. Her aunt applauded her decision to go ahead and marry despite the feelings of her parents.

"Hypocrites!" she called them. "The best answer you can give them, the pair of you, is a happy marriage – that and to come over to live in this God-blessed country of ours." Her eyes had lit with mischief. "And keep sending them postcards asking what's so bloody great about England. That's the only way of dealing with people like that."

I fell in love with Ireland, everywhere we visited, and I could happily have stayed there. For Kate though the work was back in England.

She wanted to make her way in the world, perfecting her craft all the way down the road to London's West End. In those days she had urgent, limitless ambition, and I found that a little frightening, wondering if fame and glory and money would one day take away all that we had together.

Every night that I wasn't working I would watch her treading the boards towards her goal. I watched her growing in confidence, playing bigger, more demanding roles; bringing the house down in Sheffield, drawing fine reviews in Nottingham. She played *Juliet*, *Hedda Gabler*, *Mother Courage*, *Lady Macbeth*, youth, age, tragedy and comedy. Every night I watched her become someone else, and every night she would break my heart, or capture it, and usually both. *Shirley Valentine* was a favourite. It was one of the few that didn't go over my head. It was glorious seeing her on that small Buxton stage all alone, breathing life into Willy Russell's script, and the audience not knowing that the fool sitting in the third row, with tears of pride rolling down his face, was her husband.

Salome cost me my job. My boss wanted me to work on the night that Kate was demanding the head of John the Baptist in Leicester. I went back to beg the next day, my tail between my legs; but unlike talented actresses, barmen came ten-a-penny. I didn't worry too much though. With the lights of London looming, it seemed as well not to be tied down to some dead-end bar job. I wanted to be with her through all of it. I wanted to be there as her dreams came true, and we both sensed that the day was coming.

The following week she was due to play Sybil in a stage adaptation of *Fawlty Towers*, in Manchester. A lot of important people were rumoured to be interested. It was looking like the break that she had worked so hard for. But fate had been tuning in; real-life erecting the props it generally saved for tragedy. Two of the cast, Court Jesters, were killed driving back from a performance of *All's Well That Ends Well*, in Birmingham. Instead of watching the birth of a star I stood at the graveside of two of Kate's friends.

The company never found its feet again after that, and disbanded. *Fawlty Towers,* at least in that incarnation, was destined never to be. We settled near to Leicester, and Kate teamed up with an amateur company sharing her enthusiasm. It never worked out, for some reason, and the lights of London grew a little dimmer.

Life seemed to have changed direction. If something could go wrong, it did. What we had once sailed through we now had to wade through. I found a job as temporary bar manager, and started drinking, really shifting the stuff; an old family weakness. They used to call my father 'Meths' in his later years, and in that respect I was at last becoming a true son and heir. It took another sacking and the sight of Kate crying one miserable and angry night and threatening to leave me, to finally kiss goodbye to the bottle.

"Mr Tolle?"

The words snatched me out of my reverie and I looked around to see a young, poker-faced doctor beckoning me. "Might I have a word in private?"

I followed him down the corridor, thinking what it might be like to be a prisoner on death-row walking towards the Chair.

He took me into an office and closed the door. His manner seemed to bear every indication of bad tidings.

"How is she?" I asked him.

"She's off critical, but still a poorly lady." Then he said something that shot a spike into my heart. "She needs to see a specialist. I can arrange -"

I'd already made my small mind up. The word 'specialist' could only mean one thing.

"Not Buck-Bradbury," I said.

The doctor looked at me, his mouth open and eyes wide. Then he roared with laughter. "I was thinking maybe a real doctor," he said.

"You don't rate him?"

"Does anybody rate that dollar-machine?"

I hadn't thought such honesty possible from a man in a white coat. "Well, I was under the impression -"

"Makes a lot of money, does *Professor* Buck-Bradbury. Personally, I wouldn't let him mend my cat. Not even a cat I didn't like. Does a great TV show - you should see it sometime. No, second thoughts, take a rain check on that or you'll never trust the medical profession again."

The doctor was smiling out some golden Buck-Bradbury memories, and though I didn't wish to ruin the party, I had more pressing matters.

"Do you have someone here at the hospital who could see my wife?"

"Buck-Bradbury ..." The young doctor let his smile break out into a grin. "Once knew a guy, professional baseball player, damaged some ligaments in his pitching arm. He could just about afford a consultation, and in those days Buck-Bradbury was thought of as something of a messiah. Takes a while for the truth to emerge in these matters, wouldn't you say?"

"Yes, I'm sure. But like you said, my wife's seriously ill and -"

"Anyway, this guy goes to see The Buck and asks him, 'Hey, Buck! Do anything for this arm? This arm's gotta be worth fifty grand a week.' Well, apparently Buck-Bradbury took hold of his arm and yanked it. The guy screamed out, 'Hey, Buck, what y'doing?' And you know what The Buck said?"

I shook my head impatiently.

"He said, 'I'm showing how you can double the value of that arm. I'm talking litigation, boy'. It turned out the guy made millions suing just about everybody under the sun for just about *every-thing* under the sun. The man was permanently crippled when The Buck had finished with him, but he was a sight richer."

We got back to the matter in hand. Having established that neither of us would allow Buck-Bradbury within a mile of Kate, the doctor outlined the procedure for a senior medic to examine her. Then he asked if I would like to go through and see my wife for a few minutes while he made arrangements.

She was in a side room, and when I saw her I felt my heart go down to my shoes. She was hooked up to a confusion of tubes, and there were half a dozen electronic pulses bleeping around her and as many monitor screens. I didn't know what any of it meant, but it looked serious.

I held her hand. She wasn't conscious, but I could feel her warmth. She was breathing more easily, and there was no screaming and no contorted features. Whatever stable meant, she looked it. I gently stroked her forehead and told her how everything was going to work out fine. Even as I was trying to reassure her, my voice full of hope and optimism, my mind was waging war on the injustices. She shouldn't have been lying there, suffering; she should have been out treading the boards under the bright London lights, even Broadway. She deserved success.

And yet her life had already been successful, even with a dead weight like me to keep her feet on the ground. She had done things that most couldn't even dream of, and she had let me be a part of that without making me feel inferior. I suppose that's part of what I've come to call *love*, though I'm sure I don't know what I ever did to deserve it.

I looked at her, beautiful even in sickness, and wondered what the future held. I knew that we wouldn't be going home that day. I also knew that I couldn't leave it any longer before making contact with the people back home.

That wouldn't take much doing. It occurred to me, depressingly, that Kate's aunt in Dublin was the only person we'd written to, and that had been nothing more than a brief note telling her where we were staying. We hadn't even thought to notify Aunt Helen or anyone else about the last-minute change in the arrangements, upgrading from the Indigo rooms to the International.

Did anybody back home know where we were staying?

Aunt Helen hadn't been well lately, according to her last letter. Maybe we were overdue a visit. I decided that we would go back to Ireland as soon as Kate was well enough. In the meantime, I would grab half an hour to write Aunt Helen a letter, telling her of our plans to visit, thanking her again for the note she sent us when she found out we were heading to the States, and thank her for the St. Christophers, which had stayed behind in England because we left in such a hurry.

In her letter she had reminded us that ill-health was only to be expected when you stay away from your homeland - your real homeland - for too long, and that a dip into the countryside and shorelines of the Beloved Isle was better than any amount of trips to see a Californian quack.

My letter to Aunt Helen was never written, same as the telephone call promised to the fund organiser when we left England was never made. Maybe I'm wrong to blame the press for the assumptions they made about us. We knew their tendencies, yet through our silence, we declared open season on ourselves. Kate was ill, but what excuse did I have?

The doctor was back.

"I've arranged for a specialist to see your wife later today. She may need to stay with us awhile. Do you need help with your accommodation arrangements? It could get expensive in town." The wad of money nudged against my heart, letting me know it was still there. "We could get someone to have a chat with you." I thanked him. I was going to need all the help and advice I could get. "Oh, I almost forget to mention. I believe there's somebody in reception asking after you both."

With one hand I stroked Kate's hair, and with the other I felt again at the wad of money in my jacket pocket. Then I let go of both and headed to reception.

Merle was waiting.

He would know about accommodation.

He would know about everything.

The events of the previous evening seemed more than ever like a dream. Merle had taken me out of the hotel to show me something, though I hadn't understood what it was that he was showing me. On the face of it he had saved a young girl's life; saved her from dying of a drug overdose by blowing cigar smoke into her lungs. It briefly occurred that he might after all be a colleague of Buck-Bradbury, specialising in alternative treatments. But I let the thought go, though I had nothing more credible to replace it with.

So close I had come to the truth.

Or part of it.

I saw the familiar white suit standing in the mild sunshine just out of reception. Merle was shaded underneath his black hat, and smoking a cigar. He turned before I reached the automatic glass doors, revealing a bow tie and button hole of mouth-watering orange. The doors between us puffed open.

"They told me that I was constituting a fire risk," he said. "And then they made me stand outside like a naughty boy. Is that any way to treat a concerned visitor?"

He asked how Kate was, and I told him. He considered the news carefully, all the time drawing heavily on his cigar, and letting enormous rings of smoke float back through the doors that he'd now wedged open with his foot.

The woman on the main reception desk was watching the rings with an icy disdain.

"There is no way she can go back to England, Ben. I will make arrangements, there's nothing for you to worry about."

Producing a monumental smoke ring that wobbled its way across reception with considerable attitude, he said, "Would you look at that beauty go!"

The receptionist was on her feet, waving her hands furiously at the resilient ring and stampeding towards us. "This is a non-smoking area," she barked.

"Correct," said Merle.

"Either close the doors or extinguish your cigar."

"Door closes by itself, got a mind of its own." Merle pulled back his foot and the doors closed abruptly between ourselves and the receptionist, who jumped back, snarled, marking us with her eyes before returning to her desk.

But the smoke ring was still full of the devil, clinging to the ceiling directly above her head. We watched her nose twitch, her look of disgust re-igniting, transforming what was already a sour countenance into one of near-apocalyptic rage. She would not take her steely eyes off the smoke ring that was stubbornly hovering above her like a mocking halo, not even to glare at us.

"Don't like hospitals," said Merle. "Don't like the smells. Cigar smoking should be compulsory. You can't conduct your business in a hospital, not properly. Still I keep coming back."

The last sentence struck a weird chord, though I heard it faintly.

"What annoys me, apart from the infernal smell, is the chronic subordination. Everybody smiles at the doctors, and everybody brings out their best manners like unused bone China tea-sets, as though politeness might somehow make a difference to the diagnosis, or the prognosis. Nobody dares risk it. Rudeness might cost lives, or at least an arm, a leg, maybe even a couple of good years - a couple of million dollars." He pointed his cigar hand towards reception. "Look at that, will you? Isn't it beautiful?" I watched the smoke ring keeping watch, its wide eye out-staring the hostility beneath it. "And the pecking order! Every hospital has, at its heart, a junior league Buck-Bradbury. Maybe not always about the money, sometimes the glory and the status, the reputation, too - even the occasional love of an admiring nurse. But it comes to money in the end, once they get old and wise and cynical enough." His face screwed up into a repulsed grimace. "But never upset the lady with the big ones, who manages the ward. Not even a doctor's gonna risk doing that."

He stamped out the small remainder of his cigar, closed his eyes and made a brief, curious imitation of prayer. Then he rested his hand up on my shoulder and said, "Time to go in. Even in a place like this I have people who need me. Bet you didn't know that the beds in this place get more expensive the more floors you climb. That's America, my friend. I'll talk to you later about arrangements. Don't worry. I'll take care of everything."

The doors puffed open and he made his way over to the reception desk. I followed him inside.

What happened next happened quickly.

As Merle approached the receptionist, who at first appeared satisfied that at last the insubordinate smoke ring had lost its powers of rebellion, I saw her nose start twitching. I assumed that she was sniffing at Merle for evidence of a hidden, burning cigar. Then I saw the look of concern begin to escalate into something far more urgent. She looked poised to press the security button at any moment, and I was smiling at the scene ... *when it happened.*

A tremendous explosion followed by the sound of screaming.

The hospital burst into frenzied action, people running in all directions, raised voices, alarm bells mixing into the general chaos.

Now I could smell it.

Smoke. Burning. *Fire.*

SEVEN

Four people died in the fire. Kate wasn't one of them. She was unharmed. In fact, there was a good deal more to it than that. Out of the panic and mayhem in the hospital that day walked a new Kate. And I mean *walked*. She breezed into reception like she was walking onto a stage. She was radiant, her eyes sparkling with excitement. Despite my relief at seeing that she was unscathed, the effect was unnerving.

Seeming to be unaware of the confused chaos around her, the pandemonium and fear, she came up to me and said, "Ben, are you okay? You look tense." I was too stunned to answer her. "You're pale, too," she said. "I don't think America's suiting you. I'll tell them we're leaving. Best book a taxi to the airport. England, please, and driver don't spare the horses. Do you need to sit down for a minute, Ben? I'm quite concerned about you."

She wandered over towards the reception desk, like a tourist in search of information. Bodies, uniformed and otherwise, were scrambling in all directions. I don't know how many alarm systems were being activated. It sounded like a thousand bells ringing over Bedlam.

When Kate reached the abandoned reception desk, she turned around, shrugged in my direction, shaking her head as though she was unable to comprehend such a dereliction of duty. "Nobody home," she mouthed across the chaos.

I wanted us out of there, somewhere safe, somewhere sane. I watched her merrily charting a course through the confusion, as though none of it concerned her.

It wasn't like her to be removed from the sufferings of others, so aloof and careless. That's what scared me the most. She was clearly in a state of shock. Shock could do strange things to people. People died of shock.

She needed checking over. Under any other circumstances being in a hospital might have been ideal. At that precise moment she was hardly going to be anybody's medical priority. She was making her way back towards me when the second explosion ripped through the hospital, causing a fresh wave of screaming to pierce the cacophony of bells and sirens. We had to get out of there before the whole place exploded. We could do nothing to help ourselves or anybody else by adding to the general confusion and danger.

That's how easily I discarded my sense of public responsibility.

Still dressed in her night gown and amidst the panic and mayhem, she smiled at me sweetly and twirled around. "So what do you think?" she said.

"We're getting out of here," I said.

"I like the sound of that. Good day for a picnic. Taxi sorted, Ben? They're very busy here today. Come on, slow coach."

She moved towards the exit and I followed her out into the frail sunshine. A cab was already waiting. I knew it was for us, and who had arranged it. I looked back at the hospital as I opened the cab door, ushering Kate inside before joining her. The car pulled off, heading for the beckoning highway.

Kate looked content, serene. It didn't add up. It was not the response of an intelligent and compassionate woman who had witnessed tragic, terrifying events. *Shock,* I reminded myself.

I noticed that the driver was talking into his radio. I couldn't hear what that was being said, but his lack of curiosity struck me. His failure to enquire about what was happening at the hospital, as people fled from the building, many in a state of clear panic. And he hadn't felt the need to check out that he had the correct passengers aboard.

A feeling of unreality descended. "Kate, are you okay?" I asked her.

She didn't answer, and then she nodded. "Why do you ask? I'm fine. How are you? I think they're a little distracted today. We could come back tomorrow, if you like." She patted my hand. "You worry too much." She closed her eyes, and a few moments later I heard the sound of gentle snoring.

She slept until we reached the hotel. We went up to our room, and she didn't mention what had happened at the hospital. She seemed alert, more her old self. I asked if we shouldn't unpack, insisting that we were not travelling anywhere until she had been checked over.

"I'll tell you what we'll do," she said. "We'll check into a cheaper place for a couple of days. Then we're going home."

I didn't argue. So many things had happened that I didn't understand. Powers beyond our control appeared to be deciding things. And now she seemed well again, almost too well. Who was I to interfere? *How* was I to interfere? How was it possible to be a cause for medical concern one minute, and a picture of health the next?

She agreed to rest while I tried to find out some more details about what had happened at the hospital. The way she agreed re-ignited my concerns. A shrug of her shoulders, followed by a nonchalant: "Okay, whatever." Kate, who once cried for two days over the death of a cat in the road, and who then spent a week tracing the owners and a further two days mourning for the child whose pet had been run over – now shrugging off a fire and two explosions in a hospital full of sick, vulnerable people?

In the hotel lobby I found all the details I needed. He was sitting at the bar sipping iced water. His buttonhole had turned to pale lilac.

Merle told me that an electrical fault had been discovered, occurring in the vicinity of the flammable storage units on the top floor. Heads were going to roll, he said. "Big heads, fat heads." The majority of the patients had been redistributed to other local hospitals. There were no injured, though there had been four fatalities. I lowered my eyes in respect for the dead.

"Lighten up, my friend," he said. "The way of the world: one dies, another's born. You have to trust enough for both of you, and accept the truth when you hear it, though it might not be an easy truth to bear."

I was getting used to not understanding, and I let his cryptic words pass through me, wondering if they might do better down in the dim underworld of my subconscious. It seemed preferable to allowing headspace to the obscene thought growing inside my head.

That Kate had gained strength from the deaths of four people, just as she had benefitted from the death of the old lady on the hotel steps.

I stopped the thought, pushing it away, down and out of range. It was crazy; it had nothing to do with the way of the world, the real world. It was totally implausible; fantasy of the worst kind, and it recalled how I had thought about things in my youth; the result of too many horror films too young, no doubt, and bad ones at that.

"Tell you what, Ben. They'll make sure that they resite those units on a lower floor. The four fatalities were seriously rich. Top floor jobs. There'll be lawsuits flying that will damage health care services around here for a decade. The big lesson to be learnt here, though it will be passed around in private whispers, is gonna be: *put your richest patients on the ground floor and let the paupers fry next time.* And don't think I'm kidding, not for a minute." He took another sip of water and dabbed his mouth. "Okay," he said, "let's go see the dischargee."

As I stood up I felt the wad of money nudge against my heart and the sickness of uncertainty sweep back over me.

"Something wrong?" he asked.

I shook my head, and we made our way to the elevator.

When we reached the hotel room I put my head around the door while Merle waited out in the corridor. Kate was lying on the bed reading. "You have a visitor," I said.

"You'd better let him come in then," she said. "Has he brought me grapes and flowers? Hello, Merle."

I glanced over my shoulder to catch the diminutive stranger raising his eyebrows, obviously impressed at Kate's perceptiveness. I moved into the room and beckoned him to follow.

Before he had a chance to speak, Kate said, "We're moving to a cheaper hotel for a couple of nights, and then home. It's good of you to take such an interest, but I'm feeling better now and it's time to move on." She flicked her eyes up from what she was reading. "I'd leave tomorrow, but Ben worries about me, isn't that right, sweetheart?"

Merle closed the door. "You're brave, and you're right. It is time to move on. But where are you thinking of moving to?"

"There are places all over town charging a fraction of what they charge here, regardless of who's footing the bill."

"Can't argue with that," he said. "There's a place I know offers rates better than any, if you're interested."

"Does it have a bed?"

"It has a beautiful bed. And I can have you installed within the hour. What do you say?"

Kate looked at me. "What do we say?"

"I say we take it."

"We'll certainly look at it," she said.

Merle smiled. "I'll send a car over."

He left to make arrangements, and I sat on the bed. "How are you feeling?" I asked her.

She swallowed, hard, and I saw her eyes beginning to mist. "My God, Ben, what happened at the hospital?"

I told her what I knew; that four people had died. Her tears came down like a storm breaking, her face buried hard into my chest.

The car arrived promptly to take us to our new accommodation. We sat together in silence in the back seat, Kate's hand tight in mine. It felt strong, and her outpouring of grief earlier gave me hope that she was recovering from the shock of what had happened.

The drive was a short one, and in no time we were standing by a four poster bed, looking out over the San Francisco Bay. "There's your Golden Gate," I said. I could see that she was distracted. I guessed that she was back at the hospital, reliving the horror. I led her out onto the balcony. "Would you look at that," I said, surveying the panoramic view of the Bay. I kissed her. "You know, I think everything might work out."

"Those poor people, Ben. Can you begin to imagine?"

I let her cry. She was too good at holding things inside, though God knows I was a fine one to talk. Still, I recognized the problem in Kate better than I recognized it in myself. It was her way of dealing with tragedy, storing up the emotion for an outpouring. Maybe it was part of what made her so captivating on the stage.

As she sobbed her heart out, I felt the relief of all that pain being released. She was a human storehouse sometimes, and I'd wondered if that had been part of what was wrong with her: the accumulation of past grief; the responsibility that she took on for the suffering of others. Had she become so saturated with it that even the release on stage had ceased to be enough? Was that simply the burden she carried; the size of the angel inside her?

I hugged her, and felt blessed beyond measure that someone so good and pure could have found something in me to love. I would have done anything, would gladly have given my life and soul to save her, to see her restored and well again.

Was this the beginning, the healing?

My thoughts darkened and a cold tremor raced the length of me. I recalled what Merle said about one person dying and another being born. I felt a moment of gratitude that Kate couldn't see the fear in me, or know the thoughts that were running through my head.

That evening we watched the sun fall down over San Francisco Bay. Staggered by the beauty of the scene, our silence at last gave way, and we talked about our lives together, the people we'd known and lost, our dreams and fears through the years. Kate laughed so much that night, with such abandon, as we brought a multitude of memories back to life, mingling sorrows and joys.

"Ben, do you ever wish we had children?"

Not long after we were married Kate thought she was pregnant. The prospect scared both of us. It was bad timing. There was too much going on in our lives already, and too little money. At the same time, I was excited at the prospect of having a child, and wondered if she was too, though neither of us ever voiced it. Then she began bleeding. We had been on the threshold of a gargantuan decision, and on a miserable afternoon in February we came out of the doctor's surgery with no decision to make.

Kate's tubing had been badly fitted, and was beyond repair. There was no health risk, and no baby risk, either. I had little doubt she would have made a wonderful mother. And that night, as we looked out over San Francisco Bay, I finally I told her that, and we wept together.

Our lives that night stumbled out to the crossroads. Looking back and forward merged into a menagerie of lived and unlived memories. If there was a right time to die, it was that golden night when everything was said, everything felt; and in our unremembered dreams our spirits crept out together to stare into infinity.

Except that the time and place of death had not been booked for that night or for San Francisco. Merle's plans for us were only just starting to unfold, and fate had already marked out the killing ground. The road before us, that we couldn't see, was leading out into the desert.

To a place called Las Vegas, Nevada.

The following morning brought the hounds of fate early to our door. Merle had arranged a little surprise, and he hoped that we didn't mind. The car was booked and waiting; a little sightseeing trip, free of charge, naturally. He wanted us to look back a little more fondly on the fiasco that had been our trip to the land of promise.

In one day we saw so much that we almost forgot that we were not on holiday at all. I made it to Alcatraz, and even got a book signed by an ex-inmate. It wasn't anyone famous like Al Capone, or the man with the birds played by Burt Lancaster. Rather, it was some retired murderer who'd discovered there was more money in writing than in armed robbery.

On the boat ride back from Alcatraz I quietly slipped the book into the water. I didn't wish the man any harm; he had a living to make. I just knew that I'd never get around to reading it.

Merle came and stood at my side on the deck. "Quite a place," he said, looking back at the retreating prison. "Kind of fires up the imagination, doesn't it?"

He took the pea-green curiosity out of his buttonhole, dropping it into the water. "Can you keep a secret?" he said.

I didn't want to hear about secrets. I still didn't know what was supposed to happen with the guilty one already hiding in my jacket pocket. I made some inane observation about the value of harsh prison regimes, but Merle was not a man easily derailed from his mission, and he let the observation die its own peaceful death.

"Heard of Luxor?" he said when I'd finished.

"Egypt?"

Surely, I thought, even a creature of such peculiar impulse would not whisk us away to Africa.

He reached into his pocket and pulled out a beautiful yellow rose, inserting it into his buttonhole. I noticed then that his bow tie was yellow. Had it been a moment earlier? I couldn't remember. "Luxor," he said, "is also the name of a casino in Vegas. A glass pyramid, fronted by a sphinx. Inside the pyramid you can, for a few dollars, be taken on a Nile cruise. This is not make-believe, my friend, it's what America has created for itself. It's the new kid on the block. And like its neighbours on the Strip, it's there to sell dreams. The turn of a wheel, the fall of a dice, the pulling of a handle, and your life is changed forever."

I could see that he wanted a response. I said, "Las Vegas isn't a place I've ever fancied."

"That's because you have no idea of what it can offer."

"I was never fond of Blackpool."

Merle laughed. "Blackpool it ain't, not even times a trillion."

I started to speak, and he held up a hand. "Please don't say something like, 'Maybe next year.' That always means never."

"I can live with that."

"Maybe you can, Ben."

He looked back towards Kate. She was out of earshot, and staring out across towards the Golden Gate. "You can't live cheaply over there," he said, pointing to where Kate was looking. "Sausalito. It would be good to take her there, one day. But I'm not sure it's your kind of town."

When we got off the boat the car was waiting to take us back to the hotel for what Kate believed would be our penultimate night in America.

I knew that Merle had other plans. I was learning quickly about how persuasive he could be. But still I doubted he could talk Kate into going to Las Vegas.

As we drove through the busy heart of San Francisco, watching the cable cars glide up and down the impossibly steep streets that I had seen so many times on television, both as a child and as a man, I felt a sense of perspective returning; so many familiar sights bringing back a sense of reality, blasting away the dark imaginings that had been taking hold of me.

I was starting to relax, breaking the habit of a lifetime.

We left town and headed around the Bay towards Merle's hotel. As we pulled off the main highway I was allowing myself the indulgence of optimism, when the car suddenly swerved. There was a thump and I heard the driver groan. We pulled over.

Lying a few feet behind us in the road, was a golden retriever, little more than a puppy. It was whimpering, and barely moving. Merle leapt out of the car, and in an instant he was kneeling by the side of the injured animal, carefully inspecting the damage to the poor mutt. It looked to me as though he was talking to it. Whatever he was doing, it seemed to be comforting the dog.

Kate joined me at the side of the road, wincing every time the dog whimpered. She loved animals, loved them, she once said, too much to ever own one. I think she could see that the dog was in good hands.

At last Merle got back into the car with the dog draped across his knees, and the driver turned the car around, heading back towards the highway. All the time Merle was talking gently to the wounded creature in-between giving directions to the driver.

At last we pulled into the grounds of a large estate boasting an impressive mansion at its heart, and everybody got out of the car. Merle, his clothes covered in blood, carried the whimpering animal to the huge front door, which opened on cue as we approached, revealing a formally dressed butler who by the look of him probably answered to the name *Jeeves*.

Inside the house, in the wildly exotic entrance hall, the butler saw to our comforts, while Merle disappeared into a side room, with the dog in his arms. The driver sat with us.

"I take it this place belongs to Merle?" I said.

The driver curled his bottom lip in a gesture of ignorance. "I'm just hired for the day."

"You didn't pick him up from here?" asked Kate.

"Picked him up at the hotel, same place I picked you up. Didn't know this place even existed."

It was some place not to be known by a local driver, yet our amateur detective thoughts were soon displaced as Merle reappeared, looking grim.

"As representatives of a nation of animal lovers ... brace yourselves." Then he whistled, and out trotted the dog, now a picture of tail-wagging health. "It looked a good deal worse than it was," said Merle. "All that remains is to return him to his careless owners."

Back in the car Kate asked about his extraordinary veterinary skills, but Merle's modesty was remarkable.

"Many years ago," he said, "I was witness to the needless death of a horse. It was hit by a tractor up in the Oregon woods. And you know what we did, the driver and me? I'll tell you what we did. We stood there watching, all the while cursing our inability to do anything to help that beautiful beast.

"But that didn't ease that horse's pain one iota. So when we couldn't tolerate its agonies a second longer, we did the only thing left to do – the only humane thing that was left in our power to do – and we drove the tractor back over its head."

There was so much emotion on his face and in his voice that I thought he was about to cry.

"I promised myself I'd never feel such helplessness again. You don't need to learn much to save lives and ease suffering, and what greater knowledge is there?"

We rode the rest of the way in silence, Kate's hand squeezing into mine.

I was already wondering what Las Vegas would be like.

CHAPTER
EIGHT

As we entered our room, after thanking Merle for a wonderful day, Kate reached around and pulled down the zipper on my trousers.

"Do you mind telling me what you're doing?" I said.

"I'm saving time."

We were both naked before the door had finished swinging shut. It was like the days after we first met, and it was my kind of nostalgia.

I showered early the next morning, trying hard not to whistle any tunes with Las Vegas in the title. My fine spirits needed no justification. It was all going to end happily. Kate was her old self again, full of passion and humour, and she was returning to England cured. Better to leave everything to Merle, and that included breaking the news about where exactly we were heading, and why. Something in America had done the trick, and I couldn't help give it a name and a face.

Such a simple thing is faith.

When I came out of the shower, Kate was stirring. She smiled at me, her eyes twinkling like wishing stars.

"And who gave you permission to abandon your duties so soon?" she said.

Climbing out of bed, she walked over and kissed me, long and slow. "I'll freshen up," she said. "And then I'll be back."

I watched her walk into the bathroom, winking back at me over her shoulder. "The next course will be along in fifteen minutes, Ben. Don't let me down."

The shower kicked in, and I wandered downstairs, in typical literal-minded fashion, double-checking what time it would be in fifteen minutes, calculating how long it would take to retrace my steps.

I found a small lounge area tucked around the corner from reception. A few guests were taking advantage of the free papers and coffee.

Pouring myself a drink, I picked up a newspaper, and made for one of the vacant armchairs.

"Friend of Merle?"

I turned around to meet the friendly smile of a man in his mid-thirties, a medium built six-footer with little in the way of distinguishing features. A lot like me, you could say.

"You know Merle?" I said.

"Most people here do. This place belongs to him, don't you know?"

I didn't.

"He prefers to keep this place quiet and available for friends who need somewhere inexpensive and safe. Some might say that puts it in the minority here in old California. From England?"

I introduced myself.

"Pleased to make your acquaintance," he said, shaking my hand. "The name's Gus. Say, that was a fine thing Merle did yesterday, healing that dog like he did. I hear the owners received one of his complimentary lectures on pet care."

I laughed. "They certainly did."

"Guess they'll be keeping a closer eye on that little doggie of theirs in future."

I indicated my scepticism, and Gus looked surprised. In my experience, telling people how to look after their pets, or their children, usually guaranteed a rude response or else made things worse in the long run. I shared my thoughts, and Gus looked shocked. "You mean to say, you think they'll beat that dog for causing trouble?"

"They might," I said. "It's that kind of world."

His shock turned to a grin. "You may be friends, but you don't know Merle, do you? Let me tell you: that dog will spend the rest of its life feeling like one of Cleopatra's cats. And before you ask me if that's a good thing, let me tell you: that's one hell of a good thing. Those owners are going to spend the rest of that little doggie's natural lifespan working so hard at keeping in that critter's good books that they ain't ever going to know again what it's like to go to bed anything other than ... *dog-tired.*"

Gus hooted with laughter, and went to get himself some more coffee. I took the opportunity to look at the newspaper, and came across a piece on the mutilated old lady.

Under the heading, *Latest on Butchered Corpse,* I discovered that a nationwide hunt was underway to find the person responsible for a series of killings stretching over two decades. The investigation had led to the re-opening of nine other unsolved murders, all of them carried out in almost identical fashion, though in none of the other cases had the corpse been dumped in a public place.

Ten murders, equidistant in time and location, the times and locations itemized, with two years and two-hundred miles separating each one. Every victim had turned seventy, each having, at the time, a sick and dying partner. The grislier details were identical in all ten cases, and in the first nine the partners were known to be still living and in remarkable health, despite their considerable ages and previous health problems.

"Bad business." Gus was back, perched behind me, reading the article over my shoulder. I agreed with him, that it was indeed a 'bad business' and refreshed my coffee.

The guy was nice enough and just being friendly; but anyone making sudden remarks whilst reading over my shoulder was guaranteed to leave me with ambivalent feelings. There were a few questions that I wanted to ask him, and I had a few minutes to spare before my 'appointment' with my wife.

"You know Merle well?" I asked him.

"Well enough. He's a hell of a guy. Can be a dark horse, plays his cards close to his chest, but you can't help but fall in love in the end. I've never known anybody else quite like him."

I began to quiz him about who Merle was, what he did, where he lived. I couldn't seem to slow myself down, wanting to know everything at once. Gus recognised my hunger, and I caught his discomfort.

"Let me tell you," he said, cutting me down and ending the inquisition. "Merle's a guy you have to make your own mind up about. Nobody else can do that for you."

He drank up his coffee. "Nice meeting you. Enjoy Vegas."

He knew about Vegas?

Had Merle confided, or did he take everybody he met there?

I headed back up the stairs, carrying two fresh coffees. My fifteen minutes were up.

When I got back to the room, the shower was still blasting away. I waited, but without my earlier feelings for company. The doubts had kicked in again, the questions mounting. I sipped at my coffee and pondered it all, without making any progress.

Kate was still busy in the bathroom, humming merrily at a medley of tunes that comfortably covered three generations of adolescent romance. If *Teenager in Love* put a temporary smile on my face, *Can't buy me Love* wiped it clean away.

I took the packet of money out of my jacket. How many times had I dreamt of having money? The good it could do us, the chances it might open up.

Nobody gave money like that away for nothing, not even someone as evidently wealthy as Merle. Not without good reason.

I felt the poor remains of my earlier optimism crumble and dissolve. What did he want? What were we getting ourselves into? He claimed to be a healer, and he'd come up with the goods somehow. Wasn't that enough? If he'd cured her of whatever had afflicted her, did I need to know more?

But I couldn't leave it. It just wasn't as simple as that. Hadn't he referred to himself as a magician? Did that make him insane, dangerous? What kind of healer, or magician, for that matter, cured with cigar smoke? What kind of anything organises the death of its own parents, and tells a stranger in a bar all about it? He talked about there always being a price to be paid, and about the books having to balance. Had he been talking about the butchered corpse of an old woman? About the four people who had died in the hospital fire?

And what of the other nine who had been butchered in the same fashion as the old lady, what might he have to say about them? Were they merely balancing books somewhere – and what did he know about those deaths?

Why did Gus need to know we were heading for Las Vegas? Was everyone in the hotel on Merle's payroll?

What's waiting for us in Vegas?

Maybe Kate would insist that it was time for home. She was strong again, and that meant stubborn. Then all that was left for me to do would be to slip the money quietly back into Merle's hand, and thank him for an interesting time and *please forward the answers to all of my questions to the following address.*

Stand by your Man struck up from the bathroom. I was starting to feel lonely.

"Nearly done in there?" I shouted. "I've brought you some coffee."

"Why don't you ring the airport and find out what flights are available? Today's the day, Ben."

Relief surged through me. If Merle was as sinister as my imagination was suggesting, we'd be reading about him soon enough over a glass of beer in an English pub. My guardian angel was back and on the case.

She emerged at last from the bathroom, wrapped in a towel. "Did you ring the airport?"

"What about our appointment?" I said.

"After you've made the call, Ben."

I pulled playfully at the towel. "You shouldn't make promises -"

There was a knock at the door. "Now, who do you suppose that can be?" she said.

Slipping on her dressing gown, she answered the door. "Come in," she said. "I still can't get over what you did yesterday. I've never seen anything like it."

Merle nodded over at me as he entered the room. "You mean the dog, I take it?"

"Do I mean the dog?" said Kate, beaming at him like a star-struck child. "Yes, I mean the dog! And I thought that what you said to the owners about taking responsibility – well, it should have been recorded and shown every night for a week on prime-time."

"Shucks," said Merle, grinning infectiously. "Who wouldn't have done the same?"

"Who are you, the King of Modesty? Anyway, I'd like to apologise for being so stand-offish."

He raised a hand. "No need for any of that. I understand completely. Anyway, I'm the one who ought to apologise, for the inconveniences my country has caused you and your good husband in the shape of that imposter Buck-Bradbury."

"There's really no need -"

"Oh, but there is."

"I think yesterday made up for that," said Kate.

"Yesterday was nothing," said Merle. "Don't take this the wrong way, but do you feel half as good as you look?"

"I'd have to say ... *better.*"

They both laughed, and I was starting to feel uncomfortable about the way Kate was dressed. I caught Merle's eye, and he touched his hat. Then he looked straight back at Kate. "The *Queen* of Modesty has spoken. Something here in San Francisco has hit the right button and that's for sure. Nevada might agree with you even more, though."

"Nevada?" said Kate.

"Permit me," he said, sitting on the bed, directly in line with a dazzling shaft of sunlight that illuminated his succulent pink buttonhole and bow tie. "I suspect your good husband hasn't told you much about me."

I swallowed hard and felt my forehead prickle. The money whispered in my pocket.

"I'm a healer," said Merle. "Does that surprise you?"

"I thought maybe you were a vet," said Kate, deadpan.

"You've been gifted with one hell of a sense of humour and that *is* a fact!"

"And you say you have the gift of healing?"

"I do. But unlike you, my gift has limitations."

"Wait a minute," said Kate. "Let me get this straight. Are you suggesting that you're somehow responsible for how I'm feeling today?"

"That's a tough one. If you like you can thank me for the temporary restoration of your health. But I can't guarantee that you're cured. Not yet. Not quite."

Kate sat down on the chair opposite the bed. "You're winding me up, right? You're telling me – what are you telling me?"

Merle glanced at me before returning his full attention to Kate. "I'm saying that I've started the healing process, nothing more than that."

She looked at me. "Did you know about any of this?"

Coughing, lamely, I eyed the back of my hand like there was a story written on it. I didn't know what game Merle was playing, or my part in it. I glanced at him, and he was looking back at me. I settled on the truth, though I had to look down at my shoes to tell it.

"That's why I wanted us to stay, Kate. I had ... faith."

In the silence I looked up. She was looking at me hard. "*Faith?*" She turned back to Merle. "But you say I'm not cured? I don't understand."

"It's not easy *to* understand," said Merle. "It never is."

"Who are you?" she asked him.

"It's enough that you know that I'm a healer."

"No, it isn't. What do you want?"

"I can see you're a person of faith," he said, "same as your husband. And I can see that you've lost sight of what you once believed."

"You must have good eyesight," she said, "I'll give you that much!"

"What matters is that you have the *facility* to believe."

"What is this, mind-reading or a psychology seminar?"

"Maybe a bit of both," said Merle. "Whatever gets the job done."

"You still haven't answered my question."

"Which is – remind me?"

"What is it you want?"

"To see you healed."

"Why? What am I to you? Are you a faith-healer? Do you believe in God?"

"Okay," he said, "this is the deal. Everything that happens is, at the end of the day, God's will, and there's no getting past that. Everything in this world is pre-ordained, and that includes *my* interventions. In a way that none of us can fully appreciate in this life, everything is perfect. Life is nothing more than a process of understanding the perfection of God's creativity. I struggle with faith like everybody else, and I have done for a long time. I do what I do the best I can and hope that on Judgement Day God will forgive my inadequacies."

Kate took a minute to digest what he was saying. She looked far from convinced by any of it. "But why go to all this trouble to help *me*?" she said. "And what's wrong with me?"

I watched him closely; he didn't miss a beat. "Mind if I smoke?" he said. "My hotels are not sensitive to a good cigar. Anyway, if I get caught smoking I'll pay myself the fine, deal?"

He lit up and blew a few smoke rings up towards the ceiling. No alarms rang.

"I guess you must have a thousand questions to ask me," he said, "but I want you to be patient. I don't have all the answers."

"At least tell me what was wrong with me!"

He shook his head. "I don't have the answer to that. I was pointed in your direction for some reason - some divine reason, I guess - and the healing process has started for you. But I can't say that you're cured. I don't know enough. There's someone else I'd like you to meet."

It rang a false note. Merle even suggesting the existence of someone more powerful, or in higher authority, than himself – it was like a bum note in a symphony, and it jarred the same way that his insistence that he didn't know what was wrong with Kate had rung false.

"You want to introduce me to, what, another healer?" she asked him.

"That's right."

"And where is this other healer?"

"Lives out in the Nevada desert, just outside Las Vegas."

He got up off the bed and walked over to where Kate was sitting, kneeling down before her, and placing his hands gently over hers. "I'm sorry I wasn't more open with you before. Talk of healing can find people running for the first plane-ride home. And that, in your case, would be a tragedy."

He let the pressure of his hands slowly move away from Kate's. "I've taken the liberty of arranging transport to Vegas. I hope you don't consider me presumptuous."

Kate looked over at me. "Did you know about this little trip?"

Before I had chance to answer, Merle said, "You're not at the centre of some conspiracy between your husband and my good self," he said. "Ben is a decent man, and he had faith in my powers to make you well."

"Shame he didn't think to mention it."

"He knows nothing about travelling to Vegas."

Another lie, though at least the money hadn't come up yet. I felt my hand move, involuntarily, and rest over it.

"But how do you or this other guy heal?" asked Kate. "What are you offering?"

"I can see that's troubling you." He stood up, took a few longs puffs on his cigar. The room grew misty, while the smoke alarm held its peace. "Like I suggested, everything ultimately is down to the Big Guy in the Sky. I don't have a specific religious mission, and I don't subscribe to any particular denomination, if that's what you're asking. I heal in the name of love for my fellow creatures - and I include dogs, cats and canaries in there. I'd even cure a rattler if it promised not to bite me."

"But where do you get your healing power from? Are you on terms with God?"

He opened out his palms. "It is a gift, and I choose not to question it. I have it, I use it, and I'm a thousand times grateful. You have to trust me."

"And this other guy, the one in Vegas – he can tell me what's wrong with me?"

"If anyone can, I believe so, yes."

Kate turned to me. "What do you think, Ben?"

Merle knew it and I knew it. We were going to Las Vegas.

Doubts, I was full of them, and not least the talk of another healer. But the evidence of my eyes was undeniable. Kate was getting stronger, and her symptoms had disappeared. Whatever methods he employed, Merle had succeeded where all others had failed.

I'd trusted him this far, how could I begin to tell my wife about the reasons for my doubts now? I didn't understand them well enough myself. I wanted him to persuade her, but seeing it actually happen took the ground from under me and I was suddenly less sure. The truth is, I didn't know what I believed, or what I was feeling.

Merle suggested we pack a few overnight essentials and meet him in reception.

We left our room and walked down the stairs to find the area deserted. A television, out of sight but not earshot, was announcing the fresh atrocities of the morning. Nineteen people had died less than two miles from Merle's hotel, a coach and a lorry meeting fatally beneath the disabled traffic lights at Quarters Crossroads. Nobody seemed sure of what exactly had caused the lights to fail, though what was certain was that there were no survivors. Emergency services were reporting appalling carnage at the scene, and officers were already receiving support.

I felt the blood draining out of me.

"Are you alright?" asked Kate.

I swallowed hard and tried to smile. The news report became the weather report, and then the sound of rotor blades obliterated everything else as the hotel car park transformed into a helicopter landing pad.

I kissed her. "I'm okay," I said.

The main door out of reception opened, and Merle beckoned us out onto the tarmac, where the huge dark silver bird waited beneath the deafening beating of its wings. A bright sun was starting to edge its way through the clouds, but looked uncertain. If I had been a gambling man I would have said that I didn't much fancy its chances.

We climbed aboard the helicopter.

CHAPTER
NINE

Merle took us by the "tourist route," flying over Yosemite and causing Kate to wax lyrical about believing in God again, her words tugging at something inside me. God hadn't featured in my life for a long time. He had been relegated, as far back as I could remember, to some abstract and vague possibility that I might get around to exploring one day. Life at home growing up had been too Old Testament, or maybe I was still too good at fooling myself with convenient excuses.

My mother rarely had the Bible out of her hands, quoting from it on a daily basis. We never went to church though. She said that those places were too full of hypocrites who wouldn't know the Lord if he was up there in the pulpit.

Kate had been brought up differently, and church had been an important part of her life. It was one of the paradoxes of our relationship that I, a stranger to the habit, would have felt happier if she had continued to attend. To think that our marriage had derailed her from her Christian journey through life and on into a blameless eternity, was something I didn't like to dwell on. It was partly superstition, I suppose. But there was more to it than that.

In my secret life I wanted to be preached to by the one I loved and who loved me. My mother, devout in her own way, until mental illness and a husband's thirst for the bottle had finally drained it out of her, had sown an early seed. It just hadn't been nourished, and there was unfinished business.

Perhaps, in hindsight, that's how Merle had got such a hold: promising, in the spaces between his words and actions, nothing less than the restoration of faith.

As we flew beyond Yosemite, he said, "I never heard so many superlatives. As one of our actor-cum presidents was fond of saying, 'You ain't seen nothing yet.'" On cue, the helicopter changed direction. "Nothing to worry about, folks," he said, "but for the sake of a little detour it would be a shame to miss the Daddy of them all."

It turned out he was talking about the Grand Canyon; some detour by anybody's standards. We took a look at Death Valley along the way, and he opened up a conversation about Kate's career as an actress.

"I should have taken you to Hollywood," he said, and I half expected him to change direction again and point the helicopter towards Los Angeles. "Maybe we can call in on the way back." He made it sound like calling at Marks and Spencer on the way back from the supermarket. "So what's the best role you ever played? I don't mean the most successful, or most critically acclaimed, and I don't even mean which one you thought you played the best.

What I mean is: what was the *best role,* you know, the best for *plumbing the depths of your art, man?"*

"Well," said Kate, "seeing as you put it like that ... I haven't a clue. Maybe if I'd played Sybil Fawlty."

"Doesn't sound like a Shakespearean heroine to me," said Merle. "One of the metaphysical poets?"

Kate laughed so loud that I temporarily lost the re-assuring hum of the rotors.

"I take it by your answer that *metaphysical poets* is heading a little off track," he said.

"I think you know exactly who Sybil Fawlty is," said Kate.

"That sounds to me like an accusation," said Merle.

"So, you still get the reruns in the States?" I said, feeling an idiot even as the words left my mouth. But they took pity on a poor fool, and neither of them laughed. Merle even gave my comment its due minute of silence before saying anything further.

"For what it's worth," he said at last, "I reckon you would have played Sybil to perfection, Kate."

"I'm not sure I like the implications," she said.

"What I mean to say is, you've got a certain 'formidable' quality that the part requires. Of course, you have infinitely more style, and looks-wise you knock the otherwise to-be-admired Prunella into a cocked hat, God bless her. And you'd have to work very hard to downplay your sensual - no, I'll say it and be done with: your *sexually charged charisma.*"

"If you say so," said Kate.

I was feeling uneasy about the tone of the conversation, and at the same time waiting for the turnaround. Some joke about husband Basil, perhaps. I braced myself for the punch-line, but the joke never came. Merle rarely did what I expected.

"You'd hate Hollywood," he said. "The endless brown-nosing, back-slapping, self-indulgent, self-applauding ass-hole scent of the place - you'd hate it."

"Produced some great movies."

"Can't deny that. Just so many shit people."

"Does that matter?" she asked, giving me the wink. "Doesn't the end product justify whatever it takes to get there?"

Merle glanced back at her. "If I thought for one minute that you believed that, then we wouldn't be having this conversation. We wouldn't be taking this ride."

"Does that mean that you're only interested in healing people with the right attitudes? Do you interview people and give them a rating before you decide whether it's worth having them cured?"

That was Kate; full of provocation, getting to the truth with that swinging sword of a tongue. I groaned inwardly. I wanted to see the Grand Canyon, and I wanted to put a dollar on a roulette wheel in Las Vegas.

When Merle didn't answer her question, I felt the fear grow. There was more at stake than a tourist ride.

"Who deserves to be healed?" he said at last. "Who deserves to die? All I can say is, I have an instinct to heal, and I follow that instinct wherever and to whoever it leads. It's a good question, though a difficult one."

"The best ones always are," said Kate.

"You mean like, *what's the best role you ever played*?"

And on we flew.

Later, after he'd spent forever talking us through every control in the helicopter, we came to an endless highway of trees. "Coming up over there," he said, pointing towards the suggestion of a gap in the land. "Be warned, my friends, it always outdoes expectation."

"I bet it says that in all the guide books," said Kate.

We turned and headed towards the hole in the ground that I never thought I was destined to see. He was right, *my* imagination, at least, was dwarfed. The gap in the ground kept opening up, and every time we looked we saw deeper into it. It seemed unfathomable.

We spent some time flying around the Grand Canyon, mesmerized by the scale of it; and then it was "full speed ahead for Vegas," though we did circle the Hoover Dam and put down briefly at a place that he affectionately called 'Shitcreek Canyon.'

Landing at 'Shitcreek', Merle left the rotors running while he ran into the only store in the only street in town, returning with "the only item in the western world worth having that's not available in Vegas." He held up a small carrier bag. "Shitcreek's own brand of fortune cookie. Listen to me: you should never arrive in Vegas without getting the truth out of one of these little doozies. But then I guess I'm just an old fashioned kind of guy."

He handed the cookies around and was the first to read one out.

"*A fortune waits for he who dares. For him who don't, the truth, who cares?*"

He whooped a few times, loudly, and punched the air. "Come on, slow-coaches, get to the programme."

Kate was next up. "*A fortune waits for he who dares* - do I need to go on?"

Merle looked mortified. He turned to me. "Come on, pal, restore my faith in Shitcreek."

I extracted my message. "*A fortune waits -*"

"That does it," he said, leaping from the cockpit, before disappearing back inside the store.

I looked at Kate. "You know me," she said. "Try anything once." The twinkle in her eye spluttered and went out. "What are we doing, Ben? Travelling America in search of some desert healer? This is madness. The whole thing's bizarre, and anyway, I've never felt fitter. It's all good fun, and it's very kind of him, I'm sure ..."

I trusted her instincts better than I trusted my own, and I was clinging to the idea that she would smell the first sign of danger like an angel smelling brimstone. I tried to reassure her that we were doing the right thing, though in truth I needed a good deal more reassurance than I was giving.

Merle reappeared with a huge grin. "Problem solved. That kind of mistake could get a place a bad name, and that's exactly what I told them. I said, 'Sloppy service like that's gonna give Shitcreek *a real bad name.'"* At this he erupted into barking laughter before handing out fresh cookies.

He thought Kate should read first this time.

"Fortune waits for an English Girl. Eat Shitcreek cookies and rule the world."

"Damned advertising," said Merle. "Your turn, Ben."

"Fortune's on the roulette wheel. Midnight, table four, the Silver Steal."

His eyes lit. "Give me that, would you."

I handed him the slip of prophecy. "That's a real one and no shit," he said. "I had one like that the first time I ever came here, and I won fifty times what I was worth in one night!"

Eagerly he opened his own message and read, *"A fortune waits for he who dares -"*

He screwed up the paper. "We're back to that again! Let's beat the hell out of town."

As soon as we were airborne Kate asked him two questions: what was the Silver Steal, and who was the healer? Merle was perfectly open about the latter, but vague about the former. I was, naturally, expecting the opposite.

"Name's Tobias Goldhorn, and he resides in a caravan five miles from Vegas. Has gifts enough to be the richest man in the United States, except he decided, many years ago, to follow the teachings of Jesus Christ. Strange thing about Tobias is that, for a self-professed Christian man, he never heals in the name of Christ. Reckons his soul just isn't pure enough to do that. So he heals like he's always done, in the name of wanting to make people well, and having the gift of doing it. He's never questioned that gift, never dared to tamper with it for fear of losing it. That's what I like about him. But his healing power is awesome, nonetheless. And that's his caravan down there."

We looked down to see a speck of dirty white in the distance, and not for the first time I felt something start to tie knots in my stomach. "Does he know we're coming?" I asked.

"Not unless he's started on the crystal ball."

"How do you know he'll be in?" I said.

"He's never out."

Merle concentrated on putting the helicopter down before he said anything more, and then it was to tell us nothing. "... As for the Silver Steal, all I can tell you is this: it's like nothing on the Strip. That place is full of rattlesnakes."

"I can't wait," said Kate.

The mention of rattlesnakes made me a little uneasy when it came to getting out of the helicopter. We were still a good hundred feet from the caravan, Merle looking unconcerned as he stood on the ground, waiting for me to join him. I took some deep breaths and climbed down.

The heat was savage, and I heard Kate wince as she climbed out from the air-conditioned cabin. I took her hand and we walked behind Merle, watching the ground carefully as we went, and hoping that Tobias Goldhorn's stoical lifestyle allowed for such luxury as an ice bucket and a fan.

We made it to the caravan without meeting a single rattlesnake, scorpion or man-eating spider. The curtains, seeming to depict a night sky sprinkled with stars, were closed, which seemed a sensible precaution against the brutal sun. "Hey, Tobias, open up!" shouted Merle, hammering on the scorched timber door. Then I saw him take something from one of the curtained windows. "Well, look at that," he said, showing us the hand-written sign.

Gone to Vegas.

An awkward silence accompanied us as we flew the last few miles. And what seems obvious to me now was a million miles from my thoughts then. Looking back I can see that the man at the controls was an actor of such calibre that even Kate couldn't have held a candle to him. How it would have worked on the screen or on the stage I don't know, but there in the flesh as we flew over the scalding desert sands, the man was nothing short of a genius. He played many parts, but he never played any of them better than he played seething, embarrassed anger that day.

We arrived in Las Vegas with a cryptic promise of finding our fortune in some unlikely gambling den called the Silver Steal, and a mission to find a healer by the name of Tobias Goldhorn, a man who had abandoned his designated post when he might have been using some of those amazing powers of his to intuit that special guests were arriving.

I climbed out of the helicopter and stepped on to the tarmac, catching Kate's look. We were clearly thinking the same thing. That we had arrived in a town that had never been on either of our maps, flown in courtesy of our very own healer and self-confessed magician, via some of the world's most awesome natural beauty ... and the cost of all this? Not an American cent and not an English penny. And we believed it. *Didn't we?*

We had no inkling of his power; hadn't witnessed more than the merest hint of it.

And he had bewitched us into thinking that we were in the middle of the most amazing adventure of our lives when all we were really doing was taking the scenic route to hell.

CHAPTER

TEN

THE FIRST MIRACLE I WITNESSED IN LAS VEGAS HAD NOTHING TO DO with Merle. And even if his later claim to be "a magician of historic destiny" had been true, what I witnessed in the fading of that day confirmed that there existed a magical order against which Merle could never be more than a dabbling child. The sunset that we saw that evening was an utter transformation, as night turned the cheap desert glitz into a priceless glitter of dreams.

He checked us in at the Luxor, a huge pyramid of a hotel casino, one of the new kids on the block, and featuring the strongest beam of light in the world shooting more than two hundred miles above the Earth. Merle took us along the Vegas Strip, casino after casino, all essentially the same but with little else in common. From each one we emerged dazzled and amazed, only for the next to take us deeper into disbelief. It was a fairy tale for children who believed they'd become adults, and every word was true. *And every word was a lie.* It was the beginning and end of civilization, according to Kate. Not her kind of town, and not mine.

Despite our reluctance, we spent the evening and the long night that followed imitating insignificant elves in the giant's playground, and laughing with our mouths open. At every flickering instant when my mind surfaced from its waking world of laughter, I was thinking that whatever became of us Kate had at least tasted a mouthful of the good life.

And all the time Merle was watching me think those thoughts; watching me watching her and plotting how he would use it all; how he would blackmail me with my own emotions, turning the screw that I had forged for myself, turning me into his dark apprentice. Changing me into what I blatantly was not, and was never meant to be; carrying it out like the worthy master of forbidden knowledge that he aspired to be.

Now, too late, I know it. Sometimes even a fool can find the truth; eventually; at a price.

We might have been vampires the way he ensured that we were safely inside a casino before dawn broke. He didn't want us to see the spell unweaving before our eyes as the day light mocked the illusion.

Inside the casinos there was no dawn; inside the casinos there was only the unending spinning of a million wheels of fortune. How well we knew this wasn't our world; outsiders looking in, standing on trash cans to peer in through diamond windows. The spell wouldn't hold us long, and Merle knew it.

Late the following morning we awoke in our casino suite at the Luxor. It was impossible to forget where we were: the fruit machine in the corner of the bedroom, the roulette wheel taps, the dice curtains, the playing card motif bedding and wallpaper.

While Kate showered I switched on the television. After long minutes of in-house advertising, I watched an 'educational' feature on the rudiments of poker, switching it off with a sense of relief when the phone rang.

Merle was inviting us to join him for a late breakfast.

Nothing seemed to have changed from the night before as we walked through the casino towards the gigantic food hall. The machines gorged the same notes and coins as they had done in the early hours, and the zombie faces (maybe the same ones, who could tell?) watched with bored expressions as their change buckets slowly emptied, filled, and then emptied again.

"Las Vegas calls all souls," Merle explained over breakfast. He told us how the rich spin a million dollars, and then come back and do the same the next night, and the next. How those of humbler means eat greedily in the food halls for a fraction of what some lousy diner charges, before settling back down to watch the dreams of another whole year die. "In Vegas they cater for every size of wallet. They want you here and they want you to stay here. Cents make dollars and they always will."

According to Merle, "... In Vegas everyone can dream while there's still something rattling in the bucket. Vegas will love you almost as much for your cent as for your dollar, because it knows that when you leave you'll only have one thing on your mind. And you'll go and get yourself a better job, work harder, learn to save your money, trim down on those unnecessary outgoings, and, before you know it, you'll be back. All over town the unwritten billboards proclaim: *you don't have to be rich in Vegas, but if you are we're going to love you for it.*

"Enjoying your breakfast?" he asked me, as he carefully sipped from a glass of fruit juice. I was enjoying it, as a matter of fact, and at the same time I was beginning to grasp something of his method. Merle wanted us to witness the weirdly distorted equality of the place. He wanted us to become a part of the spell that already exists, and save his own brand of magic for later on.

The economy of the great magician.

He could have bought us breakfast costing what I couldn't earn in England in a month. If he'd thought that would have impressed us, I have no doubt that he would have done it gladly. But Merle wanted us relaxed and guards down, at home in the easy comfort of self-service, eating the cheapest and most sump-tuous breakfast of our lives.

Sitting in that food hall, stuffing myself to the gills with fresh fruits, cereals and the constituents of a fine full English, some-thing else occurred: either Merle had an endless supply of the same clothes, or else he'd devised a laundry service second to none. The same immaculately pressed white suit never seemed to leave his miniature frame, while the black hat and shoes faith-fully maintained the contrast. The buttonhole and bow tie alone continued to defy expectations, now becoming a blue so deep and dark that it threatened at any moment to proclaim itself midnight.

Breakfasted, we began the first leg of our mission to find Tobias Goldhorn. We set off for Camelot. Merle had a hunch.

As we approached the casino I noticed a change in him. It was subtle, and I didn't attach much significance to it at the time. He seemed quieter than usual, and as we walked towards the entrance to the vast construction I caught a look in his eye; an expression of restrained bitterness. I can look back now and see it: he loathed the place.

We'd barely set foot inside the casino when our self-appointed guide excused himself, and went off to make enquiries. He left us alone to wander the square miles of gaming tables, and the medieval theme park extravagance.

"Is it wearing off, do you think?" Kate asked me. "Is it all beginning to look a little pathetic?"

I couldn't decide. It was wondrous or else ridiculous, and quite possibly both. It might be anything, anything at all.

"*Merle*!" said Kate, suddenly.

I turned, quickly. "Where – where are you looking?"

"Don't you see?"

"What?"

"Look around you, all of this Camelot shit. Merle – *Merlin*."

I thought about the book: Mark Twain's *Connecticut Yankee*. Camelot. King Arthur.

"You think he's named himself after King Arthur's mate?" I said.

"Maybe his parents had an odd sense of humour."

Mention of his parents brought with it a cold shiver of remembrance, and I recalled his tale of parenticide related to me back in the bar in San Francisco. But like the money, it was something I saw fit not to mention.

"We've got to ask him, Ben."

"You sound like one of the girls in a Famous Five adventure."

"Which adventure did you have in mind?"

"The one where they make up a mystery to pass the time, and then the whole thing comes true."

"I like the sound of that," she said.

"So did I ... once upon a time."

We spent the rest of an hour making critical observations about the way other people choose to enjoy themselves, proving, or trying to prove, our superiority. It's an easy thing to do, which might explain why so many people spend so much time doing it. At the same time we were reassuring ourselves that Las Vegas wasn't affecting us; that it wasn't corrupting *our* souls. After all, we were only tourists, incorruptible innocents abroad.

Merle had said that he'd catch up with us, but finding anybody in Camelot was a needle in a haystack job. "This place goes on forever," I said, checking my watch.

"Relax, he'll find us. And then we'll ask him to name his" ... Kate grinned ... "favourite magician."

"He might think we're taking the rise. It's a long walk back to San Francisco. I'd rather go by helicopter."

"A wise choice," said Merle.

We turned around to see the diminutive figure standing there, and I wondered how much he had heard. "Let's go get a drink," he said. "There's something I need to tell you."

At one of the casino bars he told us a story from the days of King Arthur. It was the story of Merlin, funnily enough, though it was hardly the tale that I remembered reading as a child.

When he began telling it, Kate glanced at me, and I knew that we were back on the same wavelength. Merle was yanking our chains; having fun at our expense. We settled down to hear the tale, consigned to let the guy enjoy his playtime.

Merlin, it turned out, was the most misunderstood figure in human history. Merlin, apparently, was not British at all, but American. He had flown over the water from his homeland like a migrating swallow - albeit a swallow in search of bad weather - to reveal his great gifts as a magician and prophet, to a people misled by their own false visions of progress.

"Fresh from kicking Cheyenne and Cherokee butt, Merlin was called, in a dream, to rescue the peoples of a distant, enchanted island from the grip of tyranny and oppression. Then he met up with King Arthur and company, and you probably know most of the rest, except that much later he found his real quest, and succeeded where every other magician had failed. I'm talking, of course, about immortality."

"So what's *your* quest?" asked Kate.

"Nothing so grand, I'm afraid to say, at least, not yet. I want to heal, and to develop my gifts of prophecy. That's enough for the time being."

"You have gifts of prophesy?" said Kate. "I thought you just relied on Shitcreek cookies."

"I might as well. As this afternoon's proven, my *gifts* are a little hit and miss."

"You mean the Tobias business?" I asked.

"I mean the *Tobias business*. Merlin would turn in his grave if he could see this fiasco." He looked up, casting an eye around the place. "Or this shit hole."

I felt the bitterness radiate, though he was quick to contain it.

"Turn in his grave?" said Kate. "I thought you said he was immortal?"

"Good point," said Merle, with a sparkle of darkness in his eyes that I didn't care for. "We will return to it another time ... and at a more appropriate location."

"More appropriate than Camelot?" I asked.

The darkness in his eyes lingered, and I chose not to push it. Then Kate broke in to ask about his gifts of prophesy, and I felt the burden lifting, the relief permeating down through my bones.

"... Varies," he said. "Sometimes I consult the tarot; other times I simply meditate on a question until the answer arises. Prophesy's something you have to work at."

Mention of the tarot set off another chain reaction of thoughts, and my mind flashed again on my first meeting with Merle in the bar at the International, and then back twenty five years to the carnival crone who had read my fortune.

... A book, an angel, a journey, a magician ...

I tuned back into the conversation. Kate was asking Merle whether he could use his gifts to win money. "Is this a request?" he said. "Are you succumbing to the spirit of Las Vegas so soon?"

"I'm curious, that's all," she said.

"Then why don't we find out."

"You mean you don't already know?"

He looked at me. "She's sharp, Ben." Then, looking back to Kate: "Okay, let's do it, tonight. Remember the cookies: table four, Silver Steal?"

"Don't you have to find Tobias Goldhorn?" I said.

Merle appeared to consider my question, and then he said, "If, Ben, I have any gift of prophesy at all, then I believe that I know where to find him. Tonight, my friend, we can accomplish three things: we can find Tobias, test out my gifts on the tables, and evaluate those Shitcreek cookies."

This said, he disappeared to the men's room to freshen his buttonhole.

"So, what do you make of that?" I asked Kate.

She shook her head. "Same as you, I suspect. I don't know what to make of him. I'm intrigued, though."

Merle came out of the men's room bearing a subtle message that I didn't understand at the time. No longer did his appearance bear the stamp of unity. The bow tie and buttonhole had finally gone their separate ways, with gold around his throat and a filthy grey over his heart. Perhaps he was indicating that the honeymoon was over, and that the darkening of our fortunes was about to begin. But, then, hindsight can be a wonderful thing.

"Come on," he said, "let's get going."

As evening fell we made our way across town, the miracle of night descending fast, and bringing the glitter down on us once again like a neon blanket of deceit. We left the Strip, and an hour before midnight found ourselves on the edge of town, where the desert comes in to lick around you like the first exploratory waves from a predatory ocean.

Leaving the playground of the rich behind us, we entered the carnival of demons. Our apprenticeships had been served without our knowing, and we walked into the Silver Steal laughing.

CHAPTER
ELEVEN

Unlike Camelot there was nothing medieval about the Silver Steal. It was like something out of a B movie, gangsters of every shape and size looking suitably corrupt, the women exuding cheap glamour. The place didn't seem to contain an atmosphere of threat, more an air of the ridiculous.

Merle suggested we wait by the main bar while he made further enquiries regarding Tobias Goldhorn. After he had fixed us up with drinks we watched him head for the door marked 'Private.'

"Bit seedy in here tonight," I said, as Merle disappeared into the smoky crowd.

"You're getting too used to fantasy land," said Kate.

It still seemed like fantasy land to me, only a different kind. A few weeks earlier and a job behind the bar in a place like the Silver Steal would have seemed like a royal appointment. Yet, for all the Bogart and Cagney gestures, and the hints of grittiness hammed up close to parody, it occurred to me that one hearty round of machine-gun fire, St. Valentine's Day style, and the whole place would be lying under the tables pretending to be dead. And who could blame them? There didn't seem much in the Silver Steal worth dying for.

"What did you think about all that King Arthur stuff?" I said, sipping my beer, starting to feel more at home.

"Camelot?"

"I meant about Merlin flying over from the States."

"I don't know, Ben. *What did you think*?" Her eyebrows were raised. "You don't think that perhaps he was enjoying a harmless flight of fancy, and testing our capacity for sarcasm?" She put on a face. "You don't think that he was being serious?"

"Of course not."

"*Ben?*"

"Did it ever interest you, you know, the Knights of the Round Table?"

"Well, I once played Morgan Le Fay in a school play. Can't say the story ever appealed that much. Maybe the kid playing Arthur was too spotty for me. That kind of thing can leave a lasting impression on a young girl."

Her eyes had narrowed and there was a faint smile that she was trying to keep a hold on. "All of that baloney about an American Merlin has set you thinking about the Mark Twain book, hasn't it? And you're putting two and two together and coming up with, oh, let's see: six six six?"

"Very droll," I said. "I have a theory, though, if you want to hear it."

"Go on, then. What have I got to lose?"

"Well … maybe Merle's hot on the trail of the Holy Grail. He's planning to kidnap us and take us to the real Camelot."

Kate laughed. "There's a book inside you, Ben. It's just a matter of getting the thing written. Anyway, what happens when he gets us to the *real* Camelot?"

I shrugged. "That's where my book stalls, I'm afraid."

"How about he wants to make me his queen, and together we will rule the kingdom?"

"That could work. So what about me? Where does that leave me?"

"You, Ben, get to write the book, of course."

"What a fine idea."

We turned around to find Merle grinning at us. "I like it," he said. "Matter of fact, I think that you might be on to something …"

"Any news on the elusive Goldhorn?" Kate asked him.

"He was here earlier," said Merle, ordering another beer for me and two mineral waters for him and Kate. "Might be back later, apparently."

That's the art of good lying: simplicity; no elaborate details to trip up on later. You either had it or else you didn't. Merle had it in spades.

"While we're here we might as well set about testing out those cookies?" he said. "I'm in the mood for a little old fulfilment on those Shitcreek prophecies."

Unlike the magnificent and monstrous theme parks on the Strip, the Silver Steal catered only for gambling and drinking. There was less distraction, and I felt the wedge of money fibrillating over my heart.

"I thought the appointed hour was midnight," said Kate.

"Nothing wrong with getting a little warmed up," said Merle.

We followed him around the tables like children following a teacher around a science museum. He pointed out this, explained that, warned about the dangers of those and extolled the virtues of a hundred ways to lose money fast. At last he reached for his wallet with a gesture that reminded me of the old western movies, the gunslinger reaching for his six-shooter. He flicked open the biggest wallet I'd ever seen, examining the contents before sweeping his gaze across the casino floor, end to end, side to side, capturing the ruthless focus of a condensed Jack Palance.

He took out an assortment of notes and presented them at one of the change kiosks, and then he sidled up to a roulette table and showed us how fast you could lose a hundred dollars. With a nonchalant smile he moved on to Blackjack, promptly doubling his losses. Kate was a little open mouthed already, but then she still had no idea how much of Merle's casual money was nestling next to my own thin wallet.

"Takes a while to warm up, especially in the Steal, I find. The stiffness is going, though. I can feel it shaking loose now."

"Glad to hear it," said Kate. "What shall we play next?"

"We? Itchy fingers at last?" His eyes lit. "I know something you'd love."

We trotted along behind him, less like children now and more like a couple of faithful poodles. At the far side of the casino we came to a section that had been roped off. Beyond the ropes stood a row of gold-coloured machines; fancy one-arm bandits. Nobody was playing them.

Merle signalled for an attendant and turned to Kate. "Care to join me? It's a straight-forward game, you can't go wrong."

The attendant, dressed in a sober dinner suit (which made a change from the medieval armour of Camelot and the Roman bedsheets of Caesars, I suppose) came over and, with a simple appreciation of ceremony, took down the rope. We stepped into the arena, and I heard Kate catch her breath. It seemed the machines were picky about their diet: they ate one-hundred dollar tokens and nothing less. There was an up-side, of course, there always is: they paid out up to half a million. *Cash.*

"Not the kind of one-arm bandits we're used to," said Kate.

"You can get used to anything in Vegas," said Merle.

He fed in the first coin, and quickly followed it with a second, and then a third. By the twelfth I was busily converting his losses into second-hand cars and maybe a down payment on somewhere half-decent back in England.

It was the fifteenth hundred-dollar token that brought home the bacon. Not the whole pig, perhaps, but certainly a few hefty slices. When the endless clattering of coins finally ended, he calmly gathered up thirty thousand dollars and asked the attendant to have the money converted into bills. "No good for my back carrying that kind of change," he said.

Back at the bar the beer turned to champagne, on the house, while Merle sipped his mineral water, and Kate did the same. We watched some more as Merle lost here, won there, and steadily, invisibly, midnight crept upon us.

The smoke grew thicker, and the noise around the tables grew louder; the Silver Steal working up to its own zenith. It was beyond the limits of flesh and blood, mine at least, not to be infected by the growing sense of possibilities. At one minute to the sacred hour, Merle handed Kate six one-hundred dollar tokens.

"Time," he said, "for those Shitcreek cookies to come home to roost. Take it," he said. "You people have brought me good luck tonight. What you win you keep, that's the deal."

Kate looked at me and I shrugged, hoping that she would take the money and win our fortune.

What if we won thirty thousand - half a million? What we could do, what good we could do with that.

How easily we deceive ourselves ... and set foot amongst snakes at the glint of gold.

I said nothing and hoped that greed wasn't taking its clothes off and parading naked across my face.

"It's up to you, Kate," I said, as coolly as my billowing desire would allow.

"Looks like I'm outnumbered," she said at last. "But there's one condition."

"Name it," said Merle.

"I'm playing for fun."

"It's the only way."

"What I mean is, it's your money; you keep whatever we win."

"We'll discuss that later. But come, the hour of prophecy is upon us."

"What am I playing?" she asked him.

"Table four, if I remember correctly. Roulette."

We moved to the appointed table. There were a dozen or so people already busy around it, and as many looking on. We quietly took our places, keeping our eyes on Merle for our cues.

The stakes had risen. Whatever we won was ours to keep, despite Kate's protests. I wanted to win, almost as though life and death depended on it. As though a switch had been flicked, transforming the nature of reality from sitting in front of a television screen, warm and safe, imagining how exciting it would be to swim amongst sharks, to suddenly being transported to the deep ocean, squeezed into a wetsuit, feeling the pressures change, plunging down through the water, catching the first sight of the circling fins, and wondering whatever possessed me to enter the water.

We watched the wheel spin a couple of times, and the outcome manifest itself in the pushing around of tokens and the accompanying myriad of signs and gestures.

"Okay, let's do it," he said. "Step to the table if you please."

"Do I bet it all on one?" Kate was waving her hands around nervously as she asked, and there was a quiver in her voice.

"It's your choice," he said. "I don't want to interfere with the cookies."

She placed a hundred dollar token on one of the numbers. I couldn't be sure which. Then the wheel spun, and at last the wheel stopped spinning. I waited, holding my breath, waiting to find out what it all meant.

The money went down.

I saw Kate look back at Merle, horrified and bent on apology. Merle said nothing, offered nothing. People were waiting. Here people didn't like waiting. Kate hurriedly put another hundred on a different number, and again the ball stopped. "Hey, this is great," she said, drily. "How much do you want to lose tonight?"

We watched the next two go down, Merle maintaining a look of indifference. But I could tell he was enjoying himself.

Kate was placing the bets faster now, entering into the spirit. It wasn't long before I could sense her discomfort rising again. The fifth bet went down, and the responsibility started to bite at the thought of losing somebody else's money, despite the fact that it seemed to be what the man wanted.

She held up the last token. "I don't suppose Shitcreek cookies ever think of giving out the winning numbers?"

"What's your lucky number?" he asked her.

"Thirteen."

"Didn't it just have to be?"

Someone said, "You betting, Lady?"

Merle's presence moved. "You say something? The lady's playing, the lady's taking her time. The lady's got a right, every goddamned right to take her time."

A silence froze around the table, and Kate placed the token on number thirteen.

The wheel was spinning again.

For me there was no thrill. For me the spin of each wheel was unbearable torture bounded by the desire to win.

And that sixth play did it.

Kate threw her arms in the air and shrieked; and Merle was there to throw his arms around her, and the first to congratulate his "Lady Luck."

I stood watching them, wondering what all of a sudden was so special about a few thousand dollars, when there was a sight more than that sitting quietly in my pocket. How in that instant I wanted to take the money around the tables and on towards the gold section, take the jackpot, give him his money back and still fly to England a rich man; Kate by my side, America forgotten, Las Vegas forgotten, King Arthur and Merlin and the whole fucked-up lot of them forgotten.

Tobias Goldhorn? *Forgotten.*

I caught Merle's eye and tried to smile. But I couldn't manage it and looked away. I took on more champagne. Kate was still sipping mineral water along with her sugar daddy, while I was wolfing down the bubbles. My glass never emptied try as I did to drain it. At some point Kate made a reference to the quantity I was shifting, and I replied along the lines of didn't she want me to toast *Lady Luck's* Magnificent Success? Secretly I was toasting nothing, but God if I wasn't thirsting for gold.

Kate excused herself. We watched her walk towards the rest rooms on the far side of the casino floor. Merle didn't waste the opportunity.

"Your turn, my friend," he said. "It's what you've been waiting for."

My heart was thumping as I offered him a blank expression.

"Come on, Ben. Knock it off, will you. You're itching for it. I've seen the way you've been looking at those machines. You're a man in love, and you've got to get it out of your system or you're not going to be any good to anybody. It's in your pocket, right?"

Of course it was.

"Then let's take it out and set it to work."

I hesitated, looking across to where Kate was disappearing into the crowd.

"What are you waiting for - your wife's permission?"

I took out the envelope containing the money.

"That's more like it," he said. "Counted it yet?"

"I've counted it."

"I bet you have. Then you'll know how much to ask for at the kiosk."

"*All of it?*"

"You may never come to Vegas again. Can you live with the might-have-beens?"

"What if I lose?"

"And what if you win? You think too much, and it doesn't get you anywhere. Where's your spirit, Ben? Where's that immortal sense of adventure that once made your nation so *great*?" He patted my shoulder. "Do it for Kate. Don't you think she deserves a little excitement in her life, a little success?"

I changed the money, all the time eyeing the door to the rest rooms. Then I hurried back to the bar where Merle was waiting to hand me a small glass brimming with something ominously unfamiliar. "Down in one and you'll get the job done," he said. "You could be flying home in your own plane yet. Come on, it ain't gonna turn Jekyll into Hyde ... least not on its own."

I needed something. My heart was beating like a psychotic hammer. I poured the drink down my throat.

I scarcely remember scrambling my way to the machines; only dimly can I recall the relentless feeding of the hungry metal mouth, and looking with disbelief at the white plastic bottom of my empty change bucket.

The last thing I remember about that night, was turning around to see Kate returning fresh from the rest room, looking at me as I stood like a toppling fool, one arm draped across the top of the machine, then looking around for Merle, who wasn't there, my arm slipping from the machine, and all light fading to black.

I awoke the next morning with a desperate need to throw my guts into the toilet bowl, which I did, repeatedly. It brought only the faintest relief. Later, some semblance of life draining back into me, I remembered the money, and then I wished I was still vomiting. Or better still, dead. Kate brought me some sweet tea and insisted I try to get something into my stomach. It helped, a little. I felt myself emerging from a jigsaw of guilty feelings, and that was entirely down to Kate. As far as she was concerned, if there was anything to forgive, I was forgiven. I wasn't the next Meths Tolle. I had merely let the occasion get the better of me and got myself roaring drunk. It happens to the best, she assured me. Though the best, she added, only allow it to happen occasionally. As it turned out, she still knew nothing about the money.

"Thought you'd go for the jackpot? Out of the ring in one: Ben Tolle and his amazingly empty wallet, risking a fractured skull for one dance with a gold-painted fruit machine. What were you doing up there? If you had any money, you were too drunk to get it from your pocket into the slot. It took four doormen to get you into the cab. It's a good job you weren't rich last night, because you were drunk enough to lose your soul."

I wished that she hadn't said that.

"If you'd had the money I won in that change bucket you were holding onto so tightly, I swear it wouldn't have lasted a minute."

"Thought you said I was too drunk to get coins into the slot?"

"You would have tipped up the bucket and lost the lot over the floor, you fool."

I needed more sweet tea. It came with a smile and a kiss.

"You were so funny, Ben, with one arm around the machine, the other holding your plastic bucket. I didn't realise it was you at first. I came out and saw Merle over by the Gold Bandits, talking to someone. I wondered if it was this Tobias guy, and then I saw you standing there, a few machines away, swaying like you were standing in an oil slick. Then you turned the wrong way and said,

'Merle can explain it all, sweetheart' and bang, you were down and out."

I winced at his name, and the connotations it raised in my banging skull: Merle, owner of the fortune that I, Ben 'The Prince of Fools' Tolle, had thrown into that insatiable slot.

"He reckoned it was the best slapstick since" - at this point Kate put on a heroic attempt at our host's drawl - "Mr C. Chaplin. Why, even that hellbound mother couldn't have done a headfirst to share a mattress with Mr B. Tolle when he's fixing to dance with one of them *perty little gold babes.*"

Laughing hurt, though it cleared my head. I asked for her latest ideas on Merle and the Tobias Goldhorn business, and if she thought we were on a wild goose chase.

"Shitcreek geese, you mean? What were you drinking, Ben? I know you were shifting that Champagne, but I've never seen you anywhere near that before, not even in the bad old days."

"God knows," I said.

"I'll tell you what *was* funny."

"Tell me. Get it over with."

"The look on your face when I came over. You looked like a man who'd lost a fortune and found a summons. You looked *terrified.*"

Rushing to the bathroom, I heaved the few sips of sweet tea back out of my stomach, and made it back to bed to wallow in self-pity.

"Sorry," she said, kissing me gently. "I'll change the subject."

"I would appreciate that."

"What were you saying about wild goose chases?"

"I don't know, Kate. Maybe it all seems a little too good to be true."

"It's certainly that."

There was a gleam in her eye that I wasn't sure of. I said, "Why would he spend all this time and effort on us? Why go to all this trouble for a couple of strangers?"

"Perhaps he likes our company."

I was close to saying it, close to coming out and telling her about the money, and about all the crazy facts that filled my head but made no sense. I was firmly in the stranglehold of hope; desperate enough to believe in anything that I could cling to, and afraid that too much truth might shatter whatever was holding Kate's illness in remission. I don't know what I would have said if she hadn't opened her mouth at that moment and knocked the stuffing out of me.

"I know why he's doing all this, Ben."

"You do?"

"He has the heart of a saint."

I sat up. "He has what?"

"The man *is* a saint."

She didn't laugh, and there was no punch line. If she was being ironic, then it was too deep and too subtle for me.

"Come on," I said. "It was generous of him to let us keep the money you won - and he's fixed up this room for free, but -"

"He's flown us to Vegas to find a healer, too, but forget all that. After what I saw last night – you're not going to believe it."

"What are you talking about?"

"I'm talking about what happened after your lights went out."

"In the casino?"

"On the ride back."

I was intrigued, but mainly I was scared. "What happened?"

She told me, from the beginning. I lay there trying to digest it all, stunned into silence.

And so the reversal was complete, with me occupying the sick-bed while Kate attended to my sick-bed needs, convincing me that we were in the best of hands. Now it was me filled with cynicism, and a good helping of dread into the bargain, while my wife, no longer seeing the friendship of a stranger through suspicious eyes, had fallen under his spell, as I had done. I had played the fool like I was born for the part, letting Merle into our lives and giving him free rein. There was nobody to blame but myself and there never would be.

Kate was playing the wonderstruck adolescent mesmerised by the magical secrets of an eccentric uncle - an uncle who was looking younger than both of us, though his age remained as much a mystery as his purpose.

After she told me what Merle had done that night, I had to endure enough hero-worship to make me wish I had something left to vomit.

CHAPTER
TWELVE

FEAR AND LOATHING WERE FIGHTING A BATTLE INSIDE ME. AT LEAST greed was keeping its head down. Greed was out of its depth. I would have happily slunk back to England, content with my empty pockets, and comforted in the knowledge that whatever dangers I was storing up had the Atlantic Ocean to navigate. I was too distracted thinking about the fortune I had thrown down the mouth of the gold machine, and about the possible consequences, to care anything more for the perils of wealth. The money had been a guilty secret, and one that I should never have kept. I was certain that its loss would expose my deceit in all its sordid glory. That Merle intended me to lose the money all along.

There were patterns, and I could almost feel their shapes.

The loathing was edging the battle. It held in its artillery the belief that Merle was manipulating us. But it went deeper than that, and its claws grew long and dug to the bone in that hour of hero worship, finding feelings in me that I would prefer to deny existed at all.

It struck me that the likes of Merle held sway from the beginning of time. Go back to any pocket of history, and if you look for him, he's there, waiting. I never went looking for him, not in any obvious way. And at the same time I must have. That's the way he operates.

The master and the fool.

I wondered how many fools it took to make one Merle. I formed a picture of the type of fool that he fed on; the type he needed to survive. There was no question: the portrait was *me*.

Dissecting the image I exposed every characteristic, peeling off layers like I was tearing open a rotten vegetable. The fool would have to be desperate as well as gullible; cursed with the burden of hope, and crippled with the insanity of love. A generous topping of naivety would always be welcome, along with a powdering of guilt and the full measure of insecurity. It was all there, in the right proportions, waiting for the master. *Poor Ben Tolle.*

The cascade of thoughts began as Kate told me what happened after we left the Silver Steal.

They'd manhandled me into the cab, and Merle had given the driver instructions. It was late, but the heat outside the air-conditioned casino wasn't letting on. The cab driver apologised that his air-con had broken down, and said that we were welcome to open the windows. Kate did so, only to be greeted with a blast of warm dry air as refreshing as boiled beer. A few minutes into the journey, she started to feel nauseous and asked the driver to stop. He pulled over, and Kate got out and squatted on the sidewalk. Behind her she could hear Merle getting angry with the driver, demanding to know why he couldn't keep the means of his livelihood in a decent state of repair. The driver insisted that the air-conditioning had been in perfect working order until right before the pick-up. At that point Kate heard a loud bang.

"Well I'll be ..." she heard the driver say. Then Merle gestured to Kate to get back inside the car.

"Are you sure it's safe in there?" she'd asked him.

"It's safe," he grinned. "And this husband of yours could sleep through a hurricane at sea once he's got the spirits inside him."

Kate approached the car, still feeling sick.

"You'll be okay once you're in here," Merle reassured her.

As she climbed into the back of the cab, sitting herself next to my snoring bulk, she was surprised to feel a blast of refrigerated air.

"How did you do that?" the driver asked Merle.

"You can do anything if you put your mind to it," Merle told him. "You can knock it off the fare. Now drive."

Merle had asked the driver to head out towards the desert highway. Soon, and with me still not stirring an inch in the back of the cab, they came upon a small crossroads, where he instructed the driver to pull over.

Merle got out of the car, walked to the crossroads, perched up on his tiptoes, and removed his hat. His head, as smooth as a billiard ball, bore the weird tattoo that Kate thought might represent the magician of legend, Merlin himself.

Having exposed his baldness, along with his love of mythical magicians, Merle pointed his nose into the air, twitching it in the fashion of a cartoon rabbit. After a few moments, he changed direction and continued in the same manner. When he'd finished, he got back into the car and told the driver to call an ambulance, giving him the precise location. Then he told the driver to turn at the crossroads and to proceed along the track.

We met the flashing lights of the ambulance about half a mile up the road. Kate told me how the driver started repeating, "Christ, oh Jesus Christ," as we approached the flashing lights that were grotesquely illuminating the scene. "*Christ, oh Jesus Christ. Christ, oh -*"

"Will you please shut the fuck up?" Merle had told him. "There's only one guy by that name, and I reckon he heard you the first time."

There were two mangled cars and five mangled bodies lying beneath a canopy of stars illuminating the dark desert night. None of the bodies were moving.

Kate paused for a moment in the telling of the story, as though she was still trying to process this next part. "He said a really weird thing, Ben. After we'd watched the bodies being loaded into the ambulance, he told me that he would visit the one who would make it, the following day, after praying for the souls of the four that wouldn't. Then he gave the police his number, and told the cab driver it had been a long evening and that if he wouldn't mind, please to get the job done and get us all to our beds. And short of the business of getting your oblivious bulk into a bed, that concluded the events of an extraordinary night."

When Kate had finished, she waited for my response. I could see that she was expecting a round of superlatives, but I wasn't in the mood. I said, "Sounds interesting."

"*Interesting*? Have you heard a word I've said?"

"I heard it. What am I supposed to say?"

She took a long, slow breath, her eyes filling up with clear exasperation. "I've just told you about the most incredible experience - something that has kept me awake all night wondering if I'm going insane – and you ..."

With her eyes busily searching mine, presumably for clues that might explain my apparent nonchalance, I made a grave mistake. I said, "I just thought that you were, I don't know - impressed with the guy."

"What?"

"You know, following on from the dog episode ..."

My words petered out and silence followed. She broke it. "Have you really nothing else to say?"

I went for it. Call it foolish pride. I said, "Perhaps it was the excitable schoolgirl tone that threw me."

Her eyes were blazing. "You don't think that my *excitable schoolgirl tone* has anything to do with the fact that I've just witnessed an out-take from the Twilight Zone?"

I'd heard enough. My mind was made up. I would tell her about the money and let her come to her own conclusions. I would tell her about the girl and the cigar-smoke cure, and what Merle had told me of his childhood and all the business with the mutilated old lady.

I got as far as "Kate -" when she opened up the bomb doors and pressed the release button.

"Are you going to ask me if I bedded him while you were out cold? Go on then, ask me. Let's get it out of the way."

The heart drained out of me. I felt my resolve to tell her the truth beat its frail wings and die.

I couldn't say how long I lay there, letting the feelings of loathing build. If those feelings hadn't been bounded and qualified by fear, the bloodshed would have come earlier, I have no doubt. It might have come moments after a familiar tapping was heard at our door.

The tapping brought fear, and the fear held the loathing in check. And when Kate opened the door to greet him, I lay there. And when he made some joke about sex being a lousy cure for a hangover, I politely smiled and played the wounded part. And whether it's possible for fear and loathing to actually cancel each other out, or merely that I was falling victim once more to the bewitching charms of the Master of a Million Fools, all I know for sure is that when he extended a hand to me as I lay there, stagnant on the bed, I received him with a warmth that chilled me to the bone.

CHAPTER
THIRTEEN

HE CAME INTO THE ROOM ON TIME AND LEFT WITH NOT A SECOND TO spare. It's just that we hadn't seen the timetable, or even known that one existed.

How long did he allow himself to enter the room, make his hangover joke, and extend a hand my way? How many minutes to deliver the plan for the day, disguised as a series of random ideas and possibilities? How long set aside for bringing a sense of ease and peace to a room full of gnawing tension, a healing hand to the growing discontent? Healing that only lasted while he was in the room, making the discontent that much more apparent once he'd left. Making him all the more indispensable once the echo of his footsteps had faded.

He suggested a short trip into the desert to view the Hoover Dam, and a dip in Lake Mead. Kate thought it a wonderful idea, and so did I. After all, there wasn't a reason in the world not to.

Merle left the room and took the spell with him. Alone again, Kate and I danced cautiously around each other, as though we had become strangers. When at last we had exhausted the silence with a play-and-a-half worth of unspoken dialogue; when our bloodless duel had worn our patience into the ground, she said, "If you didn't fancy the trip, why didn't you say so to his face?"

I had no answer. While he was in the room, I couldn't think a single reason for not accepting anything and everything. Now I could think of a dozen reasons.

"I thought you wanted to get back to England," I said, lamely.

The silence was vicious. To set foot inside it seemed as inviting as swimming across a swamp to try out anti-aggression therapy on a family of crocodiles. The silence grew so thick, so intimidating, that I had to try something to rescue my head from its teeth; to puncture the thing with sound. "Whatever happened to this great healer?" I said. "Whatever happened to Tobias Goldhorn? A bit convenient, don't you think?"

"Convenient?"

"That's what I said."

"I know what you *said*, Ben. I just don't know what you *mean*. You're talking in riddles."

"So you believe there is a Tobias Goldhorn?"

"Yes, I do. I've even seen where he lives!"

Her tone drew blood. I tried to keep the venom out of my voice. "That could be a set-up," I said.

"Don't you think you're becoming a bit paranoid? Look, if you don't want to see the Hoover Dam, why don't you tell him and we'll go back to San Francisco. And then we'll fly home, if that's what you want."

"It's not what *you* want, though, is it? Not anymore."

"What's changed?" she said. "What is it that you're not telling me?"

Another opportunity ... and I let it pass.

"Tell you what," I said.

"Tell me, Ben," she said, wearily.

"Let's forget this morning ever existed. I'll get dressed. *Merle will be waiting.*"

We saw the Hoover Dam, we dipped into Lake Mead, and we arrived back in Vegas to see another night fall from the sky.

Merle hired a car and did the driving. The Hoover Dam was magnificent, but it didn't impress Kate as much as the incident at the ice cream van on the way back to the car.

As we waited for the bulbous man in the sunburst shorts to order the triple king size with four flakes and raspberry sauce, Merle gave us the history of the building of the dam, and the birth of Las Vegas as a place for the workers to blow the hot dust of the week out of their chests. He was looking resplendent in his wild strawberry buttonhole and violent purple bow tie, and we listened as he painted a vivid portrait of the teething years of America's illustrious playground. He knew how to tell a story.

The bulbous man, meanwhile, waiting for his change, took a long and hungry look at the giant's feast in his sweaty fist, before diving open-mouthed towards the flakes. Kate and Merle didn't seem aware of the mighty display of gluttony taking place inches from them, but I was there, watching in awe as the man tipped his head back and attempted a hole-in-one.

A second later, his face was turning the colour of Merle's tie. It looked like a flake had lodged in his gullet.

The ice cream seller came back to the hatch with the man's change, but the guy was already down on his knees, out of sight of the ice cream seller, gasping frantically, pitifully, for air. The ice cream seller shrugged his shoulders and pocketed the change. "What can I do for you, sir," he asked me. I pointed down at the man on the ground. Panic overwhelmed me. I had never seen anybody die. I had never been there at the moment of actual departure, to witness the transition. My arms paddled the air as though I were treading water at the scene of a shipwreck, having spotted the first fin.

Kate was on top of the guy in a flash, pushing him forward and thumping at his back. Nothing was happening, though. At least one of the flakes was holding its ground with murderous intent, and I saw the panic begin to rise in her as she beat at the poor man's back with desperate fury. "Oh, my," said the ice cream seller, finally recognizing the dangers that came with his profession. "Not had one of these situations in a while."

Still the flake held dominion, and the recognition of a premature and stupid death entered into the victim's eyes. Then Merle acted.

With a calm certainty of movement, the man was pulled onto his back and his arms pinned to the ground under Merle's knees. The man's face was a mass of sweating, purpling veins, and that seemed destined to be his parting look on an absurd world.

Merle leaned into the purpling face. I heard a tremendous sucking sound, followed by a loud POP!

The man was breathing again. Merle turned around, proudly revealing a large chocolate flake poking out from his own mouth. Removing the innocuous looking item from between pristine teeth, he handed the man his troublesome flake, and said, "In future I would try them one at a time, buddy boy."

At Lake Mead I was better prepared. I waited vigilantly for the calm paradisiacal scene to turn to cataclysm. Surely a coach load of schoolchildren would arrive at any moment and instantly become a mass of helpless screaming, going down for the third time in the middle of the lake as frozen onlookers gazed on the scene. And then, at the last and most desperate moment, Merle would command the witnesses to stand aside, before plunging in to rescue every last one of the drowning children, the state of Nevada applauding wildly from the surrounding hills.

The coach never came, and I joined him and Kate in the water, swimming idly under the hot sun. No daring rescue necessary, nothing all the way back to Vegas.

I was still buzzing from the drama at the dam, and I wanted to talk about it. I needed to confirm that we had actually witnessed it. Instead we listened to Merle telling us more of the history of Las Vegas. The lack of acknowledgement of such an extraordinary event served to add an extra pinch of unreality to the unreal day.

He took us back to Vegas under the thickening veil of darkness. The sudden glow of lights erupting out of the hushed desolation of the Nevada desert had an irresistibility about it that was hypnotic, with a billion snake eyes drawing victims to within striking distance.

"Isn't it beautiful?" he said. "Our very own Milky Way."

I wondered which star was calling us that night. It turned out to be the Silver Steal.

Twenty minutes was all it took. We watched the roulette wheel pluck numbers from the air and dollars from wallets. Merle was calm, relaxed, like an athlete weighing up the opposition, confirming his own supremacy; limbering up, unzipping his tracksuit, waiting to flex his muscles, honed and unstoppable. He placed three bets, all straight winners. Then he handed a hundred dollar token to Kate and another one to me. "Pick a machine," he said. "I ask only that you choose the *winning* machine."

Once again we were stepping inside the roped area of golden dreams. Kate wanted me to go first. I did and sure enough the money went down.

"Don't worry about it, Ben," said Merle, patting me on the back. "Invariably it's the ladies who bring me the best luck."

I didn't doubt that.

Kate placed the token into the hungry mouth, and we watched the machine burst into a frenzy of lights. After the lightshow came the first sounds of mechanical indigestion, and then the sight of gold as the machine began spilling its rich guts.

I could see that the payout was going to dwarf what she had already won, but the gold was pouring too fast for me to gauge the full extent of it. It was like heaven had sprung a leak.

In the pit of my stomach there was no joy, and I sensed the nose of hell's legions starting to twitch. He handed Kate his car keys, and asked us both to wait in the car while he collected his money. It seemed there was to be no Champagne in the Silver Steal that night.

As we walked out of the casino, the dark heat hit us, and we climbed quickly into the car. Kate started up the engine and switched on the air conditioning. We basked in the chilled air for a few moments, and then I felt Kate's hand come into mine. I watched her cheekbones widen towards a smile.

Our eyes locked together and I felt the healing. I wanted to apologise for everything that I'd said that morning, every stupid thing. I could see the same thoughts riding across her face. The bursting silence was electric.

"How much do you reckon?" I asked.

"I daren't even think about it."

I looked out towards the entrance to the Silver Steal, waiting for something to happen.

Tell her you're sorry. Tell her now. TELL HER.

I said, "How do you reckon he'll split the money?" I tried to take the words back, squeezing her hand. I felt her look and then her hand leaving mine.

"What kind of a question is that? You mean because we - no, *I*! Because *I* put the money in ..?" She was shaking her head. "What's happening to you, Ben?"

"Will you stop asking that stupid question? Nothing, do you hear? That's what's happening to me - *nothing!*"

"I think it *is* time we were going home," she said. "In fact, I think we've left it a little late. This place isn't good for us."

I heard the catch in her throat as she quickly turned away from me, and in my loneliness I resumed my watch on the door of the Silver Steal, and waited.

Merle came back to the car, his face beaming. Climbing in, he said, "Cold in here, cold as hell." Then he turned and looked at us. "Am I intruding on a matrimonial dispute, by any chance?"

I tried to smile. "How much have ..?"

The words failed me.

"How much have *I* won? I'll tell you how much *I've* won. Seventy-five thousand. But don't you want to know how much *we've* won?"

I looked at Kate, but she was busy looking at him.

"We?" she said. "Look, I'm pleased to have brought you some luck, if that's what I've done. But we couldn't possibly -"

"You can possibly and you will. You can't expect me to spend a quarter of a million bucks all on myself, now, can you?"

We headed back to the Strip, and Merle dropped us at the Luxor, before heading off to "attend to business."

Kate and I had so much to talk about that we ended up saying nothing, undressing in the darkness, afraid of what the light might expose.

I knew she wasn't asleep; that she was turning it all over the same as I was. I lay wondering if we were rich or merely being suckered further into something that we didn't understand.

Whether I was destined to drink Champagne again and throw an even bigger fortune into the gold mouth, for whatever purpose. I wondered whether the newspapers back home still had anything to say about us, and if anybody was suggesting that we were living it up on other people's money. I wondered if anybody was speculating yet about whether we were alive or dead.

It occurred to me that if we were to die, nobody need know. They would never find the bodies or discover what really happened.

I moved closer to Kate and felt for her hand. I held it lightly, hoping that forgiveness might pass both ways between us, in the silence and in the darkness, where guilt and shame could whisper their confessions. I longed for her warmth, and for her cooling touch, and to know that what was broken could be gathered back and recast.

And then I was back to wondering if the road we were on would finally provide a cure, or if my wife was cursed to spend forever in the shadow of Merle, following him around America in the midst of some extended and fragile remission.

Remission from what?

Were we destined to find out what was wrong with her, find out about the mutilated old lady, the deaths surrounding us, the truth about Tobias Goldhorn - *Merle himself*?

Before heading into the night to attend to 'business' he'd said, "Sleep well, my friends; tomorrow you get to see the main feature. Once in a lifetime, boys and girls: we're going to Angels Camp, Nevada. We're going to finish the job."

When I finally found sleep, it was with those words echoing around the inside of my head, and with a vague image of England growing ever smaller.

And dimmer.

And distant.

CHAPTER
FOURTEEN

I FELL INTO A LAND OF DREAMS. AS I WENT DOWN THROUGH THE PEELING layers of consciousness, I sensed that everything was connected; all of it laid out before me, waiting for me to make sense of it. If I could rise above it far enough, high enough to look down, I would see it, the whole picture. It was in me to do so, and my responsibility.

As I went down deeper through the layers of sleep I came across the curious image of my thoughts being taken to the cleaners, dropping them off, one by one like so many soiled garments. All of my suspicions, my half-realisations; the splinters of truth, moments of significance - they were all treated to a good long soak, and then pummelled vigorously against a hard stone; mangled, steamed, and pressed ready for collection. And I was already standing outside, clutching my ticket, scared to go in. Then the door opened and it was like the dream was beginning.

I had an impression of myself hovering above a swimming-pool-sized float in the shape of Great Britain. I was overcome by a sense of wellbeing and power, as though I was the lord of all that I surveyed. The float began to grow, and I could no longer make out the familiar shape of the whole. Soon the coastlines were beyond my sight. I was lost and I knew it.

I hovered over the heart of England, aware of Merle's account of Merlin flying over the Atlantic. I was preparing to make the return flight back to America, and crying so hard that all of England was awash in the most incredible storm since records began. My homeland, now beloved, was awash with my tears, and threatening to sink under the remorseless deluge.

I set my course for Ireland and met Kate in the sky.

She was smiling down over Ireland while I flew in circles around her. She was torn between two worlds. As I beckoned her to hold my hand I felt one world falling away behind her, and at last we were on our way across the roaring ocean towards America, Aunt Helen receding beneath us, her distant voice feebly calling us back.

The next clear image was of Professor Buck-Bradbury standing at the gates of the New World, beckoning us in. But all we could see of him was his face. He was partially hidden behind a curtain. We rounded the curtain, our eyes full with what I first took to be anticipation and then recognised as something vastly more tragic.

Hope.

We navigated the last of the gigantic curtain and looked on at the exposed scene before us. Buck-Bradbury was stoking up a fire. The fire became the hospital. People were dying inside the hospital and Buck-Bradbury was warming his hands over the blaze. We watched, helpless to act, unable to speak.

Hearing a noise above us we turned to see Merle descending from above the flames, water coming out of him as though his entire body had been punctured a thousand times; a falling colander. The hospital hissed as the water killed the flames.

We were in Las Vegas, Caesars Palace, listening to Little Anthony and the Imperials performing to an empty bar. The band became the Beatles, John Lennon singing about a walrus eating strawberries, and we wondered what it would take to get people away from the gaming tables. We ordered drinks and watched the waitress turn from a Roman into a medieval English girl with an American twang, and we grew excited, believing that we had at last found the way home, before realizing that we were back in Camelot.

Longing for Las Vegas to be done with us, we fell to our knees, shamelessly begging to be set free.

The drawbridge opened, and freedom beckoned. In walked a stranger with a kind face, and he held up a hand. "Hi, my name's Tobias Goldhorn. I believe you're expecting me. Sorry I'm late." Goldhorn laid a hand on Kate's head, and then something caused him to jump backwards. "How long have you been here?" he asked. "You've already been to the Silver Steal? No - no! I'm later than I thought, God forgive me!"

Then Goldhorn started to change, his face melting into a different set of shapes, and slowly he transformed into the Robert Powell image of Jesus Christ, already wearing a crown of thorns, his face bleeding. We were crying for him and then he held out his hands and placed them on top of Kate's head. He started to speak, and though I couldn't hear what he was saying, I could see that he was crying for joy, that he was healing her.

I woke up.

Kate was sleeping peacefully next to me. I lay there in the corridor between sleep and waking, my mind drifting over the substance of our lives together, bombarded by disembodied details of conversations and incidents that formed the crazy mosaic of our existence. Part of me was asking another part questions, and I didn't like the questions and I didn't want them answering. Was my heart blackening like a cinder, set on fire with jealous loathing and avarice? It was better not to know.

I looked into the darkness, my memory running over the contours of the shape that lay sleeping beside me. I remembered what she'd told me on our honeymoon, when we'd visited that strange place in Ireland, the small fishing village where an unmarried young woman's third visit was said to result in marriage to an all-powerful magician. And I guessed the lateness of the hour because my thoughts had all the hallmarks of the forbidden centre of night.

This was all about Merle.

In that dark hour my imagination was capable of anything; in that hour it loved to torture me while it professed, at all times and in all places, to be my friend.

As I lay there, guessing the witchery of the hour, I couldn't and wouldn't give credence to thoughts so blatantly absurd.

This was all about Merle.

This was madness, I reminded myself, as though there was some comfort to be found in that. I tried to distract myself from the haunting thoughts, at least until the hour had passed; and I found myself wondering what Aunt Helen would have said if I could have voiced my thoughts to her. I imagined her sucking the air, waving a finger and putting the healthy fear of God inside me, and I almost felt her slap my back heartily and set all of Ireland laughing at me for being the gullible fool.

I was the young boy lost at the carnival, the old crone promising me an angel, foretelling a fantastic journey ... and a magician. Had my parents attempted an exorcism that day, using the basic tools, a kitchen table and a strap, trying to save my mortal soul?

The feeling crept back over me ... that it was all starting to make sense, connecting in ways that I could never have imagined, the image trying to break through yet still too complex for me to see and make sense of.

I looked again at the vague shape of Kate, hidden from me in the darkness, beyond my reach; and I wondered what dreams were responsible for the sublime peace that I could hear in her breathing. I felt the sweat rise to the surface of my skin as I let in thoughts that appalled me; thoughts of death and destruction, Kate's dying heartbeat lingering to infinity and I, poor impotent Ben Tolle, waging war against the God who'd abandoned her.

I beat against the dark thoughts, tearing at them as though they were an immense spider's web of neurotic fantasy.

As the hour finally passed I was left with the image of the carnival witch, staring at me with immense pity. Knowing ...

At some point during those long and sleepless hours I thought about the victims of the road accident out near the crossroads. Were they still alive, any of them?

My thoughts turned to the promise of the new day, as the desert sunrise began to break through the curtains of our room. *Angels Camp, Nevada.* I'd never heard of the place.

I fell asleep at last and dreamed of a handful of tents.

Angels Camp, where every dream came true, every wish unconditionally granted. Angels Camp, where perfect bliss reigned day and night and fear was no longer a recognisable word.

What else could possibly be waiting for us in a place called *Angels Camp?*

CHAPTER
FIFTEEN

ANGELS CAMP, NEVADA IS NOT MARKED ON ANY MAP. IT IS A REAL PLACE, though, there's no doubt about that. I've been there. I've seen it. It's where all my nightmares finally came true.

We left Las Vegas by helicopter. It was the last time Kate would see the place.

Merle told us that we would be back the next morning, and so what wasn't already left behind in his hotel in San Francisco was left in our room on the Strip. We took one travelling bag between us; a change of clothes and a few basics. For some reason I took the Mark Twain book with me. The flight took an hour, and Merle spent most of the time in rampantly autobiographical mood.

"I had what you might say was an unusual childhood," he said, glancing at me.

You know that part already, don't you, Ben?

But your wife doesn't.

My stomach tightened. If I had told Kate everything, including all the stuff about his childhood, we could have sat down and laughed or else packed our bags and headed for the airport. Either way, there would have been no secrets, no guilt, and no suspicion. I could have thrown the money on the bed at the same time, and together we could have decided what to do next.

But that voice inside me kept on asking, resilient to common sense: *would there have been any hope?* Common sense had become the enemy, the antithesis of delusion and therefore, to my distorted way of thinking, the antithesis of hope. Perhaps, above all, it was the bizarre secret-mystery of it all that *fed* my hope. To have let Kate in on the whole charade might have let in the cold light of reason and destroyed all that I was holding onto.

I don't think, at any stage, I could have coped with the spectacle of it all unweaving and crumbling to dust in the cold light. I didn't want to know about truth; I only cared for the comforts that hope could provide no matter how blind and desperate.

Kate was busy looking out of the helicopter, while I let the strange tale of Merle's upbringing shoot through my mind like a half-dreamt ghost. When he'd figured I'd had long enough to reacquaint myself with the memory of the tale, he started to spill a few more spectral beans.

"I was telling your husband, back in San Francisco, that my real education in life started and, well, you might say ended out here in the desert. California, to begin with, before I, as you might say, *graduated.*"

He laughed, as though he had said something funny.

"Not that one state differs much from another when you're out here in the wilderness. But I always thought there was something special about Angels Camp, and that's why I want to end our little sightseeing excursion by showing you something that you will most definitely never see advertised in the brochures." He laughed again, and Kate smiled along with the genial mood. I could see that she was all geared up for a perfect last day, photographing it all with her eyes, not wanting to forget a second of it.

I wondered if the day's chosen colour scheme of chessboard tie and gun-metal complement held any special significance. If it meant anything, it was lost on me. My short reverie came to an abrupt end with Merle's next sentence.

"You might have heard of Angels Camp, *California*, in connection with a famous writer of ours by the name of Mark Twain." I looked at Kate, and she didn't bat an eye. Maybe by that point I was looking too hard for evidence of the miraculous. "Twain once wrote a very famous story about a jumping frog. I guess he was taking the juice out of the people up in the Gold Country, making out that they would gamble on just about anything, and go to such lengths as to fill a frog full of buckshot to make sure of winning a bet. Well, to show that they don't hold any hard feelings, and that they have a sense of humour up there, they hold an annual frog jumping competition at Angels Camp, just to give Mr Twain something to laugh at. Give him a break from poking fun at the Devil all day long.

"But, I digress: wrong Angels Camp."

I decided that I wasn't looking too hard after all; it was blatantly obvious: his sole reason for contriving the whole Mark Twain link was to show me some more of his power.

I don't need to look to see what's in your *bag, sucker. I already know same as I know the secrets of your heart.*

"Funny you should mention Mark Twain," I said. "I'm reading one of his books at the moment."

"That a fact?"

"A Connecticut Yankee ..."

"... In King Arthur's Court ...? Enjoying it?"

"It isn't the King Arthur I read about at school," I told him.

"Well," he said, "that's Twain for you. Took a lot of liberties making his point."

"What point was that?" I asked.

"Wouldn't want to spoil the book for you, Ben. Books like that are rare."

"That good?"

"Best he ever wrote. In my opinion, the best book anybody's written with American blood in their veins. Got my copy tucked in between the *Egyptian Book of the Dead* and a little known masterpiece from the thirteenth century on magical practices on the banks of the Congo. *That* good!"

"That's praise indeed," said Kate, a wicked glint in her eye as she said it.

Merle cleared his throat. I could feel another story coming.

"I'll bet you want to know why I rate the book so highly, and I'm going to have to try and explain it to you without giving away the plot."

I was about to add that I was *re-reading* the book, so that he needn't worry about spoilers. I caught Kate's look, convincing me to let him get on with it.

"I'll try to satisfy your curiosity," he said. "But if I give too much away, well, don't say I didn't warn you."

"Go for it," said Kate. "Sometimes in life you have to take risks."

"Okay," he said, "here goes: Twain gave Merlin his due."

We waited a moment, but nothing followed.

"Twain gave Merlin his due," repeated Kate. "No, I don't think you've given away the storyline entirely."

"Good," he said. "I would hate to have done that."

"Could you," she said, "possibly elaborate? I don't mean to be greedy ..."

He let an in-rush of air whistle through his teeth, and scratched the back of his neck. The gesture reminded me of a tradesman preparing to deliver an outrageous estimate. "There's a risk to it," he said, "but if you insist. You see, Merlin was really bad ass, and I mean *big time* bad ass."

"The baddest ass?" asked Kate, entering into the spirit.

"And Twain gave him his due. Merlin was the most powerful man who ever walked this planet, and the most dangerous. I like that about a guy, and I like Twain for having the insight to see it and the balls to say it."

I had the feeling that even in the weird and wonderful world of literary criticism, what we were hearing might be classified as unorthodox. But Merle wasn't really talking about Mark Twain at all; he was talking about himself, and I didn't like it. I wanted him to stop, let us off the ride. Yet down below us was nothing but the relentless burning heat of a slow and unimaginable death, with only snakes and scorpions to crawl in reverence the length of our bleached bones.

The sense of an unfolding pattern struck me as it had done before, though this time it came with the conviction that the moment of revelation was close at hand. He was showing us the corners of the picture, nothing more than that; but already I had the feeling that I had started to watch a film, a particular kind of film; one that was making me aware once again of the mirror on the wall. Already I was thinking that when the film was over I would have to walk to the cold bathroom and brush my teeth, and then walk back towards the stairs; and that without meaning to I would catch sight of the mirror, the forbidden oracle, and see all the terrors that it held; all the terrors that it had stored up for me through the years.

I sensed that every nameless fear from childhood was about to be given a name.

"Camelot must have been quite a place," he said, looking back at me with a grin. I could see in his eyes that he knew pennies had been busily dropping for me, and he was as good as licking his lips when he turned back to the controls. "Anyway, all this King Arthur jive has taken us a little way from Angels Camp, and I'd like you both to know a little about the place before we get there. Kind of *prepare* you for it, as much as anybody can."

I saw the tremor of laughter rising through his shoulders.

"Many people live there?" asked Kate.

"That's a difficult one," he replied.

"You haven't visited for a while?" she said.

"That's not why it's difficult. It's kind of abstract – you'll see what I mean. Do you know much about the tarot?"

My miserable heart was missing as many beats as it was catching.

"I learnt about the tarot in the desert. It played the kind of role in my education that's usually reserved for science, literature and religion. For me it was all three. The first deck I was ever shown was Egyptian. The owner of those beautiful cards was an old Indian wise man, and he told me that mankind would do well to relearn the secrets of the ancient Egyptians.

"That old man spent time with me because I was willing to learn, more than willing. I had a thirst and he could see it. That old man opened up the top of that vast Egyptian pyramid of knowledge and allowed me to look down into the richness. But it was dark in there, and he told me that I had to learn to illuminate my own way, instigate and maintain my own search for knowledge. He instructed me that the secrets would yield if I wanted them badly enough.

"And I did want them. And they did yield to me. And that old man eventually decided there was nothing more he could pass on, and that it was time for me to leave. And he pointed me towards Angels Camp, and that's a true story."

"And what did you find there?" asked Kate.

"I found another old man."

"You seem keen on old men."

"And every young man should be, that's if he wants to learn anything."

"What about young women?" she said, playfully.

"I've never been one, least not in this life."

"Oh, come on," she said. "Not the reincarnation routine! I mean, I like a good yarn, the same as anybody else. But some things are just, well, you know – plain hokum."

"You think?"

"It's always so damned predictable."

"Well," said Merle. "Now you've set me a challenge. Tell you what: let me finish telling my story and then we'll decide if I'm predictable - that okay with you?"

Kate was rubbing her hands together like she was about to settle down with a good book. "Okay with me," she said.

"Back to the old man, then," said Merle. "Let me warn you, this ain't no children's tale."

Kate pretended to bite her finger-nails, stifling a snigger.

"Now, this old man was a strange one," said Merle. "But he took to me almost the minute he clapped eyes on me. Told me how he was a descendant from a survivor of the *Battle of the Little Big Horn.*"

Kate clamped a hand over her mouth. I could see her arm quaking, trying to hold in the laughter. I tapped her ankle with my foot. It only made matters worse. Her body was starting to vibrate as she fought to keep it inside.

As we continued to fly across the empty desert Merle went on with his story. He appeared oblivious to the mutiny developing in the seats behind him.

" ... He'd made his way through the wilderness in search of a new homeland. One of the first things I asked him was what he thought of the Egyptians. I wish you could have heard the laughter. I bet he didn't stop for thirty minutes." At this point he broke into loud and sustained laughter of his own, disarming Kate's urgent need to release the same stuff.

She lowered her hand, and looked at me. We both shrugged, wondering if we had missed the punchline.

Merle went on laughing, and if it didn't last the full thirty minutes, it was long enough to give us the idea. Then he turned back to Kate and winked, before banking the helicopter suddenly to the left. "Anyway, I was eager to talk Egypt to someone, and there wasn't anybody else around that day. So I took the pack of cards out of my pocket and showed them to him. He didn't laugh again, and I could see that he was full of respect for what he was looking at.

"After a long time of just sitting and looking at the cards, he went away for a few minutes, and came back with a pack of his own. My God, I remember thinking: every mad sucker out in the desert has a pack of the damn things. I was even more shocked when I looked at them."

"Not naked girls," said Kate, faking a yawn.

"Naked girls would have been easier, and you people wouldn't have had any trouble believing me. Now, I'm counting on a little of that suspension of disbelief from you, folks, do you hear? You see, that fella was only holding a pack depicting King Arthur and the rest of the gang."

The helicopter began its descent.

"The best of it was still to come, though. From out of the pack - and looking at me all the time he did it - the old man extracted a single card. He showed it to me. It was a portrait of Merlin, and the card was the devil card. And the old man just kept looking from me to the card and back again until I thought he was going to make himself dizzy. Now, that kind of thing can unnerve a person."

We were descending, though I still couldn't make out anything indicating a settlement below.

"Then the old man came right out and said it. And while I'm damned if I can remember his exact manner of speaking, what it amounted to was this: 'Hellfire and damnation, boy, if you ain't the living breathing reincarnation of old Merlin then I'll cover my gonads with honey and swing them over a bees nest.' Not the exact words, I'm pretty sure of that. Close enough, though."

The helicopter continued to approach some as yet invisible destination. I could see that Kate was as puzzled as I was. The featureless waste beneath us stretched emptily and forever in all directions.

"Spooked me when I heard it. But I've spent the rest of my life fascinated by that character - Merlin, I mean. Guess you could say I was at an impressionable stage of my life."

Now we saw it.

There wasn't much to see at first, though still enough to make me wonder how I had failed to see it earlier, given the perfect visibility of the desert air and the lack of any obstructing features. Every time I blinked the settlement beneath us appeared to have multiplied, a few huts becoming a small town, with pretensions to turn into a small city.

"But the best thing about Merlin, and the thing that most people don't even know about him, is that Merlin was a great healer.

"You see, he wasn't interested in the petty interests of other magicians. He didn't waste his time and talents searching for the Philosopher's Stone and all that shit. After all, why make gold when you can steal it? And why fool around looking for an elixir of eternal life when it's far more practical to reincarnate yourself at will? And more fun, too, as a matter of fact. Like I said, Merlin was a healer, and he understood that you've got to take the blood from somewhere."

I felt my skin starting to contract as we made our final descent.

"There's no way around it. You've just got to take that blood from somewhere. Ain't no such thing as a corpseless cure. And I know that because Merlin told me."

CHAPTER

SIXTEEN

As we moved over Angels Camp I developed an obsession with definitions. I had already discarded 'small city' and was chewing over 'large desert town'. It seemed important, somehow, though all I was doing was picking dead skin.

The town led the helicopter over its bordering huts, and on to the first of two graveyards. I couldn't seem to get a perspective on the graveyard, its angles seemed all wrong, out of kilter, somehow; as though what I was seeing was not real, and not even logically possible; a distorted projection conjured from a multitude of carefully placed mirrors.

It wasn't a place that I wanted to visit.

We moved on, the town's weird gravity dragging the helicopter towards a handful of larger buildings at what appeared to be the centre of town. Again, everything seemed out of proportion, weirdly distorted; then the strange architecture gave way to a second graveyard, rising up at us before we had a chance to gain any perspective on it.

Finally we touched down.

"Welcome to Angels Camp," said Merle. "The state of Nevada's best kept secret."

I heard the hum of the rotors change pitch as they started to slow. "No transport of any kind allowed in town, so I'll have to show you the sights on foot. Don't mind, do you?" We didn't, though the idea seemed less appealing once we stepped out of the helicopter and into the frightening furnace of the desert sun. "Fond of graveyards?" he said. "I think you're going to find the two we have here to be about the most memorable you're ever going to see in your entire lives. But there's time for graveyards later. Better get ourselves checked in first. You know, you're going to just love it here ... and that's guaranteed."

We followed him down past the side of the vast graveyard, and on towards the buildings up ahead.

The hotel didn't seem to be a hive of activity. There was no-one coming, and no-one going, either. Not a soul out on the street and no sounds of anything, leaving an oppressive stillness filled with heat and loneliness. The day had become a blinding dead of night, and *dead* seemed to sum up the place better than any other word I could think of.

We walked into the hotel and the relief was instant. The heat outside was like a rain of scalding knives across our backs, and moving inside was akin to falling into a cool stream. Behind the desk in the entrance hall sat the first sign of life; a middle-aged man with a thin pointed face that had been completely overrun by the most ridiculous moustache I had seen in a long time. The man's eyes were shining our way. "Hey," he said, hurrying from behind his desk to shake hands with Merle. "What kept you?"

"Long story," said Merle. "I'd like to introduce you to a couple of friends of mine. Meet Kate and Ben."

The man turned to us and shook our hands. "I won't ask what brings you to Angels Camp," he said.

"You can if you like," said Kate.

"Only one thing ever brings folk to Angels Camp - and that's Merle." At that he broke into cartoon laughter that recalled Deputy Dawg. I silently winced, while Kate turned discreetly away. "Now, what kind of room would you folks be wanting? You got the place to yourselves, so you can name it. We got doubles, twins -"

"Camelot," said Merle.

"Camelot?" repeated Kate, another smile forming.

"*Camelot?*" said the moustached man.

"Kate and Ben are very special friends," said Merle. "They deserve the best that we have to offer. They deserve nothing less than ..."

He looked at Kate and a mutual smile broke out between them.

"No," she said. "Let me guess." She closed her eyes, placing an index finger theatrically to each temple. "Wait a minute. I think I'm getting something. It's coming through ... *Camelot?*"

Merle had used images from his vast collection of tarot decks as themes in the decoration of the suites in this, his flagship hotel. Camelot, it turned out, was his most lavishly realised theme to date, the jewel in the crown. As all the suites were unoccupied, he said that he would be thrilled to give us a quick tour of the highlights.

"I'll save Camelot for last," he said, "We need to build up to that or else it's going to blow your mind. Probably will anyway."

The hotel was like a greatest hits compilation; Las Vegas in miniature, and all under one immense roof. We visited the Caesar room, with stars projected by lasers onto the ceiling in the pattern corresponding with the sky the night that Julius Caesar was killed; the Anthony and Cleopatra suite, very popular with newlyweds and second honeymooners, apparently; the Nile suite boasted a crocodile tank, a Nile cruise similar to the one at the Luxor back in Vegas, a beautiful statue of the supreme god and judge of the dead, Osiris, and came with optional opportunities to be entombed for the night; the Transylvania suite incorporated all the traditional trappings of the vampire myth; the Graceland suite featured an Elvis hologram and fully authenticated jungle room, while the Treasure Island suite turned out to be a carpeted desert island with a raft that the occupant could propel around the ocean-simulated leisure areas.

Kate saved her most momentous "wow" for the Haunted Opera House suite, and said that she particularly liked the luminous headless corpse that somehow propelled around the bedroom when the lights were switched off.

For my part, it was hard to beat the Hollywood suite, where I shook hands with a life-sized rubber Spencer Tracy, and pressed a button to inflate Frank Sinatra, who responded with a rendition of *My Way*.

If it was all a little hard to take in - and it certainly was - then Camelot was a crowning impossibility.

We stood outside the door in the glow of Merle's evident pride and awaited the turn of the key. Ceremoniously, he handed the key to the moustached man, who accepted the honour with such quaking humility that I thought tears to be only moments away. Merle, spotting this, brought the man back to Earth. "Hell, whatever possessed you to take on a cookie-duster of those dimensions? Explain yourself, Goddammit!"

The man, embarrassed and not a little hurt, fingered the curious display of facial hair above his top lip. "Thought it kind of suited me," he said.

"Kind of suited you?" said Merle. "A cookie-duster like that might *kind of suit* a nineteenth-century European philosopher whose ideas on style came from reading too much Immanuel Kant. It might even suit a twentieth-century torpedo-happy German naval commander! But there are cookie-dusters and cookie-dusters and that breed don't go with a thin-faced doorman at the Angels Camp Hotel. You want to scare my guests - is that what you want?"

We wondered how long Merle had been away from the place. Moustaches like that didn't appear overnight.

A different kind of tear now seemed imminent as the man said, "I'll get it shaved off, Merle."

"You bet your skinny ass you will, and right away, hear me?"

We watched him hand the key back to Merle, before scuttling away to do as he was told.

When he had gone, Kate said, "That seemed a bit harsh."

"Thin end of the wedge," said Merle, "and I'm not talking about the guy's face."

"Give them a yard and they'll take a mile," said Kate. "Today a moustache, tomorrow the collapse of a business empire!"

"Couldn't have put it better myself," said Merle. "I tell you, when you leave for England I want you to put some of that sense of humour of yours in a bottle so that I can take the top off and inhale when I'm feeling blue."

Without the merest hint of a smile, Kate said, "And maybe, in return, you can post me the clippings of that poor man's pride and joy."

"I'll certainly do that," said Merle, his delivery as dry as crocodile tears. "It will be my pleasure. But for now I think I'll leave you two alone to explore Camelot for yourselves. See you down in reception in an hour?" He raised a cautionary finger and put on a mock-sinister tone. "If you stay too long ... who knows what might happen?"

Kate looked at me and sniggered. "I've been wondering what happened to Vincent Price."

An hour wasn't nearly long enough, an entire day wouldn't have been. It was like stepping through the back of a wardrobe into a medieval Narnia. The room contained so many holograms that it was impossible at first to distinguish the solid from the illusory. When we closed the door behind us, a drawbridge immediately lowered, inviting us to cross the illusion of a large and impressive moat.

As we moved across towards the awesome portal on the far side of the bridge, we felt like anachronistic ghosts passing through the sights, sounds, even smells of a long gone time and place, a fantasy of historic myth. It was the work of a craftsman, and quite possibly a genius. It was thrilling and at the same time disturbing.

We wondered how anyone could ever sleep in such a place, as knights and ladies arose and disappeared before us like shooting stars. Even Sir Galahad made a brief appearance, lance in hand, looking suitably noble.

The Camelot Suite was optionally interactive, and we summoned Interactive Hologram Scene Number One from the menu. Instantly, a junior member of King Arthur's court appeared, and Kate asked the lad if Arthur was in town. According to the hologram - it had the grace to use an authentic English accent (Welsh was available on request) - the King was returning from a Grail-connected quest, leaving Lancelot to explore the delights of some maiden he had chanced upon in the woods.

Kate was reminding me that our hour was up, yet I couldn't resist a final question. "Is Merlin the Wizard around this evening?" I asked the youth.

The hologram answered, and in a voice that blew no pity on the fate of the curious.

"Merlin's time is midnight. He's waiting ..."

We walked back across the drawbridge and watched it rise up behind us. Kate pulled me to her. "I can't stay mad with you," she said, kissing me with such a charge of electricity that keeping our appointment was suddenly placed in doubt. Then, as quickly, she playfully pushed me away. "Save it for later, Ben. We don't know who's watching."

"You reckon he likes videoing his guests?" I said.

"I think we're in for a bad night's sleep, one way or another."

"That sounds promising."

"It's the *night in the haunted house* jazzed up. He's going to scare the living hell out of us, and he's not going to stop laughing until we're on the other side of the Atlantic. But after all his time and effort, can we deny him a few laughs?"

In reception he was waiting for us, but the thin faced man and his moustache had gone. Merle seemed eager to show us more of the delights of Angels Camp, and we followed him out into the brutal heat and back towards the spot where we'd touched down.

"So what do you think of Camelot?" he asked.

"Impressive," I said. "How much do you charge for a room like that?"

"There is no room *like* that. It's unique. And to answer your question, I don't charge a cent. I invite people I like to stay in my hotels. Let the crowds flock to Vegas – Camelot, the genuine Camelot, comes free, strictly invitation only."

"A curious attitude to business," said Kate.

"Why surround yourself with people you don't like?"

"Great, if you can afford it."

"I can, particularly with Lady Luck at my side."

We walked into the graveyard close to where his helicopter was resting. The battering heat seemed to make the sky wobble, and gave the illusion that the metal frame of the helicopter was liquefying before our eyes.

"I suppose your man now has a smooth top lip," said Kate.

"His top lip is free from hair entirely," said Merle. "I promise that you'll get the chance to see what an improvement a razor can make."

He stopped walking. The sun had climbed down the angles, making shadows appear behind the tallest of the gravestones.

"Wouldn't like to guess how many graves we have here. Some go back to, well, let's say they go back far enough to give you goose-bumps, even in this heat."

Kate said, "I hope they're not all the failed experiments of Tobias Goldhorn."

"Bet you're wondering about that guy."

"Now you mention it," she said.

"I can only apologise. Actually, I can do more than that. I can also assure you that he will never let you or anybody else down again."

"That sounds ominous," said Kate.

"It ought to."

"Maybe he has a poor memory," said Kate.

"That's something that *can* be cured," said Merle, and my suspicions that Goldhorn was a fictitious person, invented solely for the purpose of bringing us to this place, vanished in an instant, and I was thankful that I wouldn't be in Tobias Goldhorn's shoes when Merle finally caught up with him.

Merle showed us some of the more interesting gravestones, explaining the strange inscriptions. His explanations were more baffling than the inscriptions. Kate was fascinated, asking questions like she was on a school trip with a heavy crush on the teacher. I didn't like the analogy, but I couldn't get the image out of my head, and it fed on the poison that was already fermenting inside me.

We were grateful for the tombstones as shields against the ferocious sun that was now growing soft and fat in the western sky. It was too hot to think, too hot for anything other than trailing around behind the two of them, as Kate kept up the questions and Merle showed no sign of letting up with the answers. "Either of you worked it out yet," he said as we completed the circle of the graveyard, returning to where we had entered the vast burial ground. "The theme of this place?"

"Death?" said Kate.

"Very good," said Merle. "But apart from the fact that they are all dead, which I kind of see as the minimum entry requirement when it comes to lying under the soil in a place such as this ... let me put it another way. What do you reckon all of these former members of the human race had in common - I mean, while they were alive?"

"Judging by the grandiose statues and headstones," said Kate, "I would guess that they all had plenty of money."

"They were rich, yes, every last one of them. But they were also poor in spirit." Merle glanced at me, and maybe it was more than a glance. "Enough of the dead for now," he said. "How about a drink at my saloon bar? All drinks on the house, naturally."

We were leaving the graveyard, when he turned to Kate. "Let me tell you something," he said.

"Tell me."

"You're almost there."

"Almost *where?*"

"When I first met your husband I told him that you would find healing. He had the faith, but he kept it from you. He did what he thought was right, and there's nothing unnatural about that. But I have never seen a man so consumed by guilt."

"Don't mind me," I said. "Carry on, forget I'm here."

They appeared to take my advice. Merle didn't drop a beat.

"A wife doesn't always see as clearly as a stranger does," he said. "Ben sees a miracle and he gets hung up about it: should I tell, shouldn't I tell – what's the protocol here? He's still wondering if he's a rich man, and feeling guilty for even thinking about it. I lent him some money, and it became a dirty secret. It was really no big deal."

"Lent him some money?" said Kate, looking at me.

"Like I said, it's no big deal," said Merle. "This isn't character assassination. It's what I call opening up the secret doors. Healing is about transference of energies, and secret doors block off that process. They stem the flow. But we still love to close doors because we think it's safer. And we add chains and bolts until finally we construct a fortress. Nothing gets in, nothing gets out; we suffocate and then we die ...

"Now: how about that drink?"

CHAPTER
SEVENTEEN

THE SALOON BAR WAS LIKE SOMETHING OUT OF *TOMBSTONE*. WE walked in through the swing doors and approached the long bar.

The place was empty, but the moment we entered the pianola in the corner of the sawdust floor struck up with *Clementine*. Looking over at the staircase leading up to the rooms above I could see the ghosts of tightly corseted women being led by impressively holstered men.

The bar was stocked with every drink I'd ever heard of, and quite a few I hadn't. Merle whistled along to the tune for a minute. "Hey, Clancy," he shouted at last, "a gunslinger could die of thirst in here."

A figure promptly appeared behind the bar. A tall, thin man, dressed in black, with Lee Van Cleef eyes and the fancy dress costume to go with it.

"Sorry about that," said Clancy. "You caught me by surprise. What'll it be?"

"Apology accepted on this occasion," said Merle. "After all, we're three minutes early. I reckon a beer and bourbon for the guy, mineral water for the lady, and the same for the good looking one in the middle."

The bartender smiled, but didn't laugh. Merle had trained him well.

The drinks slid down too easily and the next round was already waiting. "We'll take these over to the corner," said Merle. "Same again in five minutes, Clancy."

We followed Merle to one of the plain wooden tables furthest from the bar. The same feeling descended over me as it had done in 'Camelot.' The feeling that this was more than mere theme park extravagance; that we had become displaced ghosts, lost in time and place, severed from an increasingly distant reality. The sense of disorientation brought with it a powerful need for a point of reference, a guiding light to lock onto. And he knew it. He had created it all.

"What do you think of my little saloon bar?" he asked.

What could we say? The day had been too weird, the surprises heaped too relentlessly. We were too dazed to say anything much about anything, and at the same time aware that the waiting was almost over. Expectation was in the air. Something was arriving.

Merle watched our restlessness ... and smiled.

And then it began.

"Angels Camp," he said, "is where I bring people to cure them. You have nothing to fear, believe me. There is a condition, though."

"There always is," said Kate. "Sign on the dotted line."

Merle waved a finger. "All I ask is that we are absolutely honest with each other. Nothing hidden, no secrets - everybody comfortable with that?"

Kate hesitated.

"What is it?" asked Merle. "Whatever it is, we need to get it out in the open."

"It's just that ... you brought us into the desert to find this healer, Tobias Goldhorn. And then you took us to Las Vegas, where we lost some of your money and won some back, but we still didn't find this man who we were supposed to be looking for. And now you bring us all the way out here, and you tell me that you've brought us here to cure me. I'm confused. Are you saying that you didn't need Goldhorn in the first place?"

"If Goldhorn was with us, like he should have been," said Merle, "maybe we'd be sitting here celebrating right now. But he isn't, and we aren't, and I'm going to have to try and finish the job on my own."

"Finish what job? I've never felt better. I'm in no pain -"

Merle was shaking his head. "I wish it was that simple. It isn't over, Kate. It's a long way from over."

"But ... *what's wrong with me?*"

"You're going to have to work with me until this thing's done, and that's just how it is. So, like I said: no secrets from now on."

The guilt string twanged inside me. I looked at Kate, but she was looking hard at Merle, trying to weigh something up.

"I want us to play a little game," he said. "A statement of truth from each of us in turn. Sounds easy, doesn't it? Well, the real tricky part is, it has to be a truth that's hard to admit. You'll get the hang of it. I'll go first so that you both get the idea."

Clancy came over with the next round of drinks, and I was surprised to find that my glass had already emptied again. I made a silent prayer of gratitude that there were no Gold Bandits in the room, and no hundred-dollar tokens in my pocket. The barman left the three of us alone again, the clunk of his heels reverberating around the empty saloon bar as *Clementine* came to an end for the third time.

"Okay," said Merle, taking a careful sip from his mineral water, "here goes. I have never had a physical relationship with a woman." He let a silent moment pass. "And the reason for that is that I have never trusted another's company without my underpants firmly in place. I hope one fine day soon to put that right."

His face as straight as his bow tie, he looked at Kate.

"Guess it's your turn."

Kate, who had been known to thrive on this kind of bar game in our early years together, took no time gathering her wits. "I love Ben," she said. "I loved him from the first moment I met him, and I always will love him. If he's kept secrets from me these past few days, I'm sure he had good reasons."

"I object!" said Merle. "Are you saying that your admission of love for Ben is a hard thing to admit to? I think that you need to try again."

Kate raised her eyebrows, and I could see the feistiness in her making its triumphant return. I wondered if she was about to tell him to stick his game where the desert sun didn't shine. But then she was never one to shrink from a challenge, and I saw the determination to go on with Merle's ridiculous game rise up in her. "Okay," she said. "Try this. I don't believe that there ever was another healer. I can't figure out why you would make him up, or what your real purpose is, but you're not being entirely straight with us."

Merle sat back in his chair for a moment, never once taking his eyes off Kate. "That," he said, "is more like it. Now you're getting the hang of the game. Ben, I do believe it's your turn."

I was looking at Kate. I had never loved her more than I did at that moment. "Merle," I said, not taking my eyes off my wife, "gave me some money in San Francisco. I kept the money hidden all the way to Las Vegas. When I got drunk in the Silver Steal I lost it all on the slots. I wanted to leave America a rich man."

Merle nodded, and then sipped at his mineral water, savouring it as though it was a fine wine. "Not bad," he said, tapping his glass on the table. The sound of leather heels on wooden boards brought the barman back to our table. "Another round from you, sir," he said, "and another round from we three champions of the truth."

After waiting for the drinks to arrive, he began again. "When I told Ben, back in San Francisco, that I was responsible for the death of my parents, I failed to add that soon after that I plunged into such an abyss of remorse that I contemplated suicide. And that I only pulled myself out of what would have been a fatal nosedive, by strangling to death a dozen or so of my peers. I have never looked back since, so to speak; and the moral, if there is one, must surely be this: that killers make the best healers."

I could see that Kate was taking his words with a hefty pinch of salt, though she still responded in earnest. "I watched my best friend die from leukaemia when she was only eight years old, and I hated her for leaving me. I wanted to go wherever she was going. I watched her lying in the hospital bed, sinking by the hour, and I asked to stay, and they all thought how loving and caring I was. They didn't know that I was busy in my head cursing her name. I've never spoken of her since because I'm still full of the guilt and the shame and the anger of it."

There was a fury to Kate's words that left in their wake a clanging silence. I breathed in the residue, feeling the strength of her spirit; feeling the hope awakening again.

It was my turn. "If we'd had a son, I would have called him David, because I've never forgotten the impact of hearing the David and Goliath story in school assembly. I always believed that the greatest thing that I could ever aspire to be was a giant killer on the side of good. It was the only time school assembly woke me out of my daydreams. As for a daughter, I would have called her Kate."

Kate's eyes were full, and the lump in my throat was bobbing up and down like a Halloween apple. Merle was sitting there, taking it all in, sucking on it like a vampire, and extracting his nourishment, wild and sober.

Were we anything more than slaves entertaining the emperor before he sent in the lions to rip us to shreds?

Yet there was something compulsive, addictive in the game: the promise of finding the key to it all, perhaps. "Guess it's me again," said Merle. "If I'd lowered my pants in the presence of a woman, and if, as a result, she'd borne me a child, I would have sued her for negligent conduct, and then I would have drowned the pair of them. Children frighten me. We don't know what they've been, and we don't know what they'll become."

There was the first sign of a slurring in Kate's voice. "I don't believe that," she said. "I think you're breaking the rules. You're not telling the truth, Merle."

I looked at her glass of water. *Had he spiked her drinks?*

"But if I'm not telling the truth," he said, "then I shouldn't be playing the game. This game's no good without truth. So let me tell you some more truth: I never cure the godless. I never waste my precious time on hollow shells that have nothing left to believe in, and nothing left to believe *with*. I don't care what a person believes in, but they have to believe in something. The godless I leave entirely to the likes of Buck-Bradbury."

"Everyone has their own specialism," said Kate.

"Yes, they do," he said. "Your turn again, I believe."

She took another mouthful of her drink. "For many years I had a big problem with envy. If I saw a great performance by another actress, stage or screen, I would brood on it. I would fantasise that they had really awful lives, or dream about tearing out their hair by the roots."

It was my turn again. I took a good swig of beer and downed another bourbon. "I once wrote a malicious letter, anonymously. I left the letter where the teacher would find it. It exposed the tobacco stores of the class bully. Trouble was, the plan backfired, and the teacher ended up with a broken jaw. After the bully was expelled, he beat up every kid in the class to make sure that he got the one that snitched on him."

Kate and Merle laughed. "You see," said Merle, "if we ain't all of us sinners and victims, one way or another."

Kate took her turn again, relating her sadness at being disowned by her family, and Merle gave an account of his attempts to heal a snake that had lost its poison. In no time it was back to me again, and I was hearing myself relating the story of how I became lost at a carnival when I was ten years old, a witch giving me a reading from her cards, and my father beating the living daylights out of me.

"He beat you for getting lost?" asked Merle. "Or he beat you for messing with witches and dabbling in magic?"

I'd said too much. Both of them were waiting for my answer.

"My parents were ill. My dad was drinking and my mum had a breakdown."

Merle leaned forward. "They were holding onto faith by the fingernails, Ben. A son playing about with the future was the last straw. Methodists, fallen or otherwise, don't take kindly to boys messing in the tarot."

Somewhere a phone was ringing.

"I, for my sins, have cured almost as many people as I've killed. So maybe my ends justify my means. I still haven't told you how I came to discover the truth about Merlin, and about my destiny. This really *does* call for a round of drinks."

The barman was approaching our table. "Phone call for you, Merle."

"Can't you see I'm busy? And while you're here, my guests are thirsty."

"It's urgent, Merle."

"It had better be." He stood up. "Excuse me, please."

After Merle had left us, Kate said, "I never knew about that stuff, Ben."

I shrugged. "It never came up."

"It's bothered you, though."

"Maybe he's right, and you don't know me as well as you thought you did."

She started to say something. But Merle was coming back and looking serious. "Something's come up," he said. "They've found Goldhorn." I started to ask where, but Merle cut in. "We have to go back to Vegas tonight."

"We?" I said.

"Your husband and I are going to meet the guy that you don't believe exists, Kate," he said. "And he's going to answer all your questions. I have someone to keep you company while we're gone."

On cue a young woman appeared, with long flowing hair and an alabaster smile. She took Kate's hand. "I'm Guinevere," she said. "You'll be more than fine with me."

I watched Kate's face gather into an expression of courage, and I knew that it was all for me.

"Why can't Kate come with us?"

"It's okay, Ben," she said. She looked tired, suddenly exhausted. "I'll be alright here. Do what you have to do. Let's get this thing over with."

I picked up the glass of water that she had been drinking, and sniffed at it.

"What?" said Merle.

I sipped at the drink. It tasted like water to me.

There was a dazed look about her. "I can't leave her," I said.

"Time is of the essence," said Merle. "Things are gathering pace."

"But ... can't you go, bring Goldhorn here ..?"

Merle was shaking his head. "It doesn't work like that, my friend. You have to make the journey back to Vegas with me."

"I don't understand ..?"

A few minutes later I was sitting behind him in the helicopter. The night was black, and I was scared. I was wishing that I was with Kate, and a million miles from there. I was wishing that we had never left England.

CHAPTER

EIGHTEEN

W E FLEW THROUGH THE DARKNESS IN SILENCE, UNTIL MERLE DECIDED IT was time to talk.

"Ben, if you don't mind me saying, I think we're overdue a little conversation. Man to man style, if that's that okay with you? Of course it is. What could be nicer, on a night like this, but two friends doing some talking? First up, I want you to stop worrying about your wife. She's in good hands, I promise you, and I'm a man of my word. I don't like to see you with your mind all clogged up with anxiety. You can't give me your full concentration, and I'm going to need it."

I stared out into the blackness, listening.

"They found Tobias in Camelot. Said he was looking for me, and that he must have got the arrangements wrong. I can believe that. He's a drinker, and he puts stuff into his veins, too. I've given a lot of leeway to Tobias Goldhorn over the years, believing that I saw talent, a healer. Seems I was wrong, and that's something to admit. More than that, I've lost a member of my team, and it's always sad to lose something close to you, don't you think?"

I kept my face turned to the impenetrable sky.

"But whenever you lose a thing, it's important that you find something to replace that loss. And I believe I have. I have lost but I have also gained. Do you know what I'm talking about? I'm talking about you, Ben."

In spite of myself I turned to look at him, and his dark grin welcomed me.

"That's right, my friend. Sometimes you don't see what's been right under your nose the whole time. See, I want you to play your part in Kate's healing. I want to initiate you, and I need to know that you can handle the pressures that come with responsibility. I'm not talking about some run-of-the-mill cheap-shit deal here, Ben. I'm talking about the *ultimate* responsibility. I'm talking about life and death."

I watched his eyes glow.

"I want you to kill Tobias Goldhorn. I want you to do it tonight."

I turned away; then, as quickly, I turned back.

"You heard me right, Ben. But don't worry: I'm going to be there to talk you through it. I'm going to be right by your side when you pull the trigger."

I was trying to get my breath, choking on my thoughts. When I could speak it was to tell him he was out of his mind. He smiled, serenely, and we plunged a little further into the blackness.

"That bully you were talking about back in the saloon bar – he's haunted you for a long time, hasn't he? I sensed that when you told the story just now, and I know you've never told it before. For all its humour it still hits a nerve, doesn't it? The fear of the bully has been there your whole life, and it's held you back. You've longed for liberation from the fears it's generated, and you want rid, you want him out of your head and out of your life. You *want* to be healed and that's the first step. And I want to heal you, Ben, and I will, too. And then you can repay that by helping me to heal Kate."

I felt his words hit me like a fist in the guts.

"*Repay you*? What are you talking about?"

"Steady, my friend, else you're going to bust a blood vessel getting worked up like that."

"I want to know what in God's name you mean! How the hell am I repaying you by helping you heal my wife? You think ... I'm doing *you* a favour?"

He didn't answer me; he still had other things to tell me, and other things to show me. Merle did things his way, in his time.

When I'd finished ranting, demanding answers and getting none, he let the slow trickle of truth begin to run its course. He knew my fears as I knew them, and he knew my dreams. He'd taken a tape measure and a set of weights inside my head and measured the length and depth of every emotion, and weighed to within a feather every ounce of regret and hope and fear buried in me. I didn't know how, but he'd done it all the same. I was no more than a controlled doll, fashioned and powerless, turned this way and that, dancing to an inaudible tune, one button for joy and another for despair, and in its own sad way, perfect.

He told me about fear and regret but most of all he told me about hope. It was, he said, the sadist's most potent tool. It blinded the victim, set the trap, kept the game in motion. More than that, it retained the potential for pain at its fullest, rawest. "Hope," he said, "can work miracles, though not generally for the victim."

We travelled into another silence, my mind fumbling around the things he'd been talking about until it was time, by Merle's invisible watch, for the next instalment.

"I think I'm due to answer a question that I know's been bugging you, Ben. You want to ascertain whether you're going home a rich man, and by my reckoning that's an honest enough question for anyone to ask, and so I'm going to answer it honestly.

"So let's say, for the sake of argument, about what exactly constitutes 'rich'; that you're coming out of this with enough money never to have to worry about money again. Not that that isn't a lot easier said than done for most people, money becoming a habit like it does. So you beware of that little old phantom that we know as greed coming knocking at your door some soulless night, that's what I'm telling you. Don't let him in, Ben, do you hear me? *Don't let him in.*"

"Are you paying me to murder Goldhorn?"

He sucked at the air like he was cooling the sting of a scorpion that had crawled onto his tongue. "I think you're getting things mixed up here. Let me explain the way money features in this relationship. You see, when we met I gave you some capital because I had to know if you could be trusted. I was hoping to invest a lot of time and money in you, and, well, if you'd cut and run, okay, I would have lost some cash, but I would have saved a lot of time and trouble too. Now I know I can trust you one-hundred percent: you're an exceptionally honest man, Ben, and all the guilt you suffered over the money told me that much.

"Which brings me to Kate ..."

He let the moment hang painfully, while he tinkered with the flight controls, making lights come and lights disappear, tweaking all the time at my nerves.

"You two were made for each other, if that can ever be said about a man and a woman. You must forgive my cynicism; it's kind of ingrained by now. Kate is what you might call a talisman for me, Ben. Actually, she's a good deal more than that, but one thing at a time, eh? Ever heard of the Holy Grail?"

I'd had enough. "I don't give a shit about your -"

He held up a hand. "This is the heart of the matter, so hear me out. I'm not looking for holy relics. But I do have a genuine plat-inum plated mystical quest that will bring me unrivalled power in this world, so what do you think about that?"

"Impressive," I said, faking a yawn, while nursing an urgent need to beat my fists into his face.

"It will be impressive, and you will play your part in helping me achieve it."

"By me killing Goldhorn and Kate being a good luck charm?"

"Sounds a little *out there* when you put it like that."

"We go home rich, but not for killing Goldhorn?" The bile was rising and it tasted bitter. "Why us? Why are you doing this to *us*?"

He touched the controls, and I felt the helicopter bump against the sky. I needed no more reminding of my position.

"Certain as I am in my instinctive powers," he said, "I never leave anything to chance. I knew Kate was my talisman from the beginning, but habit said to test things out properly, scientific style. And where better to test out a 'good luck charm', as you put it, than in Las Vegas? So, a by-product of that test was a modest payout, and wouldn't it be cheap of me not to share out my good fortune?

"There's nothing else to read into it, my friend. I'm doing what any honourable man would do, given the circumstances and a generous nature. Killing Goldhorn has nothing to do with money, not directly. If you wanted to push the point, you could say that an unreliable member of the company is always a bad invest-ment, a liability. I guess you could say that."

We were making our descent.

We arrived back in Vegas, on the dark edge of town, the immense dazzle of the far-distant Strip burning out of the desert night sky. A cab was waiting to take us the short ride to a motel, the austerity of the place distinguishing it from anything on the Strip and anything belonging to Merle.

The motel looked to me like a converted prison, and maybe it was, I didn't ask. The bright reception area at the front was patrolled by a guard the size of a truck, with a length of chain attached to his forearm that led all the way to the throat of a dog even uglier than himself.

With an effort of will I took my eyes from the vicious looking double act, and peered through the large window out back, behind reception, where the rooms awaited their occupants. Mutely they waited to be chosen, a series of one and two storey blocks with doors fronting an almost deserted car park. I knew that in one of those lonely and miserable rooms a brutal fate was waiting and that I was to be a part of it.

Merle walked over to the guard and asked him the dog's name. "Lucifer," barked the guard. "Nice name," said Merle. Then he got down on his knees and started to run his hand around the dog's face.

"Better watch yourself, pal," said the guard. "You're gonna lose fingers doing that."

Merle responded to the warning by rubbing his face around the dog's nose and mouth, riding the growls and snarls, turning them into the softer sounds of what sounded like genuine canine affection. The guard watched with ugly disbelief before pulling hard on the chain and marching towards the all-night cafe on the other side of the highway.

Merle looked at me and winked. "Nice dog," he said. "Bad breath but nice teeth."

He booked a double room, all the time looking at me and smiling, like he was concealing an almighty pay off or else a proposal of marriage. As we turned to leave he took my hand, and I saw him look back at the receptionist, his arm slipping around my waist. Together we walked out into the car park and on towards a one-storey block of rooms at the far end of the complex.

We entered the ground floor room and Merle closed the door behind us. "Sorry about that," he said. "It disgusted me as much as it did you. But we have to be professional about these things."

I eyed the miserable room, which consisted of little more than a bed, a ripped chair and a small table. "Don't worry," he said. "We've not got to spend the whole night here."

"I think there's been some mistake," I said.

"Sit down, Ben."

I sat on the bed, and Merle sat down next to me, placing a paternal arm around my shoulders. "You look about ready to cry," he said.

"I don't know what I've gotten into," I said. "Just let me go back to my wife, she'll be scared out there on her own -"

"She's not alone, Ben. She's in good hands, the best, in fact." His arm caressed my shoulders tenderly, his eyes becoming soft and full. "She'll be fine, my friend. Look, it's not easy to do what I'm asking, not easy at all. But you're big enough - big enough where it counts. And after all's said and done ... you have Kate to consider, and don't you ever forget that."

"You'd never hurt her -"

"What do you think I am? Would I harm my very own good luck charm?" He reached into his pocket. "Look," he said. "As it's your first time, I'll make it easy for you."

He held out a gun, its handle pointing towards me. "Small, I know, but then size isn't everything, isn't that what they say?" I took the gun from him. "It packs a punch, my friend. Goes in like a pin, comes out like a cannonball. One squeeze will do it, one little squeeze is all it takes. You don't have to be a marksman; we don't want any fancy trick shooting. Forget all those movies, this ain't the Wild West."

He started to laugh.

"Why are you killing him?" I said. "Why are you murdering Tobias Goldhorn?"

"I'm not killing anyone, Ben. *You are.*"

"Why - for drinking, for turning up late?"

"He let me down. Do you know what it means to be let down by someone you once trusted?"

"I can't do this," I said.

His eyes narrowed, peering so hard into my face that I felt my blood shiver. "You can because you must. Here's some advice, it may help. *Do it for Kate.* She's depending on you."

"You said you wouldn't hurt her."

"And I won't. But you seem to forget, she still isn't cured. She needs more and she's counting on you. Looks can be deceptive. You see someone in the street one day, apparently in the finest health, and the next week you read that the cancer got them. Diseases sometimes take a holiday, but they always come back twice as hungry. I want to help you, I want to help both of you, but you've got to meet me halfway."

He looked at the gun in my hand. It felt cold.

"Just squeeze," he said. "Nice 'n' easy. It'll soon be over, nothing to it."

We sat for a few moments, and then I heard a car entering the car park, pulling to a halt outside the door; voices, footsteps; the knock at the door. Two large men in suits book-ended a small, bespectacled man in his late-forties, tired and at the same time wired, with a kindly light in his eyes that hadn't quite been extinguished. The three of them came into the room, but they didn't sit down. They stayed lined up by the wall, inside the doorway.

Merle stood up and walked over, stopping in front of the short, bespectacled man who was just tall enough to be looking down on Merle, though not from any remotely tangible position of power.

"Tobias," said Merle, "once good friend and healer. Never in the course of human history was so much talent wasted. Never was so much of my time and reputation compromised. Where did it all go wrong?"

"I think I m-must have misunderstood your instructions," stammered Goldhorn.

"I think you *m-must* have," said Merle. "But never mind, it won't happen again. Empty your pockets."

Due to some initial reluctance on the part of Tobias Goldhorn to do as he was told, assistance was provided. It came swiftly from one of the suited giants, and it came in the shape of a fist.

With blood running down his face Goldhorn emptied his pockets.

Merle looked at the contents, paying particular attention to some interesting looking powder that Goldhorn had placed down next to an accompanying needle and syringe. "I think it must be time for the fix to end all fixes," said Merle. "What do you think, Tobias?"

"I won't let you down again, I promise, I -"

"Correct, Tobias. Cover him, Ben."

Nothing happened. The gun in my hand remained pointed at the floor. I was blank in my panic, struggling to keep breathing.

Calmly, and with limitless authority, Merle uttered my name and gestured for me to lift up the gun, so that it was pointed directly at Goldhorn. It was the closest I had come to an out of body experience. I was somewhere above it all, separated, watching myself act, without any possibility of intervening.

"Stand up, Ben."

I stood up.

Merle gestured for me to alter my line of fire, so that the barrel of the gun was aiming right between Tobias Goldhorn's eyes.

"Fill up that syringe, Tobias," said Merle. "And use all of it."

"But -"

"*All of it.*"

Goldhorn filled up the syringe, while the part of me that had watched from the ceiling above, slowly rejoined the greater, more wretched part that was holding the gun. I was staring at Goldhorn's shoes while both of my hands shook wildly.

I heard him start to cry.

"Have mercy, please ... all I did was - I went to the wrong casino ..."

"You certainly did that, my friend."

A lifetime later Goldhorn's face came into my line of vision as it hit the floor. I wanted to look away but couldn't. I could see that he was dead.

"You can put the gun down now, Ben. Okay, everybody, party's over."

CHAPTER
NINETEEN

A CAR WAS WAITING. MERLE MOVED A FINGER, AND THE VEHICLE crawled towards us like a large, hostile insect. I looked back to see the door close on the dead body of Tobias Goldhorn. For a second I envied him.

Then I thought of Kate, and I was clinging to life again as though I loved it. My exposed nerves freshened by the salt wind of hope.

The four of us got into the car, and a short ride later we were parking outside a block of private offices. Merle took me inside and his henchmen came along to keep us company. We walked through a dozen numbered doors and twisted along a labyrinth of corridors until at last we came to a door without a number. One of the suited thugs opened it, revealing a small study dominated, on the facing wall, by a large portrait of Merle.

The painting, in oils, mixed a dozen styles in haphazard fashion, as far as I could tell. If there was any representation of bow tie and buttonhole, I couldn't make it out.

He took his seat behind an imposing oak desk, directly beneath the portrait. "Just about the worst painting I've ever seen. But the man was dying at the time. Context in art is everything, Ben. I wouldn't sell it for a billion dollars. Now, why don't you take the weight off? It could be a long night."

I sat down while he made a few calls, the last of which was to Angels Camp. He was talking to Guinevere, the woman charged with looking after Kate while we were "out of town." He was telling her about how Goldhorn had let his habit get the better of him, calling it "another statistic to beat into the heads of the youth of America."

He asked about Kate, and glanced up at me before telling Guinevere that he was "really sorry to hear that."

I was out of my seat, and he was waving me to sit back down, with additional encouragement on hand from his attendant thugs.

"... If her condition deteriorates further, you'll have to move her to the Palace and start preparing. Keep a close watch."

He placed the phone down and held up his hands. "It's okay, Ben. Just some night sweats and a bad dream. Might have been the mineral water - I'll speak to Clancy when we get back."

I moved towards him. "We've got to go back," I said.

I felt the movement of air as the suited giants moved on me, and saw the flick of Merle's eye hold them in check. Then he gave me a look so bathed in compassion that it stopped me in my tracks. "This might be the hardest part for you, this separation. But things still need doing this end. Guinevere knows what to do, so start trusting me, will you?"

The two suits were quickly briefed before being dismissed out into the night. I didn't recognize any of the names that Merle had given them, and I could only imagine what acts of inhumanity they had marked into their schedules. The sickness of the grins on their faces as they left started my heart playing jazz rhythms again.

I waited for Merle to say something. He opened a desk drawer and took out a bottle of mineral water and two glasses. Filling them, he handed one to me. We might have been clean-living buddies about to discuss the finer points of cheese tasting.

I pushed the glass away, and he pondered over the gesture.

"You know what I once heard someone say? That if you emptied a man's pockets you would know the truth about him. We found out the truth about Goldhorn for sure, but what would people make of the contents of *our* pockets? What would they make of finding that gun hiding all alone in your jacket, Ben? You used to have a pile of money kept hidden in there not so very long ago. And now it's a loaded gun. Would they say, 'The man's a killer', or would they know the truth: that the man's doing all he can to save his sick wife?"

"What's the point to all this?" I said, taking the gun out of my jacket and throwing it across the desk.

"I see," he said. "You threw that gun down like you were ridding yourself of one more guilty secret. You've done nothing wrong, my friend, not really, *not yet.*"

"Why did you make me think I had to kill Goldhorn?"

"You would have done it, Ben; I saw it in your eyes. We can all pull a trigger; everyone in this world will kill for a price. Finding the price, that's the trick. And price doesn't necessarily mean money." He lit a cigar. "I believe we were talking about the contents of a man's pockets. Would you care to know what I have in pride of place in mine?"

He took out a silk scarf from which he produced a deck of tarot cards. "My travelling deck," he said, handing them to me. "Shuffle them, please." I hesitated. "Oh, come on now, Ben. The sooner things get done the sooner we can get you back to your beautiful wife."

After I had shuffled the deck, he took ten cards off the top and made a pyramid shape of four-three-two-one. "Had your future told recently?" he asked me.

I thought again of that remote scene from my childhood; a small boy lost at a late summer carnival.

"You're a mess, pal," said Merle, looking first at the cards and then at me. "One unholy mess. What you said about that bully, who I believe went by the name of Johnny Winterburn ... what you said just about sums you up."

I asked him what he was talking about, and how he could possibly know that name.

"I know a lot of things about you and your life, Ben. But for now, let's concentrate on this character Winterburn."

He took a heavy pull on his cigar. "You never tell that story, you never address the things that Johnny Winterburn did to you and the feelings he created in you. So, consequently, you don't under-stand the way certain people and certain situations make you feel or react. You don't explore your discomforts to find out what caused them. *Denial's* what the shrinks call it. Dereliction of your duties as a man is what I call it."

"Is this a psychology lecture or a psychiatric consultation?"

"That's very funny. But you dismiss me before you know what I have to say, and you do so at your peril, because I mean to help you. Take Winterburn, for example: the damage he caused didn't stay inside the school gates. You took it with you, out into the world where it could grow and fester. As for Winterburn, well, he gave up being a bully when he won the lottery and retired to a life of luxury in San Francisco. Small world, isn't it? Yet what kind of justice is that? Did your suffering end at the school gates?"

Merle took a photograph out of his pocket. "More of those pocket revelations, you could say. Here, take a look."

The photo showed the aged but still unmistakable features of Johnny Winterburn, complete with jug ears, freckles, and a spade chin. He was tied to a post, an enthusiastic crowd appearing to throw bricks at him.

"He enjoyed throwing rocks at people, didn't he? He used to wait for other children after school, and he would take them to an old piece of waste ground, with them pleading all the way for mercy. And then he would make them stand up against a tree while he threw rocks at them until they were crying and screaming. But it never made any difference to Johnny Winterburn. He just threw harder.

"That photograph shows Winterburn being stoned to death minutes after being told why. Now that is what *I* call justice. You might feel a moment of revulsion, my friend, but you've got relief coming. Your heart might still race when you see a guy with elephant's ears, but peace comes from trusting in the powers of *real* justice."

"How..?"

"It would take longer than the rest of your life. Suffice to say, I've been laying all your ghosts to rest."

He opened up a rogues gallery of my past, reintroducing me to the "conductors of my ill-fortunes", forcing me look on their withered corpses and sickbed screams, frozen as they were into photographs which he kept pulling from his pocket like conjurors' rabbits from a bottomless hat. "Beginning to feel a little of the real Ben Tolle creeping back? That angry guy you've been keeping hidden? Liberating, isn't it?"

"Why go to all this trouble?"

"Why, it's no trouble, no trouble at all. The immediate future and the far past are all that remain. Let's save the future 'til last." He was looking at the cards.

I said, "I thought they spoke of futures, not pasts."

"That's very astute. But the future always depends on the past." He pointed a finger at me, and then at the cards? "Bring back memories?"

"I was only a child."

"Nothing's ever really forgotten, though. It's just a matter of recall. Permit me to assist. Picture a little boy, lost from his parents. Good parents, too, in their own ways. Meths loved you more than anything in the world, but dammit if the drink just wouldn't let him be. And that's where he was that day, sniffing out the refreshments tent, and adding to your later insecurities.

Your mother, well, if she didn't have enough of a job keeping an eye out for poor old Meths, that and coping with her own demons.

"And while all this was going on, a lonely little boy was getting himself so lost that only a very old woman could find him. And when she did, she took him to her tent and looked a long, *long* way into his life. What she saw disturbed her – no, it *terrified* her. But she should never have let that little boy sense that terror; for how can a boy, or a man, face the future with all that storehouse of fear promised to him, no matter how subtly or unintentionally?

"Well, that old girl died a long time ago, though she never stopped thinking about the little boy. She died without realising the harm she'd done to him, passing on that apprehension. You can be cured of all those other damages, my friend, but a scar like that would still leave you a long way from clean. So ... I had to take another old woman, to *symbolise* her, if you will. It had to be done, you do understand that?"

"What the hell are you talking about?"

"Well, Ben, it's like this. See, this old woman was herself a card reader. She had nowhere near the gifts of the old woman who rescued you that long ago day, so I had to kind of transmute the soul of the one - the dead soul, you follow me? – into the other before I started to transfer her organs back the other way. And what we ended up with was the soul of the fairground lady in the fucked about corpse of the inferior card reader, and the essential inner workings of the latter forwarded on to the soulless remains of the former. Sounds complicated, doesn't it? It's surprisingly straightforward once you get the feel for it. Anyway ..."

"You killed the old woman in San Francisco?"

Merle's grin appeared wider than his face.

"Thought we'd never get to it!"

The rising nausea exploded. I caught the vomit in my throat.

"I thought you might show at least *some* gratitude, Ben. I did it for you and for Kate. But that's in the past, and it's the future you really want to know about. Yours, Kate's ..."

My throat was burning, and I had to take a few sips of water to ease it. Watching as I put the glass down, he nodded slightly. He knew I'd need the drink. Two glasses, not one.

"The police believe the old lady was one of a series of killings over many years. You probably know that." He picked up his glass. "To fulfil the prophecy of the two glasses, I too must take a sip." Having done so, he placed the glass back down. "Now, Ben, would you like to hear some more about the deaths of sad old ladies?"

He sighed and gave me a weary look. "At times you think I'm young enough to be the son you never had. Other times you think me old enough to be the father who was never there for you, unless he was blaming you for getting lost at a lousy carnival and beating his own demons out of *you*. And did your mother protect you, or was she every bit as crazy as he was? Too busy worrying about old Meths, and clinging to a faith that was deserting her? Righteous indignation and Old Testament bullshit ain't no substitute for love, my friend. We're orphans now, and those devout losers are paying the price. It's one thing losing your own faith, but when you nurture that loss in those you're charged with caring for ... they ain't at rest, believe me."

He looked away for a moment, before letting his gaze rest squarely on me.

"I'm hard to pin down and even harder to weigh up. I guess I have one of those kinds of faces, and the kind of twisty personality that goes with it. The truth is that I can only be one or the other: prodigal son or prodigal parent. So which would you like it to be? Would you want me as your son or your father?"

I picked up my glass again, weighed it for a moment in my hand, and then hurled it against the wall. "I've had enough of your games."

He didn't flinch, stayed looking right at me. "Choose, my friend," he said. "*Choose.*"

I stood disarmed and wretched under his glare; then a look of something - *disappointment?* - swept across his face and he lowered his eyes.

"Magicians set up patterns," he said. "Sometimes those patterns are created just to hide the true nature of their work and purpose. I'm too young, really, to have killed all of them, and in a couple of years somebody else - some other magician with access to the circle of knowledge - will be glad of that particular pattern to disguise his own darker need. And if *he* doesn't, someone else will. It'll give the police and the press something to get their blunt teeth into. Anyway, that's enough trifling with the past for one day."

He turned back to the cards, and took his time with them, at last turning them over, one by one, placing them down so that they formed a pyramid face.

"There is killing to be done," he said. "This man is on his way to Angels Camp to see your wife."

I looked at the face in the pyramid and heard the rush of air into my lungs even before I felt it.

"Whatever reservations, whatever inner controls we had to dismantle to contemplate the killing of Tobias Goldhorn ... I'm sure they won't apply in the case of the good doctor."

I couldn't hold back any longer, throwing my guts over the face in the picture.

Professor Buck-Bradbury.

CHAPTER
TWENTY

Merle went out attending to business. I could only guess what that might amount to. I was alone, the ruined picture of Buck-Bradbury for company, nourishing my worst imaginings until the sun came up.

What did Buck-Bradbury want with Kate? What game was Merle playing? *What was waiting at the bottom of all this?*

For all the talking that Merle had done, I was no wiser than I had been back in San Francisco. I was like a diver plunging down through the blackening depths of dangerous waters, sensing the imminence of revelation, periodically surfacing for air, every time empty handed, each dive deeper than the last but no more rewarding or illuminating.

I could call the police – *and tell them what?* I wasn't ready for the straightjacket, the needles and the padded cell. So I waited, knowing in every bone that the coming hours would be stamped in me, branding me forever.

The day started before the dawn. I was sitting with my head in my hands, longing for England, and praying a pagan prayer of deliverance. Wondering how a believer would fare in my shoes. I was not a believer, though I longed to be one. In that forsaken hour how I longed for that. Yet the door seemed closed against me. *Of my own accord?* I couldn't work it out. But in my unbelief I had taken Kate away from what she had once found comfort in. Had our wedding really been her farewell to faith?

I blamed the hypocrisy of her devoutly pious family for ruining her religion, and no doubt they in turn would be blaming me. Yet her spirit was purer than any self-confessed believer that *I* had ever met; and if the gates of Heaven could ever close in her face, then the universe was nothing, meant nothing, and amounted to nothing.

Still, I had played my part. Was this the price I was paying, that we were both paying?

As the night crawled on I wore out the hottest part of my fire with constructions of Merle's death, and Buck-Bradbury's for good measure; and what was left wasted itself trying to fathom the meaning, and why I should ring the police, and why I shouldn't ring them, and what Buck-Bradbury's business in Angels Camp could be.

As the dawn approached, a forlorn and undirected prayer of hope was interrupted by the ringing telephone.

Hours earlier I had picked up the phone and asked the girl at the other end for the number of the Angels Camp Hotel. She'd never heard of Angels Camp, Nevada, and there was nothing listed. I had crashed the phone down, unsurprised. And now, in the darkest hour, I picked it up again, reconciled to the playing out of fate, half expecting the absurdity of a wrong number.

"Ben, how are you doing? Sorry it's taken me so long, you must be hungry and tired."

Was I? It hadn't occurred.

"I'll be with you in an hour. I meant to give you the number back at the Camp, so you could give Kate a ring. That was so remiss of me. Got a pen handy?"

I took the place apart. In the past I had been accused of not searching thoroughly for things, mainly by women. But I put my hand on my heart when I say that there was not a pen or a crayon or a writing instrument of any kind in that room.

"How good are you at remembering numbers, Ben?"

We tried the first five until the second five threw them into chaos. We tried again, and then again. It was like juggling with too many eggs and too few hands. Merle suggested some memory system, and we practiced it, and eventually it seemed to be work-ing. Up to ten numbers, that is; the remaining five took another system and what felt like the better part of a lifetime. Finally, I felt safe enough to put the phone down. I punched in the numbers fast, praying that I wouldn't have to do it a second time. There was a delay, a mocking silence. Already I was rehearsing the numbers, already their sequence slipping.

"Guinevere?" I felt ridiculous even saying the name.

"Ben? Merle said to expect your call."

"How is she?"

In the hesitation I felt fear and rage gathering like the onset of a storm.

"She's had a poor night, Ben."

I remembered what Merle had said about moving her to the Palace. "Have you -?"

"She has been moved, and everything is going to be fine. You must trust Merle, he has everything in hand. You have to do as he tells you, everything he tells you. That's the secret."

"Can I speak to her?"

"She's sleeping. Better that you let her rest. You'll see her soon enough. I must go now, there are things to prepare. Goodbye, Ben. *Safe journey*."

"But – don't go -"

She was gone.

I tried to recall the numbers, but they had mashed into brain soup. Fury exploded and I crashed the phone down, smashing the handset to pieces.

The dawn came. And the hours rolled on ... and still I waited.

When I heard the first sounds of his returning, I thought of a cat - or a fox - fresh from the night's killings, the blood still wet around its mouth. I stood up, I wanted to be on my feet when he came through the door. He had taunted me with those numbers, playing me like a terrified, hopeless creature being pawed around before the kill. There had been a grinning face at the other end of the phone, though I had been too distracted to see it. An office without pens? *Deliberately cleared of pens!*

He came through the door and held out a hand. "Sorry, Ben - what a night! I meant to be back sooner. And about that number, I should have -"

I ignored the outstretched hand. "Where's the camera, then?" He looked blank. "What kind of a sick fucking sadist are you?"

"Ben?" He rushed towards me, embracing me. "Oh, Ben, what has the long night done to you? Do you really think I'm capable of such ... *evil*?"

If he needed an answer my eyes must have given it to him. He sat down. "When you needed me most I left you too long ... in my rush to finish business I didn't spend the time with you that I should have ... I didn't consider your hunger and your thirst, not even your anxieties about the one you love. I left you a phone and no number -"

"Are you taking the - you could have asked them to ring me, you fucking ..."

"I can see, my friend, that from your position you can only deem me a failure. But believe me, my business is your business, and you are the true inheritor. The father has sinned yet the son must not suffer for those sins, not anymore."

I let his sick parody of fatherly concern run its course. And then I watched as this little man in his eternal white suit, now adorned in scarlet and turquoise accessories, changed again.

"Don't treat me too harshly. I only mean to do the best I can. I love you both so much, and I want you to be proud of me when all this is over. I want you to be able to stand back and see that it was all done with love in my heart. When I stand on my podium and make my bow to the world I want you both to be there. If you are not, the day will be empty, the accomplishment nothing. I want us all to live happily ever after. We are family beyond flesh and blood. The father, the mother that I never had - you can't call that trash left rotting in the Oregon woods *family*. I am still young, still learning and finding out about the world. Do not judge me too harshly, for the greatest test is still to come. Have faith in me a while longer and I promise to repay that faith. You will be proud of me when you see what I've done. When you see the whole truth, you won't abandon me."

If I'd sat him on my knee, adopted the accent and said, "Hell, son, ain't your daddy always been proud of you?" the scene would have been complete. As it was, I stood in confusion, looking on this – *this what*? - captor, saviour, teacher, tormentor, father, son, healer ... *executioner*?

We left the room, and not another word was spoken until we were in the helicopter, heading back to Angels Camp.

"By the time you leave this little old country of ours, you'll have some tales to tell the folks back home. I bet you'll even write books about it, one day. And if you do, I hope you paint me fairly and accurately, and maybe with a pinch of sympathy. Time and distance can distort a person's evaluation of the truth, and I would hate to think of my good nature and character being maligned in some foreign corner of the world, with no opportunity for redress. You know something, Ben? I think you're going to have to make me the hero of the tale. Hell, I could be one of the great characters in world literature - how about that!"

We flew on across the burning desert.

"So, Ben, what do you say?"

"About what?"

"Making me the hero?"

I told him to write his own fucking story.

He put on a hurt expression. Said he would have to attain immortality by other means. "Are you not interested in what those means might be, Ben?"

"Not particularly."

"Do you know nothing of the world, of the art of diplomacy, the politics of people? You care for the patient best by keeping the doctor sweet. You look at a situation, see where the power lies, and you suck up to that power. You don't have to like it. In fact, you might despise it, but you learn to use it for your own ends."

The father was back in the chair, and the powerless son sat hating him.

"That's what *I* did, what I had to do. And now I don't have to suck up to anybody. Not ever. But I would never have survived if I hadn't let people like Buck-Bradbury think that I was full of respect. I think you'd better start playing your part correctly and showing some respect to me, Ben. I want you to like me, I even want you to love me – I'm serious about that. But more than anything, I mean to make sure that you play your part the way I want it playing. I would rather you did it for love, but what matters is that you do it. Now, any questions?"

"Why is Buck-Bradbury going to Angels Camp?"

"To meet his destiny, of course."

"Meaning?"

"A bullet."

He took the gun out of his pocket and handed it back to me. "You're going to be requiring this again later, so I suggest you take good care of it."

Once again I held the metal secret in my pocket, though this time the feeling was different. Events would likely run their course without any involvement on my part, as they done had for Tobias Goldhorn. And even if I was to be called into action, the thought of playing a role in Buck-Bradbury's demise was not exactly tearing me up.

Merle was feeling the need for in-flight entertainment. And I was it.

"Buck-Bradbury isn't a man who takes kindly to surprises. Likes things in their place, does The Buck. Nothing left to chance. He's making the journey over because he thinks there's good reason. And he's right about that, *dead right*. He's just wrong about what the purpose really is."

"So why does *he* think he's coming to Angels Camp?"

"That's complicated. It's like this: Buck-Bradbury still sees me and him as partners. He wants to see the culmination of my work because he thinks he's got shares in it. You see, me and the Buck go back a long way."

I didn't doubt it. They seemed made for each other.

But the implications were starting to buzz around my head like drunken hornets.

"Partners?" I said.

"When you write that book of yours, I'd appreciate a little re-working here. This isn't the part I'm proud of.

"See, I met Buck-Bradbury at a healing convention in California, where every hare-brained, doctorate-hopeful loony tune was played to death. The greatest minds in medicine and magic together in the dumb realisation of a common belief: that when all the bullshit is sieved out, the bottom line of the healing game is to become rich and powerful.

"We devised a system. The Buck would milk them as far as belief in medical science could stretch, and then I would come in to tidy up from a more *esoteric* perspective. Of course, I was the less visible partner, and none of his *referrals* to me were ever known to the patient."

"I don't believe you," I said.

"But you understand what I'm saying?"

"I told you, I'm tired of your games."

"This is no game, Ben."

I caught the seriousness in his tone, and the shock waves began to hit me.

"Are you telling me ...?"

"Go on, say it."

"You sick bastard," I said.

"That's only half of it, though. It's a two-way street. The Buck was only passing back what he was given in the first place. You got to The Buck through me."

My fingers traced the outline of the gun. "Why are you telling me this?"

"The partnership is over, Ben. And I want you to help me terminate the contract."

"No, wait a minute. You recommended Buck-Bradbury – you were the anonymous benefactor? *Why?* You've got no angle on us, nothing to make from us."

"You've got to pay attention, Ben: I have more than the power to heal. I have the power to create sickness. Like Christ in the Apocrypha, I can cause what I later choose to heal. Buck-Bradbury saw the potential in our partnership when he understood that I could make the richest the sickest. It was a blank cheque to him, though I had a mission beyond money. I was collecting the souls of avarice and giving them a cemetery of their own, and I was keeping one plot vacant for the greediest of them all."

He turned away from the flight controls and grinned at me again.

"You've guessed it with that speed-brain of yours. But there's more, Ben, a good deal more, that's if you're interested."

Turning back to the controls, he said, "I keep two cemeteries. The Cemetery of Avarice speaks for itself, but in the other ..." He whistled, shook his head. "In the other - boy, you're going to be impressed with this. In the other, I've amassed the souls of every great magician and healer from the humblest medicine man to the eternal spirit of the immortal Merlin. Take that in, my friend. You might call it the ancestral home of the universal magician. I'm a proud man, Ben, proud as hell!"

"You ... *made Kate sick?*"

"Before I answer that, my friend, let me tell you something else. The rich and greedy who found their way into the Cemetery of Avarice, were selected for their sins. The world is a better place

240

for their expiry. When The Buck graces that place with his presence, what I have created will be an enduring monument, and a lesson for all mankind. That has been my hobby, but not my vocation. My real work lies in the other cemetery ... with my friends."

"I said ... *Did you make her sick?*"

He held up a hand, while the other maintained the helicopter's steady course across the desert. "Bear with me a moment longer. We're almost there."

He waited for me to ease back in my seat.

"You've had to endure a lot of cryptic jive, so here's the thing. I began in Egypt, culminated in the form of Merlin, and at last found my spiritual home at Angels Camp. The cards told me that my present incarnation can restore all my parts into one, and I've spent the best of my adult years gathering my souls together.

"Yes, I made Kate sick. I needed purity to light the fuse. I had to bring her to me. The only way was via The Buck, and that meant inducing a condition that would baffle the medical world. Simple, when you know what you're doing. And now The Buck is travelling to Angels Camp because I've asked him to open a new cemetery. It's a business opportunity that's got him licking his chops like the hungry rat he is."

My fingers wouldn't leave the cold outline of the gun. But I still wasn't taking it in.

"*How -?*"

"Let me finish, will you. You deserve to hear this. You see, my friend, when he gets to the Camp, The Buck's going to get what you might call the Mother of Surprises. He's going to be reintroduced to the one that got away. And then you get to do the honours, Ben. You get to put an end to that walking piece of avaricious shit. Now think about *that*."

"You put her through all of this ..?"

"She's unique, my good friend. And I have roamed the world to find her."

"*You* ..?"

"Lost for words, eh? So maybe now you can see why I should be the hero when you write your tale. One favour deserves another, isn't that what they say?"

He looked back at me. "Put the gun down, Ben. It ain't time for the gun, Ben. *Ben!*"

I didn't shoot him. Shoot a man while he holds your life two-hundred feet above the crawling desert sand ... while my wife rots among strangers?

He knew the time to tell it.

Out of the corner of his eye he watched me place the gun down.

"Keep that hate nice and safe and fresh for the Buck. All this friction between us carries a vibe through the air, and it travels faster than a spaceship and it ain't doing Kate any good, I tell you. No good at all.

"See, every time two people as close as we are think a bad thing about the other, your good wife goes another inch down the hole. And let me tell you, she ain't got many inches left to go. She's pure, Ben, and that rare kind of purity slips the worst."

"How did you make her sick - you never even met her?"

"You've got so much to learn. Remember Salome? Of course you do, you got the sack over it. What a night that was. I was over on business, and fancied a little entertainment. I always had a soft spot for Herod's daughter, and I never saw anybody bring her back to life the way Kate did that immortal night.

"I treated myself to a programme, a souvenir of the performance, so I could keep her pretty face by my bedside. I can tell a lot from a photograph. How many nights I studied her, Ben, and how far I got inside her mind. I heard, and I watched, her thoughts, day and night. You were in there, too, and how I envied you. I had to get inside your head, and then I didn't envy you at all. Not with all of those hang-ups and all of that baggage.

"But I saw the way to Kate; the sign was loud and clear: Ben Tolle, aspiring writer ... professional *fool*."

I felt the helicopter start its descent.

"Ever heard of August Strindberg?"

I was too confused to think straight.

"Kate would know. She played *Miss Julia* – don't you remember?"

I couldn't bring it to mind.

"It's not important," he said.

It was, though. He knew something about Kate's career that I didn't.

"What *is* important was Strindberg himself. Bit of a dabbler, and I'm not talking about his playwriting. Thought he'd use a bit of late nineteenth century witchcraft to get his estranged wife back. Used telepathic powers to make his daughter just about sick enough to require a visit from Mama, and he did it using a photograph.

"The kid got sick and boy did the guilt set in. It sent old August crazy. Dabbling's dangerous in the wrong hands, my friend – and you know the funny thing? I got all of that shit from the programme notes: Telepathic Suggestion – it's been around a long time, don't you know."

I didn't believe him. Telepathy belonged in fiction. As for hypnosis - Kate wouldn't fall for that. And I told him. He laughed. "Ben," he said, "excuse my abruptness, but you don't know what the fuck you're talking about. Man, she was perfect. She was as ripe as they come. She even dreamt about a great magician coming to claim her, and all because of some half-assed legend in an Irish village. The realist in her never ousted the romantic. That's what the two of you have in common. You ought to know your own wife better than you do, and yourself, come to that."

We were coming in to land.

"We're just about there, Ben. Sit tight now."

CHAPTER
TWENTY-ONE

In the dark heat we touched down behind the Cemetery of Avarice. The gun was back in my pocket and feeling more at home there than it had done before. We walked down past the cemetery, past the hotel and on towards the Palace.

The Palace was a large, white domed building dominating the near distance, blinding the eye from catching the dark pit that lay behind it: Cemetery Number One.

Merle said, "Knowing the high price I was going to be extracting from you, and believing in wholesale justice, I did everything in advance to make it up to you. I purged you; I cleansed you. I made the till balance. I always make the till balance. I don't want your gratitude, though. I want your loyalty, in fact I insist on it."

My imagination was rioting while Merle was still barking on about loyalty and trust and faith. I had become numb to his words. All I knew was the gun in my pocket and my love for Kate.

I stood at the foot of the steps leading up to the Palace, filled with awe and dread. As I climbed the steps the fear started to melt into the relief of resignation.

At the top of the steps we came to a solid white door, almost invisible in the context of the whiteness of the rest of the building. Merle gestured and I went in ahead of him.

Nothingness greeted me as I entered the blinding whiteness. We walked along a corridor of pure white, at last reaching another door, almost invisible. I opened it and screamed.

Inside the door was a thin passage to yet another white door. This time the whiteness had been shattered. Mounted on the door was the severed head of the moustached man.

Minus the moustache.

"Looks much better that way, don't you think? Clean shaven, I mean. I guess some would say that was taking a close shave a little too far. What do you think, Ben? I mean, can you take personal hygiene too far?"

My empty stomach heaved. I was down on my hands and knees. Merle's hand stroked the back of my neck. "That's the way, my friend. Get it out of your system. Can't be much left in there to bring up now." I brushed his hand away, easing myself back on to my feet. He glanced deliberately at his watch. "Hope you don't mind me asking, but are you in the habit of bringing your wife a little something back when you've been away?"

Recovering my composure a little, I told him I tried not to leave her in the first place.

"Not even to take a beer in a San Francisco hotel bar? Not even to take a little trip to Vegas to assassinate a failed healer? If you really want to, if you think it would be appreciated, you could take our friend here and maybe get a female opinion on the trim."

I tried not to look again at the mounted head as we went through the doorway into yet another corridor of blinding whiteness, narrowing into a long, straight tunnel. In the distance I could make out a figure. The figure wasn't moving, and I began to doubt that it was a person at all. But as we got closer I could see that it was a woman.

Guinevere.

"How's the patient doing?" asked Merle.

The woman looked at me in an attitude of sympathy.

"What is it?" I said. "How is she?"

"Come, come," said Merle. "We're all adults. Answer the poor man's question."

"It's as well that you're back," she said.

"Do I detect an element of the downbeat in your voice, my dear?"

"For God's sake - *how's my wife*!"

"You must forgive my friend," said Merle. "He's had a tough night and a challenging morning. He's keen to get down to business."

Passing through yet another doorway, the whiteness ended abruptly. We entered a black room lit with candles, an archway leading through to a small chamber more dimly lit and heavily ornamented. At the far side, in a cot suspended above the stone floor, lay Kate.

She wasn't moving.

"She's sleeping," said the woman, taking a damp sponge and smoothing it gently over Kate's forehead. "It's Ben. He's come back for you. Wake up, my love."

Slowly Kate's eyes opened, and all I could think was how much this resembled some cheap stage act. The Ben Tolle who lived somewhere beyond the fantasy land of my imagination spoke to me in whispers: *We don't believe any of this, we're from a small island where up is up and the devil lives in hell. And though it's against our nature to walk out on a host, come on, Kate, let's get the plane out of here and leave this freak show.*

I held her hand. It was wet. Her mouth moved, and I could feel her breath on my cheek, her chest slowly rising and falling.

But no sound coming out of her.

"Can you hear me, Kate? I'm taking you home."

The voice in my head whispered: *Let's get the hell out of this nightmare. I'm going to take this gun out of my pocket and shoot the fucking heads off these weirdos and pick you up, carry you out of here ...*

Her eyes scared me. The wildness in them conjured images of possession and haunted graves. I thought this must be the end.

"It's going to be alright," I said, fighting back the tears.

These creeps are killing you. And I'm taking them down with us.

I turned to Guinevere, and saw her wiping her eyes. Then Merle beckoned her. "Let's leave them alone," he said. "Allow them some privacy."

As they were leaving the room, I heard him say, "I take it the good doctor's arrived?"

The door closed behind them. I kissed Kate. Her skin was burning up. "Can you hear me?" I said.

She nodded, I was certain of it, though her eyes had closed again, sealing in the wildness. I hadn't been with her, trapped instead on a fool's errand; holding a gun to a stranger. I felt my right hand snake into my pocket and finger the cold metal.

How merciful to take out the gun and end it, for Kate and for me … for better or for worse.

The gun wouldn't come out of my pocket, and my hand turned at last from the unforgiving chill, finding its way back to the scalding skin. Behind me I heard the door open. I turned, my hand squeezing once more around the cold hard metal of the gun.

Guinevere came in and sponged Kate's face again, so tenderly, lovingly, and looking at me with such concern, compassion.

"Will she live?" I said.

"Merle will save her. Trust him."

"Has he sent you to soften me up?"

"He's a wonderful man, an amazing healer. We have all been saved by him."

She continued to run the soft sponge over Kate's face as my bull-shit detector switched to overload, the anger erupting. "Is this some weird-shit born-again cult you're running?"

"We owe him everything," she said. "Merle has healed as many people as he has killed."

There was not a trace of irony in her voice; it was like she was praising the work of a saint.

"There's a price, though?" I said. "There's always a price."

"Only in cheap stories," she said. "Merle decides whether someone's worth saving."

"What about the guy with the moustache? He must have been 'saved' once."

"His soul is safe. No-one lives forever. This is not a colony of vampires. We, the saved, will all die one day, and rest in the good cemetery, not twist and turn for eternity in the Cemetery of Avarice."

"He cut the guy's head off for not having a shave!"

"He has a strange sense of humour."

"It's called psychopathic where I come from!"

"Trust him, Ben."

"I was taught never to trust a psychopath. I had an old fashioned upbringing."

"Don't mock what you don't understand."

"Kate's never going to get out of here, is she?"

"You must have faith. Merle wants to cure her. He will, if you let him."

"So he can cut off *her* head when he feels in need of a good laugh? What's he saving her for?"

"I can't answer all your questions."

"I can see that! Do you know what he told me on the way here? That he caused her illness in the first place!"

The echoes trailed off into silence, all the while the woman continuing to gently bathe Kate.

The door opened and Merle came in. With a flick of his eyes, he sent Guinevere from the room.

"Your turn?" I asked him. "Can we talk somewhere else?"

"If you'd rather," he said. "The ball's in your court now."

I kissed my wife. "I won't be long," I told her. "Then I'm taking you home."

We went back through the archway. Merle instructed Guinevere to go back into the black chamber to tend to Kate.

Standing in the whiteness of the corridor beyond, Merle said to me, "The choice is yours. I cure her tonight, or you walk out of here, transport supplied, and take her home to die. Nothing's changed; it's up to you. It has always been up to you. I will not cure somebody against their will."

He must have seen my knuckles tightening. "Easy, my friend," he said. "We are entering the eye of the storm. There are rules and they matter. They can't be disregarded because of your impatience. Tonight I will place the last occupant in the Cemetery of Avarice. Buck-Bradbury will be cutting the tape with his own shin bones."

He sighed, heavily. "I had hoped to unlock the gates to my other cemetery tonight, but I still haven't thought of a name. Nothing seems to capture its grandeur. I thought I might let Kate decide ... but if it isn't to be, if she really has to go home and die, then worry not, my friend. I'll find another to unlock the gates. I've waited this long; I can wait a little longer. And for the record: I'm not afraid of you spilling any beans. I can make you forget all of this like a ... *cheap stage hypnotist."*

I felt cold and alone.

"To put it crudely, think of me for a moment as some old witch, if it helps: pointed hat, broomstick - the works. Now, picture my vast caldron, bubbling away, full of every ingredient you ever read about as a kid. Well, metaphorically, Kate is the last ingredient to go into the pot. A stir and a pinch of pepper and salt, and the recipe is complete."

His face cracked into a smile. "I can see you're thinking about it. So let's do it. Let's go for tonight's star prize. We walk into a room, where Buck-Bradbury is making himself comfortable. He'll demand to know what's going on. Knowing that you're not exactly rich, and that charity deals tend to be cash limited, he'll smell a rat. Credit where it's due, he's pretty sharp for a quack. Anyway, I tell him you're guest of honour at the opening of two cemeteries. This will confuse him and I will have to explain. He'll still be a little confused when I'm done explaining, and that's where I'll have to call on you to clarify matters by pointing that gun, which I trust you've been taking good care of, right into his avaricious piece-of-shit face.

"Then we walk out together, the three of us, and visit Cemetery Number One so that he can dwell on the might-have-beens. He won't understand them any more than you do, but still. Then we'll move on, good friends that we are, and he will stand in his VIP plot at the heart of the Cemetery of Avarice. He will ceremoniously pick up the spade, generously supplied for the occasion, and move a few clods like he was the president. While he's doing that, Kate will be brought down to join us. And then the hero, the real prince, the noble knight will kiss the sleeping beauty until she wakes, melting with rapturous bliss into his - your - arms."

He pointed two fingers at my right temple, and cocked back his thumb.

"And then, my friend, you squeeze, oh so gently, and you fill up the hole with the crowning carcass of greedy, selfish meat. Now, isn't that beautiful? Ironic, too, when you stop to think about it: because, in a way, the Buck *will* be healing her after all. The final trade off: the final *life for a life*. Tonight the healing is complete, and then *she* decides."

"Decides? Decides what?"

"Her fate, of course: whether to return to England with you ... or else join me."

"Join you?"

"*In the New Camelot.*"

He walked back down the passageway to a side door that I hadn't noticed earlier. I followed him. "What are you talking about?" I said.

"I started out with the best intentions, Ben. But somewhere along the line I learned the most valuable lesson of all: that we waste our time trying to square the circle. I turned my back on the age old search for the Philosopher's Stone, rejecting the quest for youth and riches; and once I had given up that particular Grail, though it had bugged me for the longest time, I was liberated. But it didn't last. It was ivory-tower liberation. The desert is full of demons, and their number exceeds the grains of sand.

Only a fool would relinquish power when *they* remain hungry for it."

"You're starting to sound like an evangelist," I said.

"Is that what I am? Maybe that's my problem. Not good enough for the Narrow Way, but still preaching my message all the same; still recruiting, still converting and making it all add up to something. Philosophers of antiquity amused themselves with medicines to cure disease and reanimate old age; spells to calm the savage winds and bring down refreshing showers to replenish the earth's fruits. They wanted victory over death; they wanted wealth and they wanted prophecy. But the world has changed, and it demands a philosopher of laughter to make all its dreams come true. Even destroying the world is now admissible if you have the wit for it, if you can make it *funny*."

I began to see flashes of something that I understood later. A man torn between good and evil, teetering on the edge of faith and fighting a raging battle with the promises it offered. Genius, lunatic, saint, sinner, God and devil.

A man torn bitterly in two … he hesitated outside that room. Then he opened the door and went inside.

CHAPTER
TWENTY-TWO

THE ROOM CONTAINED A TABLE AND THREE CHAIRS. MERLE ASKED ME TO choose one, but there was really nothing to choose; identical cheap white plastic merging into plain white walls. "Business ought to have no distractions," he said, studying my reactions. "I'll go bring on The Buck."

As he headed to the door, I said, "What happened to the five at the crossroads?"

His eyes narrowed. "You think I arranged all that to impress your wife? Okay, you may have a point. But unlike yourselves I didn't get sidetracked by events and forget all about those poor suckers. I regretted my actions as soon as I reached the hospital, and I'm happy to say that all five will make remarkable recoveries, astounding their loved ones and anyone else interested, considering the state they arrived in. I do have one regret, though. The doctors on hand, who really don't know very much about anything, are going to be taking a lot of undeserved plaudits, becoming consultants that much sooner as a result of my compassionate nature. That's a tragedy for the future of health care in Las Vegas, but it's the balance we tip when we intervene. It's the nature of the world, and even I can't do anything about it."

Concern and regret crept over his face, petering into a crumpled smile. He eyed his watch. But I wasn't finished. I said, "What was going on with Goldhorn? He said something about the wrong casino. We were supposed to find him at home. You knew where he was all the time - his card was marked. You used him to get us to Vegas, and to show me what happens to people who disobey you."

"Are you asking or telling? You have been busy in that little head of yours, Ben. This is starting to sound like the tie up of some lousy dime-detective, and I think you ought to mail some of your thoughts to that retired cop back in San Francisco still sniffing after clues about the old lady. He could use the help of someone like you. A little tip, though: leave that part of your book vague: because you're still not sure, are you?"

"Is Kate going to be healed tonight, yes or no?"

"That's down to you, Ben."

He left the room. In the silence I heard my heartbeats pounding out a funeral rhythm, and I wondered how much longer they could sustain what was left of me. The sound of footsteps approaching the door brought a wave of nausea, images of Kate lost forever in some God-forsaken limbo jabbing into my brain like burning needles. As the handle of the door slowly turned I took out the gun and raised it using both hands. It felt like a cannon, heavy and brutal. I saw the shadow of the figure fall by degrees into the room, and the gun shaking in my hands.

Merle entered, closing the door behind him, keeping one hand raised towards me. He was alone. I put the gun down onto the table and fell back into the chair.

"Easy, my friend," he said. In one hand he held a black case, and in the other an urn. My feelings broke in half and formed two opposing camps. On one side, relief that my meeting with Buck-Bradbury had been at least temporarily postponed; on the other, grim forebodings as I looked fearfully in turn at the case and the urn.

He took off his bow tie and removed the buttonhole. "The curse of fashion," he said. "You wouldn't believe the lengths I have to go to avoid being seen in the same outfit twice. That kind of thing can quickly create a slapdash impression. Is it my fault that I have such a penchant for black and white, and have to find my ever shifting variations in accoutrements? But neither you nor Buck-Bradbury has ever seen me naked, if you'll pardon the image; so one avenue remains open."

He laughed. "I'm kidding, Ben. I wouldn't inflict that on The Buck himself!"

Placing his bow tie and buttonhole into the urn, he took a lighted match to them. We sat for a few moments watching them burn. He was smiling into the flames, looking sad when they finally died. "I enjoyed that," he said. "I'm going to enjoy this so much more." He placed the case on the table in front of me. "A final word before the night begins. In the last days you've seen a lot that you at best only half believe, and which you certainly don't understand. What I'm saying to you is this: don't write your book too fast."

He looked at the case and licked his lips. "You could title your book, 'Thou shalt not suffer a witch to live' - Exodus 22:18. Those were the words of another great magician, Moses, no less. Ironic, don't you think, that in the darkest age of Christian slaughter, the words of a magician were the rallying cry of 'good Christian souls' all over Europe, to burn and hang and condemn those so poor and broken that they had only the invocation of the supernatural to make life bearable."

He kept looking at the black case. "You will write your book, Ben. You'll have no choice in the end. It'll burn inside you until you have to let it out: and then you really will be a writer. Destiny - you can't fight it." He sighed and looked at me. "You can't fight what you are, Ben. You've got to let this thing soak for a good long time, and one day it *will* make sense. And that's when you write your masterpiece. To the world it will be greeted as nothing more than a work of the imagination, but you'll know better: you, my friend, will be charged with unveiling the deepest secrets of this world."

I started to speak, to tell him I wanted done with the whole damned business, and not relive it on paper.

"Wisdom changes everything," he said, cutting me down. "You're not there yet. There's more to go through: *Rites of Passage*. Nothing will ever be the same again, not for you, not for any of us. Look back from the right perspective and the clarity will appal you. *Then* you can write your book. *Then* you won't have a choice. And you'll tell the truth, my friend. It's what you were put in this world to do."

I felt my thoughts, my memories, cascading, in sequence, out of sequence ... church bells rang once for Kate and me ... they summoned us to the altar ... and I had never known greater joy than on that day … and maybe I had been too humbled to write in the presence of such divinity … the painter defeated by the first recognition of the new bursting day … and now as the day faded towards nightfall at Angels Camp everything was at stake and I would have slaughtered the world for Kate and Merle knew it.

"Time to bring on The Buck," he said, opening up the black case and placing a hand inside. "I thought, in the circumstances, that I'd make life a little easier for you."

"That's very considerate," I said.

He turned his back and the scene was like a junior school magic act about to begin.

"Abraca … dabra!"

He twizzled around and held out the severed head of Professor Buck-Bradbury. It still had its glasses on.

And it was still grinning.

"Saved you the job because I knew you'd do it, Ben. Took his head off with a scythe: one cut, clean as a whistle. Did it from behind while I was telling him about rich pickings coming all the way from Chicago. You can tell from the grin that we were talking big-time. Only thing that ever put a smile on that face: money, money and more money.

"And that double-crossing bastard never knew that I knew. All the time I was working on my masterpiece, my Camelot, he was putting money into that obscene blasphemy back in Vegas. Once I found out he was already a dead man. He took Tobias down with him and one day that wretched place will burn. That's a story for another day. Follow me, Ben. We're almost done."

I followed him out of the room, the vomit burning from my gut to my throat, the gun in my pocket as heavy as a doomed planet.

Down the steps of the Palace I followed him, on towards the Cemetery of Avarice. All the time he was swinging the head of Buck-Bradbury by the scalp and skipping along like a Halloween schoolboy.

In the cemetery, a small group encircled the central plot where Buck-Bradbury's final resting place had been marked out. There were a dozen people standing there, including Guinevere. The night was black, with no desert breeze; perfect stillness in the dark heat of the desert night. They all held candles, white candles. This was no Satanic Mass. Yet the thing I feared most had nothing to do with the raising of devils.

Around the circle of employees Merle was dancing like Rumpel-stiltskin, issuing indecipherable incantations with mounting excitement. Without warning he stopped and the circle parted. The head of Buck-Bradbury was lowered into the prepared ground.

Merle knelt down over the remains of his old friend and business partner and said, with considerable gravity, "*Money ... money ... money.*" Then he stood up and kicked dirt over the severed, grinning head. "The perfect obituary, I think."

He thanked everybody for their devotion and service over the years, and asked them to make their way down to the other cemetery for the final ceremony. Placing an arm around me, we followed the procession, past the hotel and beyond the Palace, to the vast seething area of broken angles now gently illuminated with candle-light.

As we entered the graveyard I felt his arm leave me. I should have felt the relief of it, but instead a wretched loneliness consumed me. Fear growing like a curse, every skeleton I ever gave refuge to wielding steel dipped in poison. The Children of the Dragon's Teeth terrified me as a child, and they were coming for me now. I was no Jason; I was not the stuff of legend.

Merle walked on ahead less easily now. Like a man approaching the scaffold.

I followed, solemnly, on towards the light.

TWENTY-THREE

THE STILL UNNAMED CEMETERY WAS OF EQUAL DIMENSIONS TO THE
Cemetery of Avarice. I took this to be an embodiment of Merle's
theory that the world is divided neatly into material and spiritual
ambition. But in terms of atmosphere the burial grounds were
worlds apart. This place, from the moment I entered it, affected
me; it conjured bizarre images of destruction and terror that
came from no place in my memory. There were no gravestones
here, no markings of any kind. The place hummed with death,
was *alive* with death.

The perimeter was marked out with large candles placed in
holders high above our heads. We walked beneath the light to
where Guinevere and the other eleven 'disciples' now stood,
occupying a central position. Merle began invoking the endless
names of the spirits that he believed inhabited the burial ground.

The roll call was delivered with such ponderous reverence that I
can only liken it to memorials of war dead that I had witnessed
on television. The respect was unconditional, the effect

extraordinary. If he was weeping inside for all who lay in that vast garden of death, as he appeared to be doing, then I pitied him.

The names meant nothing, apart from 'Merlin', which he saved until last. When the invocations had been completed, the cemetery fell once more into an abyss of silence. Nothing moved, nothing visible or audible crawled; again I felt the tension rising, and with it the strange certainty that an unknown, intangible world, was in motion.

He moved away from the centre of the cemetery, and signalled for me to join him a few yards from where the circle of twelve stood. Guinevere stepped backwards, out of the circle, then turned around and walked towards us. She was wearing a plain linen smock which she lifted over her head, letting it fall to the ground. She was naked, and I tried to look away. One by one, all the other assembled men and women shed their garments, simple clothes lying at their feet. I felt the weakness in me as I feasted on Guinevere. My hunger was obscene, and it repulsed me.

Unhurriedly she came, making the short distance between us last an exquisite, excruciating age. I felt the weight of other eyes burning into me, and at last I lowered my gaze to the ground in shame.

Then I felt the touch of lips on my cheek. Guinevere stood in front of me, her smile rich and flawless, and my heart caving in under the strain of it. Merle waved his hand and I watched her turn and walk back to take her place in the naked circle. As she walked away I felt myself go under for the third time, washed up on another shore.

Merle kissed my other cheek, softly. "Temptation," he said, "is what makes us human. If we were above temptation there would be no point to anything. We could all cut to the chase and go straight to Heaven. For some of us the temptation proves too great. It breaks us; and then we lie defeated: the tragedy of life."

His face remained close to mine, but there was no scent of anything on his breath. I could taste fear in my throat, smell the remains of lust in my crotch, hear the twinkling of the stars above us and the creaking of the tombs beneath our feet. But I could not detect a single odour from the physical world on him as we stood on the brink of revelation.

His voice had a calmness that sent me back to childhood, and found me tucked up in bed, waiting for the fairy tales to begin. The days before faith was shattered and the darkness spread like a cancer through the house; my mother holding in her hands the key to my dreams as she selected the night's adventure; the delicious anticipation of the magical tale, my blood beating faster at every dark twist, hoping for all I was worth that there would be a happy ending. Believing that *I* could affect the ending; developing the superstition that any lapse of concentration on my part would risk lives, the happy-ever-after lying entirely in *my believing*.

"... It isn't so much what we do, my friend, as why we do it. What magician ever used more terrible magic than Moses? But the man's motivation was plum. I too began life cast adrift as a baby, though the stream took me on a different course. Not to fight oppression in Egypt, and lead the people to the Promised Land, but to the myth of the Grail and Camelot and all of that bullshit. The cost of any fatuous existence is payable in blood, and I moved on to the ghosts of the unholy desert. I chose to seek power, and whatever good came along the way doesn't erase the motive from my obituary. Now that I know that the power exists and is within my reach, I'm less sure of myself. I wonder if I'm the right vessel after all. Maybe I'm merely the penultimate: John the Baptist waiting for Jesus. Maybe I should leave it to the one who comes after me. Maybe I have too little appreciation of the absurd to rule the world. Or perhaps I yearn, even at this late stage, for the *Narrow Way*.

"Mathew 7:13-14. Enter ye in at the strait gate: for wide *is* the gate, and broad *is* the way, that leadeth to destruction, and many there be which go in thereat: Because strait *is* the gate, and narrow *is* the way, which leadeth unto life, and few there be that find it. Beware of false prophets, which come to you in sheep's clothing, but inwardly they are ravening wolves. Ye shall know them by their fruits."

He kissed me again. "Don't be disturbed by what you see, Ben. The night will pass."

He asked the naked assembly if they had reached a decision. Speaking as one, they said, "We have decided." They held hands in one long, unbroken chain, and turned their backs to us.

My flesh tightened on the bone. None of them moved except Guinevere, turning her head to look over her shoulder towards me. I watched a single tear fall from her eye, her nakedness no longer fascinating me. I wanted to drape a cloak over her and over the rest of them.

With a gesture from Merle, Guinevere urged the others forward. Then he took my hand and we followed.

I could make out the deep shadow of a large hollow in the ground. Merle mumbled incantations in a language I had never heard, as the twelve moved to the edge of the pit. I wrenched my hand out of his and stopped. The rest of them carried on walking, Merle behind them.

The gun felt restless in my pocket. Twelve people were walking to their deaths. Would a bullet through Merle's head break the trance, or whatever it was, saving twelve lives? Would killing him destroy any hope that Kate still had?

Or set her free?

How could I know?

The twelve stopped on the edge of the pit, and Merle began handing out small objects to the faithful. One after the other fell pole-axed into the darkness. Last to go was Guinevere.

And all the time the gun remained impotent in my pocket.

Merle turned around and walked back towards me. "They wanted to be part of it," he said. "They couldn't walk away from the might-have-beens. Asking to join the reborn and I've granted their wish. It is an act of mercy, nothing less." He stood in front of me. "Don't look at me like that," he said. "I am not their murderer, rather their saviour. These were my people. What kind of monster betrays his people? I am not of the Buck-Bradbury's of this world. It's nearly over, only a little longer to keep faith, my friend."

He looked past me, and I turned to see four men entering the cemetery bearing Kate towards us. My breath caught on the burning, freezing air. I turned back and saw that Merle's white suit was now adorned with a bow tie and buttonhole as white as his clothes, almost invisible in the context.

"My favourites," he said, "on a night as dark as this."

Kate appeared to hover above the raised hands of her bearers as they moved in slow, agonising ceremony towards us, stopping a few feet from where we were standing. They laid her down.

"Doesn't she look beautiful?" said Merle.

I thought of the Hammer Horror movies, burying beautiful brides of Satan in Romanian soil, Peter Cushing sharpening the stake. We watched those films together, laughing one minute, holding back a scream the next. I once told Kate that she would have made an excellent witch, though she reckoned a werewolf was better suited to her temperament, and more fun in the makeup department. I asked what was so endearing about werewolves. "The werewolf is the greatest, the most terrifying of all monsters," she said. "To be with someone, close to someone, and not know their true nature. To be loved by the beast one moment, and ripped apart by it the next – that has to be the most tragic, the most heartbreaking horror of all. On the other hand, it's what I do every night on the stage. I transform. I become something, and then, obeying the dramatic laws, I change again into something else."

Had I changed, too? Had I transformed? Becoming an actor in my own horror movie, standing in the grimmest of graveyards, thousands of miles from Transylvania or the London Studios, featuring in a psychopath's fantasy without the vaguest idea of how it might end?

Merle beckoned the bearers forward. The four men moved towards the dark pit, pausing when they reached the edge. Merle was handing out more capsules. A few moments later the four fell silently down into the pit.

Kate lay unmoving on the ground, and I knelt beside her.

The town was empty, the graveyards full.

Almost.

Merle knelt on the other side of Kate, placing a hand on her forehead. The incantations began again.

Panic reared up inside me. I said, "We don't want any part of this."

He carried on as though my words were nothing more than soundless rushes of air.

"Do you hear me? I said *we've had enough!*"

He stood up and faced me. "Leave us," he said. "*Go*. We don't need you, Ben. Your work is done."

"You've got to be out of your mind," I said.

I took out the gun and pointed it into his face, as Kate lay unmoving on the ground between us. "I'm not going anywhere without my wife."

He let my echoes distort into a thousand voices that boomeranged back on me. Then, calmly, but with enough gravity to break the world in half, he said, "Then she'll die."

We stood over her. We might have been, to some lonely pilgrim walking past this Godforsaken place, two rogues fighting over the girl we loved.

The barest breath of sour wind stirred across the graveyard.

"Okay," he said. "So let's reconsider the options. There is a way that you can be with us tonight." He was holding up one last capsule. "It's a short and a painless ride, my friend."

"You promised to save her."

"Save can mean many things."

"Don't play any more games."

"I'm offering you a place in a new world, a better world. Don't you want the best for her?"

"I want to take her home."

"To die?"

"At least we'll be together. It's enough."

"For you, perhaps, though not for her."

"You don't know anything about her."

He laughed, and it was a dry, humourless laugh. "Poor fool, poor magician's fool, poor face at the bottom of the deck. What can you tell me? I brought her here, I listened to her dreams and I orchestrated her nightmares. And you can stand there and tell me that I don't know her! You have the face to tell a magician who has searched the centuries and every square inch of this world, that he doesn't know his own bride!"

He watched the disgust unfold on my face, and I saw it reflected on the curved, carnival mirrors of his eyes; every childhood terror the foreshadowing of this moment, the weight coming down the years like a black star falling towards me.

I pushed the gun forward, trying to hold it steady. "What are you? You talk in riddles. You're nothing but a cold-blooded killer."

"Have you understood nothing? *She is mine.* It is time for you to let go, Ben."

My finger pressed on the trigger of the gun. "You're a cheap conman turned psycho, and you're out of your fucked-up mind."

"You could still be part of it, Ben. Eternity needs fools, too. You haven't the purity of spirit to be a part of the kingdom, but you could play the fool out in the borderlands of the New Camelot."

Kate's head moved; the faintest sideways motion. She was alive ... *and she was turning him down.*

I saw his frustration, his disbelief.

"Kate," he said. "Trade in this living death. Ben can't give you what you deserve, what you were born to be. It's yours for the taking. Nod your head and we'll have the world at our feet."

"Get away from her," I said. "Or I'll kill you."

A smile rose and broke into a grin. "You think you can kill me? You think that the magician with the keys to the kingdom can be killed by the gun that he left in the pocket of his fool?"

"Let her go," I said.

He reached towards his pocket. "I thought something like this might happen," he said. "I came prepared." He held one hand up, while his other hand moved slowly, carefully into his jacket, taking out a marker pen. To my astonishment he drew a bullseye on his forehead. A second later, so fast that I didn't even see his hand move, he was holding up a dead rabbit.

"Sleight of hand," he said. "Got to keep your eyeballs sharper than that, my friend."

The wind was gathering and starting to pluck at Kate's hair, and around the thin shroud that wrapped her body. My miserable brain couldn't handle the conflicts. There was too much I didn't know. I was at the centre of my life, free to choose - *either, or*: there was no middle ground left. I could fire the gun or I could throw it down. The choice was mine, given to me alone; no-one to confer with, no-one to consult. What kind of freedom, though: freedom to make the biggest mistake of my life? How could I know what was hiding behind that choice? What, in the face of such contradictions and absurdities, did having a choice mean? Without knowing the consequences, choice meant nothing.

I held the gun as steady as my frayed nerves would allow, and I searched for the truth in Merle's half-smile.

He had no intention of saving her. Was he beckoning me to shoot him? *Why?* So that he could catch the bullet? Or had sleight of hand already taken the bullet from the gun? Was he already holding it between his teeth?

None of this mattered. All that mattered was Kate. If he wouldn't wake her from this living death, I would shatter that death along with his targeted forehead. I said, "I'll count to three. Bring her back or I'll shoot."

He was laughing. "Make your decision, Ben. But remember: it isn't what we do but why. Choose carefully, my friend: back to England as a jobbing actress ... or set free by your own sacrifice to find happiness. I'll put it another way, to clear up any doubt: a noble sacrificial suicide, or selfish murder consigning the one you profess to love to a mundane life."

"One …"

"What greater love, Ben? I believe you're thinking about it. And I have another title for your book: '*The Sad and Sinful Lives of Merle the Magician*.' I like that. Or you could just come straight to the point and call it: '*The Narrow Way*.' Laying down your life for the one you love. Maybe you can still find the entrance, Ben. What do you say?"

"Two …"

"One last suggestion: '*Notes from the Ghost Town*,' because that's where you're headed. You'll like it there. It's where you belong."

"Three …"

"*God forgive you, Ben. Forgive us all - the whole damned ship of fools.*"

I looked at Kate and then back at Merle. Then I fired straight at the bullseye.

The power of the discharge kicked me backwards. I wasn't sure that what I had seen through the screen of gun smoke wasn't some cheap illusion. The shot had taken his head from his neck, and the torso stood for a moment, as though daring me to try again. I wondered, in a lightning second, if fake blood might erupt like a volcano and the sound of laughter confirm the joke and complete the stunt.

None of that happened. The remains of Merle crumpled to the ground.

As he went down, a note fell from his hand. I moved toward it, the gun still trapped inside my fist, my hand shaking to free itself of the weapon like it was glued shut around a fistful of wasps. I bent down and picked up the note.

What choice did you have? Like this note it was already written.

I saw what I had done. What Merle had *prepared* me to do: arranging his own suicide; leaving me to pull the trigger.

But I still didn't understand why.

I went over to Kate. "It's Ben," I said. "It's over, we're going home."

She didn't stir. I could find no pulse. I began screaming. I couldn't leave her in that place. I picked her up and tried to put her across my back. We fell so many times, crushing my face into the dirt, until at last I got her across me and began my walk of pain. I looked back once, and the debris of the night remained. I had really done it, I had shot and killed. I never looked back again and walked until the night became dawn and the heat poured down like lava. At some point I lost consciousness, and when I awoke, Kate still lying across me, I lifted her up and set out again. I was on the edge of exhaustion when I buried my hands into the burning sand to dig out a resting place. I beckoned death to reunite us, lapsing into it as the murderous globe above torched my body and shrivelled what I took to be my last thoughts in this world. Yet each death gave new strength with which to look once more on the poor mound that now housed Kate's body; and each time I looked I pledged my undying love: that soon we would be together again, not in some perverted Camelot with a thousand reincarnations of an ancient magician, but in a holy place where the God I had never acknowledged could finally grant redemption.

For the first time in years I prayed, *really prayed.* All my thoughts channelled towards an all-powerful, loving deity that I now knew was watching and listening. I prayed that the spirit of Kate, pure, incapable of evil, would be granted salvation. I asked that the pathetic murdering soul draped across her might be given deathbed forgiveness, and gaze on her once more and for always.

I felt the final fall beginning, and entered the lonely darkness. The tears came like a long prayed for rain, and the brutal globe of life beat its burning hammers down to erase me from this world.

CHAPTER

TWENTY-FOUR

.

I REGAINED CONSCIOUSNESS TO FIND KIND FACES LOOKING DOWN ON ME.
I asked where Kate was, before slipping back into a lesser
darkness ...

Those who found me and took me into the shade to rejoin the
living, nursed me back to life, steering a course from death's
door. They never spoke, communicating by drawing pictures in
the sand, and in this way we learned to talk with each other.

One day I drew them a picture of Merle. It took hours to make a
few lines in the sand conform to the image in my head. At last, by
picking at a few features, highlighting bow tie and buttonhole,
hat and shoes, a murmur of recognition went up among them.
One of them went away for a few minutes, and returned with a
collection of items: a shattered hat, the fragments of a white bow
tie, a blood-stained white rose, a pair of immaculate black shoes
and two sets of cards: Camelot and Egypt. The items appeared
genuine enough.

The eldest, the man most highly respected among them, made two readings from the cards. Then he set about making elaborately detailed drawings in the sand. This took him many hours, and when he had finished he took me carefully through them as the others watched with interest.

I observed, as the story unfolded.

Two travellers had met and fallen in love while a mighty magician watched. The magician took a special interest in them; he had known about them, in his own way, for a long time. He believed in the reincarnation of past souls; believed that he had known them even before they were born. He let them grow, plucking them out through the dreams of the sick one; he made her sick, but not through magic; he used the power of mind to create sickness. Once his heart had been pure, and once he had believed in a greater good in a better world. Then that heart had blackened, and with it had grown an army of delusions. A terrible destiny arose within him that couldn't be reconciled.

The old man looked at me. I said, "He was nothing more than a hypnotist and a murderer. He turned me into his executioner."

I raved about cemeteries.

"He created a Cemetery of Avarice and he planted Professor Buck-Bradbury's head in the middle of it. He filled another with devils and magicians, and manipulated me into killing him so that he would lie forever at the heart of it. He thought he was the reincarnation of Merlin!"

They watched, listened.

"He was torn between good and evil, God and the devil. He wanted to be the culmination of the dark power of the universe, yet he wanted that power broken for good. He wanted God to forgive him."

The old man looked at me, blankly.

☙ "None of it makes any sense. He took my wife! How could a sane man look for forgiveness from any kind of God by creating sickness and leaving all that another man loved out in the desert to rot?" I was flailing, screaming the words out as though exorcising them. "It could have been anyone. We were just unlucky. A rich, psychotic conman bored and in love with my wife. Life is a lottery, a game of chance on a giant roulette wheel. There's no rhyme or reason for any of it."

Everything went black again. They nursed me, comforted me, bestowing their patience without limit. For all my ravings, I still didn't know what I really believed; it changed by the hour.

At my request, the elder began the drawings again, recapping over what the pictures had already revealed. The drawings started to become more complex. The story in the sand went on:

... The magician lost his sense of purpose, finding that he didn't possess the dreadful ambition of his infamous ancestor. He conspired against himself to end the quest unless the male traveller should, by his own free-will, consent to choose otherwise.

... The magician had shown them many things, and at the end he wanted their friendship and their belief.

... He could not crown his dreams, fulfilling all that had inspired him, unless they freely gave their consent. And so he gave the keys to the kingdom to the male traveller: a loaded gun and no spells against him. He wanted them to go with him. His soul was breaking in two.

"But how can any of this be? It makes no sense."

Still, I *had* believed. Merle had given the promise of hope and I had been willing to believe in anything if it meant that my wife would be spared.

The last drawings showed the firing of the gun and the burying of Kate.

They held my hands as I looked at the representation of her burial, and their warmth, their compassion filled me with love for them and hate for myself.

Two drawings remained.

The last of all was me. I was holding a book. I remembered Merle's talk of me writing it all down. I moved back to the picture that preceded it, but it wouldn't yield its truth.

I feared its truth.

They stayed close to me and watched as I searched for meaning. The symbols were obscure and I couldn't work out how they fitted together. Then one day I caught a flash; a hideous glimpse into a waiting epiphany.

I looked into the faces of the new friends around me and saw the awful pity on their faces. I didn't want to know the truth. I didn't think I could bear it. That awful glimpse unlocked the door, and traces of enlightenment seeped through.

I don't blame them, they were right to show me. Despite everything, they were *right*. It would have come to me in time, anyway. Better that I saw it while they were around. They would never have abandoned me.

The picture took me to my cross and was my crucifixion. It asked: would Kate have lived if I had not fired the gun?

And on my cross I found the answer: *she would have lived.*

She wasn't dead.

While I conducted Merle's suicide, Kate had remained in a trance. Hypnotism: the power of suggestion. The gunshot altered nothing. She was alive. The effects of the sun would have killed her in time, but the truth was ... *I buried her alive.*

That is the cross I nailed myself to.

She was sleeping, waiting to be woken. She was not ill, she never was ill. There was nothing to be cured.

That was the lesson that I found in the picture in the sand. That was the truth waiting for me to become well enough to comprehend, and strong enough to face and stand in the appalling shadow of all the remaining days of my life.

I remained with the desert people as the weeks turned into months. They witnessed the depths of my suffering and recognized the danger of self-destruction. I owed them my life, which for a long time meant little.

We travelled together through the wilderness, drawing in the sand together, trying to understand a little more each day. They were as puzzled by my dogged, poverty-stricken rationalism as I was by their easy acceptance of the unseen world.

The days deepened, and tiny fragments of darkness began to weaken and break off under the focus of light that their wisdom generated. Slowly I saw our differences dissolve, our thoughts begin to merge. It no longer seemed that one school of absurdity had greater currency than the other. What came to matter was not some futile yearning for an impossible, all-encompassing truth: rather, the maturity of self-knowledge. And while the pain of enlightenment is beyond my powers to describe, my reward began with the first recognition of the depth of love and forgiveness inside me. How I could go on loving Kate in death as I had loved her in life.

There was no creed to their teachings, only the wisdom of spirit. I learned from them the healing power of prayer, and the deeper knowledge that comes with the healing.

We came at last to the outskirts of the town that has now become my home, where they knew it was safe to leave me, and where I could continue to reconcile my grief through prayer and meditation. They drew again the picture of an unwritten book with my name across the front. They showed me that it was good to write it all down, and to tell my tale; that in doing so I might find greater understanding, and a way to make my peace with the world.

Before they left me, we spent more time communicating with sand pictures. They forced me to dwell on Kate's life, not merely her death. They taught me to resurrect the happiness we shared, understanding its infinite value, its eternal existence: a sacred rock never to be eroded by the rolling river of time. They proved to me that joy always leaves a trace in the dust of the earth, and in the collective psyche that is the legacy of all humanity.

I tried to recapture every moment of our lives together: the love, laughter, tears - and it all began to feel real again.

The last thing they showed me before they left me in the safety of the town was a single word in the sand. A word written in English, and the only word that ever passed between us.

HOPE.

They underlined the word, embraced me, each in turn, and then we went our separate ways.

Not long after I arrived here, an English newspaper was waiting on my bed. It was an old paper, and the page left open for me told of the unspeakable villains who squandered public money, given in good faith, across the American West, last seen living it up in the Vegas casinos, never to be seen or heard of again.

When I read that, I left my room, trembling inside, dreading that I would be sent back to England in disgrace to tell a story that no-one would believe.

I walked for hours, becoming more determined by the footstep to begin writing it all down.

When I returned to my room I found the ashes of the newspaper smouldering safely in the toilet bowl. I began writing that night.

It matters little if the book is read. What matters is that it is written, and the patterns it has revealed: a man driven by the forces of good and evil, at war with himself; creating sickness, or the illusion of it; wanting Kate, to take her from me by revealing my faults, my weaknesses; failing to take account of the miracle of love that would have held us together forever, and still does.

Between the lines on the page I can see how desperately he needed us; our belief, our sacrifice. I was his fool, yet he wanted to educate me, and to cure all that was wrong in me. He set out to use me for his own wicked ends, but came to learn from *me*.

Even now as I flick through the pages, I see an enigma too vast to be captured by the poor tools of pen and ink. In these closing pages I am still full of questions: was he merely a talented conman and a brilliant hypnotist, deluded in believing that he had occult powers gained from the tarot? Was his life ruined so completely by the past that he found it beyond his powers to heal himself? In finally glimpsing the unbreakable power of real love, did he offer himself as a sacrifice so that our lost faith could be restored?

It doesn't add up. Kate wasn't saved.

I did my best … but in these closing pages … something is wrong.

On the brink of revelation I am defeated.

Something is wrong.

I resolve to put this away now. The truth that comforts me is that the slow torturing of my mind towards insanity is not my just dessert for picking the wrong colour on the roulette wheel, and putting hope in the promises of a stranger.

I still have my copy of the Twain book. It was in my jacket pocket when they found me. It's all I have left of the material world and I read it from time to time. It has its own peculiar comforts to offer, not least because it was written by a man deeply hurt by the world, a man who never lost his rich humanity. I aspire to that, and when I read his book I think of how Merle referred to his beloved *Merlin*, and how he believed that Twain above all had it right when he drew his character. And I've come to believe that Merle found the responsibility too great for him to unleash that spirit back into the world, and left it for me, his perfect fool, his innocent and naive Percival, to decide. And if the world has been granted a stay of execution by this, then the world itself is the ongoing monument to Kate's needless death. She graced this world, and she chose me as her companion. These are the things that matter.

Words have failed me. In a tale like this, how could it have been otherwise? As Twain said: '*Words are only painted fire.*'

The pain was too great to be conjured again on paper.

He was right. He knew the limits.

I've found the ghost town that Merle promised, and I've written the pages that he said I would write. I wonder what he would make of them. And I wonder - in the last instant of his life, as the bullet prepared to shatter his brain - if he found the entrance to the Narrow Way.

I hope that whatever the truth about Merle, his torn and restless spirit has found forgiveness and peace.

So, I'll remain here. Hope can never be exploited here. The world that breeds the likes of Buck-Bradbury doesn't exist here. Here no-one gets ill. Here there is only life and death and prayer.

EPILOGUE

Today I'm setting out to find the grave and say goodbye. If fate brings me back from my pilgrimage I will leave this manuscript at the small post office in the centre of town. It will be mailed to Kate's Aunt Helen in Ireland, and might go some way to explaining what really happened. She's the one person I trust to know what to do with these strange pages.

I don't have her address. But they can find anyone from here. And they can never trace me. This place bears no postmark for the bounty hunting press to seize on.

We don't really exist here, none of us. Here we are all ghosts. Living, breathing ghosts from past lives left behind.

POSTSCRIPT

They were waiting for me. I walked out into the wilderness in blind faith and it led me to the place where I laid her down to rest and covered her with earth. They were waiting like they knew the day and the hour.

There was a simple cross in the sand. They must have placed it there. The eldest and wisest of them pulled the cross out of the ground and broke it in half. He handed one piece to me, and with the other half he began drawing. The first picture revealed Kate entombed in the wilderness. The second ...

Alive!

Then the elder drew two diagonal lines through the first picture, crossing out the depiction of the entombment. He pointed at the other, the final picture, and I looked up to see them all smiling. The elder looked at me and his eyes shone deeply into mine ... and I believed.

A short time ago we arrived back in the town that has become my home. They are sitting with me as I write this. There is the faintest movement of dust on the horizon, slowly taking form; a small party of people moving towards us.

And there, in the middle of the party, I can see her.

They're closer now. She knows it's me.

She's shouting something.

Let me write this down. Let me write this last thing down.

"Which way's Hollywood, Ben?"

FINALE

... I WAS STILL HOLDING THE GUN ...

Merle standing in front of me, his face cracking into a grin ...

Kate still on the ground, not moving ...

Days, weeks, months wiped away, and the night as dark as hell and the candles burning low ...

"Had you going there, Ben! Some trip, eh? You shoot me in the heroic style, and then bury your living, breathing wife out in the godforsaken desert. What are you on, man?"

His laughter sounded like gunfire.

"But then guess what? It's your lucky day! Some travellers happen along and save your miserable ass. And all you can do, hero that you are, is fulfil all of those ridiculous dreams you stored up about being a writer, instead of doing the *truly* heroic thing and putting that gun to your miserable fucking head.

"Do the world a favour, pal. I mean, all of those epilogues and postscripts – that shit about forgiving me … come on! Don't you understand any of it? Don't you know how to end it, *Writer Man?*"

I looked at the gun in my hand. *Was it real?* I pointed it to the ground and fired. The explosion of sound startled me, and the dust it kicked up into my face convinced me that the gun was real and the bullets live.

"You planning to shoot your beloved now, Ben? One scene missing from the book, old friend: *the finale.* For my sake, your sake - but most of all for her: *do it, pal, and this time do it right.*"

In that bullet flash I saw it, and the look on his face confirmed it: his power derived from victims, and we gave it freely.

Whatever happened I had to remain strong for Kate. There was only one ending that made any sense. Not his ending, *mine.*

I said, "You shouldn't play Russian roulette unless you know everything."

"What's to know? It can only end two ways. Kill yourself or turn into a killer. Either way she goes free."

I held the gun on him and for a split-second saw a flicker of doubt. Then the moments lengthened, and I watched the belief start to pool back into him, his power humming once again, radiating out into the pitiless night. Another second and it would be too late. This was it.

I squeezed on the trigger and screamed out, "God forgive me."

I watched the light burst in on him, the grin sliding off his face.

"Put the gun down, Ben."

"You taught me how to kill."

"Ben, the gun ..."

"You loaded it. You made this happen."

He came for me, nothing left in his eyes but fear.

"The finale," I said, pulling the trigger all the way.

The bullet took off most of his face, and he hit the ground like a cheap villain on a bad night in Hollywood. I let the gun fall.

"Ben." *Kate's voice.* I stumbled to where she lay. "What's wrong," she said. "You look like you've seen a ghost. Take me home."

"We're already here," I said.

She started laughing ...

... "Third time lucky, sucker!"

I was still standing, holding the gun, Kate on the ground, Merle grinning.

"Okay," I said. "What now?"

"It's your call. Your last chance, Ben."

But what I'd learnt still held. His power came from his victims, and we gave it to him of our own accord, out of fear and lack of faith.

"It's all down to her," I said.

"You mean that? Let me get this straight. You're ready to accept whatever she chooses? *Whoever* she chooses?"

"Let her go," I said. "Release her from this."

Merle knelt at Kate's side. He placed one hand on her head, the other across her heart. "*Which way's Hollywood, sucker?*" he said.

Kate's eyes blinked opened. She looked at Merle, and then at me. "What's going on?" she said.

"The truth," said Merle. "Ben loved you ... because he needed you. Without you he was less than nothing. You showed pity because that's who you are. But you don't know the truth about your husband."

She started to get up.

"Do you want to know why his father drank so much? Do you want to know why his mother had a breakdown and went insane?"

Kate was struggling to stand. I went to help her, but she brushed me away.

Merle went on: "Do you know why your family abandoned you, Kate? And why your faith deserted you? Do you know why you have no friends left, and no future in that old life? Why you are the vagabonds, the scoundrels, the runaways from your own people, your own country?"

Kate was down again, battling to get to her feet, determined to stand without assistance from anybody.

Merle's accusing finger was pointing straight at me. "You drove your family to drink and to madness, Ben, and you drove faith, family and friends from your door, and Kate's, too. The bullies from your childhood were never bullies at all; you formed them out of your own image - who you were and who you still are.

"Your father tried to beat it out of you, and Johnny Winterburn tried his damnedest, too. And what thanks did they ever get for the sacrifices they made? They tried, in their own ways, to help you, as everyone did. But you fucked up everybody who tried to save you. You demonized them, you wore them down, and you drained the love out of all of them. You screwed up the world and you still haven't finished ... you looked into the eyes of the witch and you accepted your destiny. You brought it all on yourself, Ben, a long time ago, and you invited me in to try and put it right."

"No!"

"They all marked your card, Ben. Got you down as a fantasist, out for himself and blaming the world for his own sins and failings. You needed a mirror to see the demon, just like in the old days. It wasn't what was hidden over your shoulder that you needed to be afraid of ... it was what was already hidden inside *you*. If you love somebody, you have to set them free. You're killing her, Ben, suffocating the life out of her with all of that baggage. You always knew you'd fall short, that one day the world would see through you, that she would see through you, and see that imposter, the con man desperate to play the hero, well now's your chance. Let her go ... allow her to choose."

Kate was standing and Merle turned to face her. "It's time to make your life again, Kate. Reclaim the future that's waiting for you. The choice is yours."

"If you're so powerful," she said, "why did you need to go to such lengths? You could have found an easier way."

"It doesn't work like that. God didn't click his fingers to save mankind, he sent his only son to die on a cross. Love means nothing if it isn't given freely."

"Are you God? Not some screwed up psycho who happened to see Macbeth and lost the plot?"

"I fell in love, Kate. You were magnificent on that stage, and I saw a greater role awaiting you."

"So you gave me the freedom to choose by ... *hypnotizing me* ... taking me to hell and trying to destroy my husband?"

"I would destroy the world for you, Kate."

"And if I choose you ... what happens to Ben?"

"He goes free to live out the remains of his miserable life."

"And if I choose Ben?"

Merle tilted his head back and laughed. "Why would you? He was damned from the start. We can rule the world, Kate. I'm no mere hypnotist."

We stood, the three of us, alone in the midnight desert. Kate turned to look at me, and I wondered what she was seeing: dead weight and disappointment?

I threw the gun down on the ground.

"I love you, Kate, I always did and I always will. But I'm no hero ... you're the hero. And you have to choose ..."

She turned back to Merle: her saviour - *her knight in shining armour?*

She held out a hand.

"Come on, Ben," she said. "Let's get out of this graveyard."

Merle appeared stunned.

I took Kate's hand, and we began walking, waiting for the bullets to hit us.

In the silence of the desert graveyard we walked, our hands gripping tightly; white knuckles and pulse and undefeated love.

We were on the threshold, about to leave the cemetery, when it came, brutal and shocking: a single gunshot rupturing the night.

We stopped, for barely a second, looking at each other, not even whispering.

And not turning back.

Never once turning back.

We kept on walking ...

Printed in Great Britain
by Amazon

16092679R00173